FLOTSY

Peggy Hogan

FLOTSY

DOUBLE DRAGON

Dedication

To Earth:

may you flourish.

Chapter 1

I was born Olivia Marie Ducharme in a little fishing village on the east coast of Canada. The Island was beautiful, but I only realised that long after I had left.

Living close to the sea, I was forever in the cold Gulf water swimming with the other children, and the fish and the crabs and the lobsters. Afterwards, my penchant was to wander off alone along the beach seeking treasure washed up with the tide and collecting anything and everything that caught my eye—rocks, shells, bits of driftwood—and string them on old fishing line or the occasional piece of rope. Sometimes I would braid these necklaces through my long, dark hair or wear them around my neck and wrists and ankles. I so festooned myself with these marvels that I looked like flotsam moving on dry land. Flotsy, the other kids called me. I loved it; it made me feel like I belonged.

One morning, just after my thirteenth birthday, I woke with a burning need to stop the village from extending the old dock deeper into the bay; I had no idea how to do such a thing, I just knew it was a very bad idea. At breakfast I pleaded with my mother and father to help; they smiled and said that I had just had a bad dream. But I could not stop myself from talking about it with everyone I met until the school mistress called my mother and said how it was distracting the other children from their lessons and would she please, please, please make Flotsy stop talking about the *bad* dock. My mother stormed over to the school and dragged me out of the classroom to the stifled giggles and wide eyes of my classmates. I was ashamed and dreaded the beating when we got home—my mother was angrier than I had ever seen her.

The dock was to be lengthened so larger boats could sell their catch to the cannery that was considering our village as the location of its new plant. The village council thought that demonstrating how well the community worked together to attract their business would impress the cannery owners.

But I knew, just knew, that very bad things would happen if they disturbed the old dock. It haunted my dreams. I saw the new tarred timbers being lowered into the water and the winch slowly working its way loose in the ancient planking. It had worked hundreds of times before, my father said to me, why would it fail now? He told me this over and over as I stood teary-eyed before him to tell him that I had had the dream again. He would pull me onto his lap, even though I was a newly minted teenager, and smooth my sleep-mussed hair with his callused hand and send me back to bed.

I begged my mother to make him stay home the day that the huge logs arrived but by now my entire family, and quite possibly the entire village, was very tired of my constant harangue.

I sat at my desk in school that day but heard nothing of what Mlle Blacquière said. The third time I was reprimanded, I blindly accepted my punishment and began cleaning the dusty, chalk-filled brushes, not even bothering to protect my good school clothes. When the alarm was raised and everyone rushed out the door to see what had happened, I just sat on the steps, tears streaming down my face. I knew exactly what had happened—the metal rivets that had been slowly working their way loose, had ripped from the dock in a sudden surge. The huge log cradled in the thick chain plunged down onto the two men who laboured at the pulley. They barely had time to look up before it shattered the planking beneath them, dragging them and the heavy winch mechanism into the water. It was over in seconds.

The foreman had his best divers in the water in moments, but it was already too late. I knew that my father's skull had been given only a glancing blow, but it had been enough to kill him instantly. Gilles, his partner, was unconscious when he entered the water but was very dead by the time he was extracted from the wreckage.

My father's body lay in the front room, but I could not look at him. Pain was etched deeply into my mother's face and my two young brothers looked scared and bewildered. No one stopped me when I left the house and walked down to the beach; I could feel their relief pushing me further and further away. It was my fault. It was my crazy dream and my crazy talk that had made this happen. Premonitions were simply never discussed; people who lived off the sea knew that. To do so was just plain bad luck. That was what everyone thought—I had brought the bad luck and it had killed my father as punishment.

The new cannery was finally located in the next village over; they said it would take us too long to repair the damage to our dock. The fishing that year was bad; there was nowhere to easily put in for unloading the catch while the dock was being fixed. Of course, all of this was also my fault. I had cursed the village.

The next four years passed like a kind of torture for me. I felt slightly dazed a lot of the time because I made myself stay awake for as long as possible night after night. I would wander aimlessly around the village, which gave me a whole new air of weirdness that I definitely did not need. But, even more so, I did not want any more dreams.

"Mais non! T'as l'air d'une folle!" my mother yelled at me one day as I was leaving for another tedious day at school. Not very imaginative of her—she always thought I looked like a fool, and she always spoke French when she was mad at me, as if I didn't understand her, as if anyone within earshot couldn't understand her. The problem was that she didn't understand me. She never saw how the other kids crossed the street when they saw me coming; she never heard the Gallant boys sneering their cruel words at me; she never witnessed the teachers manoeuvring me to the front of the class so that the other kids wouldn't have to worry about me sitting behind them, making them twist around to look at me every two seconds, though what they thought I would do to them I couldn't imagine.

My one friend, Jacinthe, thought that maybe it was because my eyes were a little spooky. When I studied them in the mirror to see what she meant, they looked like everyone else's eyes to me. She was right, though, almost no one looked straight at me, not even my mother.

As was my usual habit when I wished to ponder something, I meandered down to the beach,

10

stooping to pick up whatever caught my eye as I went. The finger-shaped translucent shells in my hand were quite lovely and I studied the beach in earnest for other bits with which to fashion I-knew-not-what. A pointy piece of driftwood looked useful as did the length of net webbing. I sat down and tried to pierce a hole in one end of a shell. Not surprisingly, it split, but right down the middle. The shell halves were about as long and wide as my index finger with small bulges at the tips where whatever mollusc who had lived in it had anchored itself. I picked apart strands from the net webbing and soon had a good length of the strong, thin material. I secured it around the bulges on the ends of the shells until I had a little curtain of dangling half shells. On impulse, I tied it around my head so that the shells obscured my eyes, and when I moved, they clicked and clacked. Through the translucent slices of shell my view of the world came and went in between the pearly light.

That was why my mother was mad at me that particular day. She hated the new fashion I had created for myself; she thought I had gotten over gathering bits of stuff from the beach and wearing it. I should have waited until I was out of sight of the house before I had tied it around my head, but I had forgotten. If my mother took it away from me, I would just make another one. She knew this.

"Vite! Je ne veux pas te voir."

That stung, and I cried, but only a little. I guess I was getting used to people not wanting to see me.

The decision came upon me in a rush. I had had all the schooling I could stand, and I was old enough to leave home. Monsieur Arsenault would be making his weekly trip to town the next day; I would ask him for a lift to the bus station. When I declared my intention to my mother, I tried very hard not to see the there-and-gone relief in her eyes. My brothers shrugged and returned to whatever it was they had been doing; for my part, they had never been more than nuisances I cleaned up after. My friend, Jacinthe, gave me a hug and promised to write when I had an address.

With some clothes in a ratty old suitcase and a few dollars in my pocket, I boarded the bus. I was going off-Island to a city where nobody knew me or my curse, where nobody shunned me, and where nobody would care about me—that, sadly, would remain the same.

Chapter 2

After the bus left the Charlottetown station, a great weariness settled on me and I slept while I was transplanted from the only home I had known.

I woke much later with a stiff neck and rubbed it as I blearily squinted out the grimy windows. We had arrived somewhere—I had forgotten the name on the ticket; it didn't matter anyway—and everyone was leaving the bus. In a daze, I followed.

There were more buildings and people than I had believed, in my *naïveté*, were in the entire world. The noise and confusion at the bus terminal made me feel small, in an alien place, lost like the bug I watched circumvent the toe of my shoe and skitter around and around the piece of detritus next to my foot. The bug probably knew exactly what it was doing, which didn't say a lot about my own survival skills.

In my peripheral vision, a bench emptied of its occupants. I shuffled over and sat down, needing to regain my equilibrium. I sat there for a long time, and the details of my surroundings began to filter through. People were in a terrible hurry; they must have very important business to attend to or perhaps they were late for supper. My mother hated it when I was late for supper.

Kiosks selling newspapers and pop and other sundries were strewn about the perimeter of the terminal. *I should buy a newspaper*, I thought. It would list places to stay. I froze. Tonight would be the first time in my life that I would sleep somewhere other than in my own bed at home.

13

Tears stung my eyes and I scrubbed them away, furious that I could weaken so quickly. This wouldn't do. I was likely just hungry and rummaged through my shoulder bag for the sandwich my mother had shoved in there as her parting gift. I bit into the mayo and baloney and closed my eyes. I would be strong and make a new life for myself. I would be someone that people wanted to be with just because they liked me. I would be a person of value.

Composed once again, I opened my eyes and, for the first time, really looked around. My gaze fell upon a homeless man. I had read about homeless people but had never seen one before. He seemed relatively content but who knew how people really felt? Not even me who, for some unknowable reason, received glimpses into their most intimate moments—their most intimate future moments, future moments in which something bad inevitably happened to them.

Reinforced by food and rest, I did my best to nonchalantly stroll over to a bulletin board crammed with bits of paper advertising all manner of things for sale and, happily, rooms to let. I spent some of my meagre hoard of cash on a detailed map of the city and wrote down the information for a few rooms that looked to be within walking distance. But, being my first time in a city, I miscalculated the size of city blocks and had to walk much farther than I anticipated, and, tired and footsore, I mounted the steps of the closest address. The woman who answered my knock looked me up and down and shut the door in my face. Stunned, I stood there not understanding for a moment what had happened. I had been judged and found wanting. Just like that. I reminded myself that it was my choice to come to a city and trudged to the next address. It was getting dark.

This time, my knock was answered by a young man. He asked me questions for which I had no answer like where had I worked and did I have any references. I think I must have looked pitiful because he took pity on me, and the money for one week's rent, and let me in.

The room was tiny and at the top of three flights of narrow stairs. Exhausted as I was, I didn't notice much else besides the bed, took my shoes off, and lay down fully clothed. The rest of my life could wait until tomorrow.

I woke early as usual and swung my legs over the side of the bed, eager to take a look at my new world. To my right, the morning sun streamed in through a dormer window that had its very own sitting bench. On my left was a chest of drawers, and beside it, a small desk and chair. Opposite the bed was the door with a coat rack of sorts nailed into it for hanging things. I was enchanted. Eager with anticipation, I stood and looked out the window. At first, I couldn't quite understand what I was seeing. It was as though a sea of grey waves had solidified and was punctuated by mysterious eruptions. Like wiping a smear from the glass, the view resolved into rooftops and chimneys and steeples.

Something wasn't right, though. It took me a moment to put my finger on the source of my unease: there was no water anywhere to be seen. I felt like I was suffocating and frantically tried to open the window. It had a locking clasp. My fingers strained to turn it; I was getting desperate. It gave at last and I pushed the window up, sucking in the air. It helped, but it didn't smell right—there was no tang of salt and seaweed. I wondered how many more unexpected jolts awaited me.

I told a little white lie to get my first job, not the best of beginnings. Who would have thought that you needed to be eighteen to wash dishes? I was seventeen and been washing dishes since I was five years old! But the job paid in food and enough money to get by. With my head down scraping at the pots and pans, I barely spoke, other than a mumbled acknowledgement when more dirty dishes were piled beside me.

After a couple of days, I was getting a bit lonely, truth to tell, and on a break later that week, one of the waiters was outside smoking a cigarette. It would have been rude not to say hello. We chatted about the weather and the work at the restaurant and he seemed like a nice fellow. He was older than me, but it was still nice to talk to someone. That is, until our eyes met for a moment. His glance skittered away. You would have thought I had suddenly grown fangs or something. He dropped his half-finished cigarette and hurried back inside.

When I walked in a few minutes later, everyone stared at me as though I was a dead rat. I hurried to the sink and applied myself to the dishes, working furiously. Before the end of the day, the manager took me aside and said that my work was unsatisfactory, and was letting me go. No reference letter would be forthcoming.

Meagre paycheque in hand, I walked over to the MoneyMart and cashed it, stuffing the bills in my bag. My first job had lasted four days.

I wandered the streets, depressed. Residential neighbourhoods morphed into a business district, but I barely noticed. They were just more buildings smelling of cement dust and the decayed detritus that gathered about their foundations.

Tired and thirsty, I went into a convenience store for something to drink. The man ahead of me at the cash register was busily buying lotto tickets. I had heard of this back on the Island but had never seen the vast array of glittery choices that were available. How did they work? How do you choose? I leaned forward and paid closer attention to the transaction going on. Suddenly, the cashier whooped and yelled, "It's a winner!" Everyone in the store cheered and the man ahead of me who had won turned around and hugged me.

"How much?" he asked the cashier, breathless.

The cashier held up a finger, the store hushed. He made a phone call, repeating the series of numbers on the ticket that the man had given him. The cashier's face lit up in a huge smile while he scribbled something on a piece of paper and handed it to the man.

The man in front of me closed his eyes for a moment, opened them, and read the number on the slip of paper. He began to sway, and I steadied him, getting close enough to glimpse the five figures on the paper. He had just won over eight thousand dollars. Wow.

He began to hop from one foot to the other in a little jig. The patrons in the store cheered and danced along with him. I squeezed through the throng and escaped into the night air.

I had never thought of gambling before but, tonight, it seemed like a good idea. Or a terrible one, a little voice whispered inside my head. I promised the little voice that I would only spend ten dollars. The little voice tried to say something else, but I quashed it.

My city map had an assortment of businesses, restaurants, and places of entertainment advertised around its border. There was a small casino called Money for Nothing about a ten-minute walk from where I stood. Inspired by what I had just witnessed at the convenience store, I strode there in record time and entered the noise and the heat and the lights of my first gambling establishment.

The ranks of slot machines were crowded with people. I continued past them and on to the gaming tables and observed the card games for a while. They didn't seem very interesting to me. A great cheer arose from a different sort of table and I went to check it out. The roulette wheel was beautiful. The spinning and the bouncing marbles made it seem like a lot more fun than anything else I had seen so far. Excited, I exchanged my ten dollars for a coloured disc. I watched what the other players did and placed my disc on a number. The handsome young man in the tuxedo spun the wheel and the marbles flew. Around and around they went, making me dizzy. When they slowed and stopped, I stood there, mesmerised. The young man pushed a small stack of coloured disks towards me. I could only gather them and excuse myself. I had to pee.

After I washed my hands, I dug the discs out of

my pocket where I had stashed them. I couldn't remember what each of the different colours was worth, but I had six of them. Feeling calmer, I returned to the table and placed two of them on a number. I won again! This time, I left all but the four I still had in my hand on the table. And won for the third time in a row.

The table was beginning to attract more people as word spread—everyone wanted to be near a lucky streak. A little warning tendril crept up my spine, and, this time, I listened to my instincts. Gathering my winnings, I brought them to the cash window. The efficient man there counted, calculated, and extracted bills from a drawer. When he doled the money out to me, it took every ounce of my seventeen-year old restraint not to scream in victory. Instead, I carefully folded most of my twenty-seven hundred dollars and placed the money in a zippered section of my purse. I then hung the purse diagonally around my body with the main part of it snug to my belly and put my jacket on over top. I bought myself a celebratory bag of goodies and, luxury of luxuries, took a taxi back to my room.

The next day, I rose early and walked in the direction of my former employment. I had decided that it would be better if my landlord thought I was still working. There was a coffee shop a few blocks further away and that is where I bought my first meal with cash money.

I knew that if I kept this up, my winnings would be gone, and then what? While I sipped a second cup of coffee, I decided to make a list for myself. Jacinthe always teased me about my lists. "How can you need a list for stuff you do every day?" she would say. "Does it say it's time to blow your nose? 'Cuz you got a big booger in your left nostril." Then she would laugh hysterically as I frantically searched for a tissue.

The spasm that squeezed my heart left me breathless. Shaking, I put my coffee cup down. I was alone in a big, strange city with no friends and no family. There would be no Jacinthe walking through the door to sit with me and gossip about the other diners. I could just imagine what she would say about the cute guy at the counter. She would say, "That one needs a good seeing to. Look at the state of him!" I smiled as the first tear plopped onto my empty hand.

The waitress was making the rounds with fresh coffee for her customers. I scrunched the napkin in my fist and blotted my face. This would never do. I flipped the paper place mat over and, when she arrived at my table, I asked her for more coffee and if she could lend me a pen. With a smile, she gave me both. There was a nice tip in her future—no need for a premonition to foresee that one.

Shrugging off the memory of Jacinthe and all things Island, I started on my list. If I was to get and keep a job, or even have a decent conversation with anyone, the first thing I needed was some way to disguise my eyes. Of course, I had seen people wearing sunglasses, but they would be too dark and inappropriate for indoors. Maybe I could get regular glasses with a bit of a tint in the lenses but without a prescription. Should be easy enough. Secondly, and while I had a little time, I would gather information about how things work in a city—my ignorance was going to get me into trouble sooner rather than later.

20

A Library would be a good, safe place to start. After that, well, it would depend on what I found out at the Library. I wrote down 'write home' as my third item and crossed it out; I wasn't ready for that yet.

With the five-dollar bill quite obvious on my table, the waitress was happy to point me in the direction of not one but two places that sold glasses. I smiled, squinting my eyes so she wouldn't be frightened, and left.

The glasses were easy, and it wouldn't take me long to adjust to the grey shading. More importantly, they disguised my hazel eyes very well. It was like they disappeared.

At home, we had a Library van that visited every few weeks. How could that have prepared me for my first experience at a city Library? Who knew there were so many books? At first, I just stood and looked at them, lined up side by side, row after row. I think I must have cried a little because one of the librarians asked if I was alright. I could only nod.

I spent the rest of the day and part of the evening there, stepping out only for a bite to eat. The same librarian who had spoken to me earlier asked if I was finding what I needed.

"I need to read everything," I answered. Somewhat abashed at my outburst, I hoped I didn't sound crazy, but she smiled.

"Is this your first time in a big Library?" she asked.

I nodded my head.

"I'm nearly done my shift, but if you can come back about mid-morning tomorrow, I'll show you around and explain how it's organised."

"Really?" I whispered.

21

She smiled. "See you then."

The next day, Moira toured me around each of the sections of the Library, which to my surprise included music, and introduced me to the Dewey Decimal Classification System. I was in heaven. When my very own Library card was placed in my hand, I felt happier than I had in a long time. The next few weeks passed in a glory of words and music. I couldn't get enough.

***

The thud of fist and boot on flesh repeated over and over. The high, tiny windows let in, thankfully, little light. Details were in deep shadow and I could not make out the features of the assailant's face. I could, however, smell his rancid sweat and hear his laboured breathing; he had been at this for some time. He didn't care that the man on the floor could not possibly be alive with his neck at such an angle.

***

I woke sick and shaken. The sick feeling lasted well into the afternoon and I made myself stay away from the Library. Moira would know something was wrong and I didn't want to have to lie to her.

This was the second time I had had such a virulent dream. Neither of them was

anything like a regular dream, the difference was palpable. I was a bystander, a witness, to a seemingly real event complete with smells, sounds, and tastes—it always struck me as hideous that I could actually taste the smell of blood—and, worse yet, the cloying miasma of fear and hopelessness, ruthless power and madness.

When the same dream came again the following night, I got up and got dressed. I needed

22

to get out. I needed to not sleep.

A pamphlet I had glanced through at the Library described a safe place where women could go at any time of the day or night. I took a taxi there. The attendant was kind and showed me to the main living area where, she assured me, there was always someone awake who wanted to talk or play cards.

Four women in the middle of a Scrabble game glanced at me as I stood at the doorway to the main living area. Another pair played Cribbage. There were some comfortable-looking chairs facing a television turned on and at low volume. A popular talk show had just begun. I sat where I could see most of the room and, between keeping an eye on any activity and the small distraction of late-night viewing, it was easy to stay awake. When I left the next morning to get some breakfast, I put a generous donation in the battered wooden box at the door.

I was at the Library as soon as it opened. There were dozens of books on premonitions, precognition, clairvoyance, and other psychic phenomenon. I studied what each of the words meant and decided that 'vision' was a more accurate definition of what happened to me. I couldn't believe I hadn't thought of visiting a larger Library before. The old book-mobile van that came to the village had a selection of battered romance and mystery novels, but mostly carried children's stories, and I wouldn't be caught dead in the Library at school—only the nerdiest of nerds went there, besides is wasn't much bigger than the book-mobile. The optimist in me must have shunted the likelihood of another vision into the never-gonna-happen-again box, so why waste my time? Right. Lame excuse. I was determined to find if there was anything out there to explain why these visions happened and, more importantly, how to make them never happen again.

That first vision I had in the city, however, seemed to act like a catalyst for others, many others, to begin their nightmare stalk through my mind. The pharmacy had a whole section of over-the-counter drugs to help me stay awake but, wouldn't you know, they either made me sick to my stomach or just plain didn't work. My research at the Library gave me a few avenues to pursue and pursue them I did. But as the days passed, sleep deprivation began to make it impossible for me to concentrate. The words just didn't make sense anymore. Depressed and frustrated, I left the Library and shuffled along the sidewalk in no particular direction.

A veil descended over my eyes. Startled out of my melancholy, I stopped; the other pedestrians broke around me like a wave. I could still see the actual world, but as a kind of faded version behind my most recent vision that overlaid it. Disoriented, I sat on the curb and put my head in my hands, forced to experience the macabre violence that might happen somewhere, sometime in the future. Lurching to my feet, my only clear thought was escape. My desperate need wrenched an iota of strength and clarity from somewhere within me and, with it, I picked up the few things in my room and made a quick trip to the casino where, thankfully, my luck still held. I had no one to say goodbye to except Moira at the Library and I regretted leaving without a word. Old suitcase in hand, I took a taxi to the bus station and bought a one-way ticket away from this city.

**

In my tiny Island village, only the lives of a few dozen people whispered inside my head. Those visions had been mostly about who was cheating on whom, who had charged a bit too much for their catch, or who had won at the fish cake contest. It had all been somewhat annoying to me but fairly innocent. Admittedly, the first few times, I decided they were just clearer dreams than normal and really wanted to believe this. But, through the ever-so-efficient village gossip, it did not take long to hear about the goings-on, and what did go on matched my dreams in every detail. These clear dreams had been true visions. When I first realised this, it felt like a fist had reached inside my chest and tightened around my heart. A moment later, I breathed a small sigh of relief. I had learned my lesson with the *bad* dock episode. I had not mentioned the dreams to anyone, not even Jacinthe—there was no knowing what the people of the village would have done to me and, maybe, to my family.

In the mornings, my mother would stare at me at breakfast. I kept my eyes down and concentrated on my porridge. Somehow, she knew, and it didn't take a clear dream or any kind of vision to figure that out. She had always been distant but, since my father's death, she had treated me like I had a contagious disease, always keeping me at arm's length and always watching me. It was creepy. The only difference between her and everybody else in the village was that, every few years, she wanted to look directly into my eyes. I wouldn't let her. Now, I wondered if she had been trying to tell me something. She could have just said it.

After that first city, I traveled in a southerly direction and kept generally to the coast where the casinos were more likely to be located. I would arrive in a community, find a room, pretend to look for work, and spend time at the Library or at the movies and, for a short time, all would be well.

Then it would start again. A single, repeated episode of violence became multiple, repeated episodes. It was beginning to seem like a straight-forward mathematical equation: more people equalled more visions. I always managed to endure it for a few weeks, thinking that maybe the thing I saw would play itself out in the real world and I would not have to preview it anymore. It seemed like a good guess.

Perversely, and over time, the visions worsened and became increasingly gruesome, showcasing the darkest of human behaviour. My theory was that very bad things must give off stronger emanations, sort of like the squeaky wheel getting the grease. Whatever the reason—and I had no idea why these visions came to me—they would soon become unbearable and I would move on to the next community, yearning for that tiny window of peace that opened when I first arrived at a new place.

I never tried to warn anyone about what I saw. It would have been a futile effort in any case since I didn't know the people in my visions, and so couldn't contact them anyway. There were times when I would recognise something in the background or could tell a bit about the timing or an exact location, especially if there was something obvious like, say, snow on the ground or a distinctive building. It was a different and often worse kind of torment when I would read in the papers or hear on the news about some crime or attack that I had seen but hadn't done anything to stop. My visions were useless in preventing the fate they foretold, and my guilt at what I should be able to do and could not, deepened.

I thought of my mother and her long list of expectations and rules: stand up straight, be a good girl, be quiet, hold your stomach in. But, ironically, she never hounded me about the overly long bangs camouflaging my eyes. I asked her about that one day, and, without warning, she slapped me across the face. "Don't ever question me," she hissed through tight lips, then proceeded to fuss with the sleeves of my shirt, tugging them down. "There, that's better," she said and sent me on some trivial errand in the village. I did as I was told, cheek stinging and confused by a mother who I tried hard to please, but I was resigned and saddened and filled with inadequacy at ever being able to do so.

My visions were real situations that I should be able to avert and real people that I should be able to help. But, once again, just like at home, I was useless and inadequate.

The letters I wrote home had become a regular part of my week, an item on my list. Jacinthe would have laughed at that. I rented a post box as soon as I arrived in a new area and sent the address in my next letter saying that any mail sent there would be held for me. I checked every day, but in the three years I had been gone, only one letter had arrived, and it was from Jacinthe. I had read it so many times that it was getting thin and frayed, and I promised myself I would photocopy it before it fell apart altogether. She said she missed me, that the village was the same, and that she was dating one of the Gallant boys. She said my family was fine and that my brothers would soon be shaving. I could barely remember what my brothers looked like and asked in my next letter if there was any way she could send a photograph. I hadn't heard back yet. One day I might even gather the nerve to call my mother.

***

The room was lit by a bare bulb hanging from the ceiling by its power cord. It was cold and smelled of urine and other things best left unidentified. There was a ratty sleeping bag on a filthy mattress and, huddled in the middle, was a woman of indeterminate age. The bones in her face were as visible as though she were a skeleton specimen in a lab. Her scrawny arms were scabby with needle marks and burns. The needle she held in her hand shook ever so slightly and she took a slow breath. Steady again, she injected herself.

I couldn't get a clear view through the dirty window beyond the woman; there was no hint of her location. It was cold. I knew this not only because my visions spared me nothing but also, when she breathed, little clouds of vapour would appear. The vision held me until no more little clouds would ever appear again.

***

Sweaty and twisted in my blankets, I woke. I didn't often see self-inflicted deaths and I found

28

them despairingly senseless. There was so much violence inflicted by others that to inflict violence upon one's self seemed somehow gratuitous.

I showered and put on shorts and a brightly-coloured top. Bright colours cheered me and the deep breathing technique I had learned cleared my head. I soon found my Zenlike calm and stepped out into the soft early morning. I continued breathing deeply, only now it was to saturate myself with the ocean's aromatic cleansing and not to distract my stomach from its post-vision heaving. A few early-morning risers speed-walked along the shore and, if I focused on the gentle waves, the city that loomed behind me disappeared.

"Excuse me," a man said.

My idyll was shattered. I jumped, my nerves on edge and heart racing.

"Sorry. Didn't mean to startle you," he said. The sun was behind him and I had to shield my eyes to see him. He looked harmless. Looks could be deceiving. I waited.

"Umm," he began

His hesitation suited me; maybe he would just go away.

"Umm, he repeated. "I just wondered if you knew if there was a coffee shop nearby that was open. At this time." He looked at his watch. "It's early." He stumbled to a halt, flustered, not encouraged by my standoffishness.

I was twenty-one years old, not a gullible child, and wary of a strange man on an almost-deserted beach. He was taller than I was—easy to do—and likely wasn't hiding a weapon in his biking outfit, tight as it was. Brown hair, brown eyes, very tentative smile. He was turning to go.

"Wait," I said. He turned back. "There's a great spot about a mile that way." I pointed north. "They roast their own beans and serve food."

His smile widened. It was a nice smile, which must have been what made me blurt, "I was heading there myself. Want some company?" I couldn't believe I'd said that. Me, who never approached anyone and discouraged even the most innocuous conversational opening, had just asked a total stranger on a sort-of date.

Without the slightest hesitation, he said, "That would be great!" He retrieved his bicycle from where he had balanced it against a telephone pole and began to walk.

A few seconds later, I followed, stunned at myself.

"I'm Peter, by the way."

"Olivia," I responded, giving him my formal name. 'Flotsy' just made people ask questions.

We chatted about the area. He was new here, just transferred in with a bank where he sold mortgages to people. He loved his job for exactly this reason.

"You love selling mortgages?"

He laughed; the warm sound of it smoothed the last of my nervousness. "No, no, not that part," he explained. "I love to meet different people, see different cities, and explore the surrounding areas. It's great! The bank pays for the move, and I don't have to go through the hassle of looking for a job." He looked over at me. "How about you? Been here long?"

This was exactly why I never was more than a

passing acquaintance to the people I met wherever I lived. It was hard work to invent a history for myself and remain consistent over a period of time, however short that time might turn out to be. Most people were satisfied with generalities, like that I'd just moved here from up east and was looking for work in a—and this part changed depending on where I was—restaurant or a fish plant or an office. This time, I used the fail-safe story that I was on a short vacation after a recent death in the family. This made almost everyone uncomfortable and eager to talk about something else, anything else. Peter was no different.

"Oh. I'm sorry," he mumbled.

"It's okay," I said softly, looking down. I held the pose for a moment, and then looked up with a fake-bright smile and asked, "So, where have you lived so far?"

Relieved, Peter spent the next hour telling me all about his life, about the places he'd been, and about some of the things he had seen. When we parted, there was no mention of a second meeting.

The death-in-the-family card worked every time. Even though this was exactly what I wanted, watching him cycle away was hard.

I had promised myself many times that when I found the right doctor or the right psychologist or the right... shaman, witch, wise-woman, whatever, that I would go talk to him or her. Books were marvelous, and I had learned massive amounts of material on all manner of behavioural disorders, unexplained phenomena, weird occurrences, and speculation. The mind remained a vastly unexplored and complex territory in which, according to some, anything could happen. But I had yet to come across something resembling my dilemma, and certainly had not found a solution.

This was why I watched him go. No one could understand what happens to me and, if I told them, they would not just walk away, they would run, and likely call the authorities to warn them about the crazy woman in town.

Chapter 3

I drifted from place to place, searching for that one location or that invisible line I would cross to silence the ever more frequent visions that assailed me. I continued my research, reading everything I could get my hands on, writing to experts, and calling help lines, still hoping to find something—anything—to make them stop. I kept copious notes and made graphs of my visions to determine if there was some kind of thread linking them together. The scrapbook where I accumulated and analysed my research had already grown to a dozen fat volumes and I was no closer to finding help or to finding someone with whom I could identify. It seemed that I was unique. Oh joy.

One very convenient thing I learned in my travelling was that if you have the money, it was relatively easy to obtain authentic-looking identification and any other papers that a person might need. I learned to drive and invested in my very own transportation which doubled as my accommodation. It had become a nuisance to pack and unpack so often, and I had a few, okay, a lot, of books and CDs that I could not bear to part with, and that was in addition to my scrapbooks and the guitar I had acquired up along the way, and they were getting cumbersome to lug from place to place.

The camper van turned out to be an excellent decision. There was always some sort of campground on the outskirts of a town and, if I didn't stay in the town itself too long, I could sleep like a normal person for a time.

One pattern I had observed was that it took a bit of time in a new location before the visions associated with that place manifested themselves. Those few days and sometimes even weeks were heaven and, even though I was lonely, I had my books and my music to keep me company.

The life of a nomad can be interesting assuming you are in fact a nomad at heart. Alas, I was not, and longed to settle in one place. Funny how a beautiful garden lit something inside me; I could feel the soil, dark and moist, in my hands and under my fingernails. I just knew that I would be happy whiling away the early hours of the morning admiring the shoots, trimming to shape and encourage growth, and, afterwards, preparing food with the unmistakable taste of fresh herbs and vegetables. Even if this was not to be for me, I took every opportunity to talk to gardeners, landscapers, and nursery employees, and to immerse myself in every place where things grew. This passion brought me to forests and swamps, to the seashore and to the hills, and to parks and botanical gardens.

It had not taken long to outgrow my camper van and graduate to my beloved Winnebago—not one of the big ones, but a smaller, sleeker version that would be easy to drive on less-travelled and more secluded roads. I called him Harvey, my own very special name for the RV—the *haitch* being a sadly misunderstood letter in my home village.

I filled my days with a regular routine that kept me both busy and sane. The years passed.

***

My visions suddenly, and devastatingly,

34

multiplied. They must have been crouching, building to some unholy threshold, and like an avalanche, I was at their mercy. They shook me like the helpless prey that I was.

Constantly changing location no longer alleviated this new onslaught of horror; the formula I had so carefully adhered to had become useless. Utterly exhausted, I pulled into a campground whose name I instantly forgot and lumbered my way to its most remote campsite.

I was desperate to stay awake. At first, I downed a wide selection of over-the-counter uppers hoping to find one that worked; I didn't care anymore if they made me sick. I drank quantities of thick, black coffee and took cold showers. I practiced on my little guitar until my fingers bled. I began a macabre ritual of setting my alarm clock at fifteen-minute intervals and pricking myself with a sewing needle. If only I could stay awake long enough, I convinced myself, the bloody savagery and unspeakable brutality of my visions would have, in actuality, occurred somewhere and would be done torturing me. Day blurred into day, and nights were an exercise in masochism.

I wandered out of the campground and into the town. I couldn't remember its name, even if I had known it at some point. Not that I really tried to remember the places I'd been—they would all soon be tainted by my curse. I was vaguely aware of how hungry I was, but I couldn't let such a trivial thing distract me. With every breath and every shuffling step, I clung to the sole purpose of staying awake. So far, and I prayed that it would remain so, I had not had a recurrence of the veil-over-my-eyes-in-the-daytime episode.

In my peripheral vision, the glare of fluorescent lights distracted me. The doors opened like magic. I smiled at myself; I was losing it. Through a haze of fatigue, I recognised the smell of a pharmacy. Funny how they all smelled the same.

"Can I help you?"

I swivelled around, grabbing onto the handy counter when the room spun about in a lazy circle. "Yes, please." I was proud at how the courtesy of a 'please' came so easily to me and I smiled at him.

He took a step back. His mother had not drilled him in the niceties of polite conversation.

I continued. "I need to stay awake." I was getting good at communicating, given that I hadn't done it in some time.

"Are you going on a trip?" he asked me.

What did that have to do with anything? Then it dawned on me that he likely thought I was driving somewhere and had to remain alert. "Oh, yes. A big trip." I couldn't look him in the eye; I could never look a person in the eye when I lied. Below me were tiers of magazines, one of which had Madagascar splashed across the cover. "To Madagascar," I added.

"All those shots," he said.

"What? Where?" I hunkered down and looked frantically around the store. A woman walking towards the counter stopped, turned around, and quickly headed in the opposite direction.

Bewildered, I glanced at the store clerk who looked at me with disgust.

"NA meets at the Y."

He was speaking in code.

36

Slowly and enunciating with emphasis like I was a moron, he clarified. "Narcotics Anonymous. At the YMCA on Sherwood Street." He pointed to the door.

My reserves of polite interaction came to an abrupt end. "You don't understand." I glared at him through the flush of embarrassment I could feel heating my face.

He continued to stand there with his arm out and his index finger pointing towards the door, as if I hadn't spoken. A second clerk walked purposefully towards me.

The brief flare of energy and clarity that had sustained me through my discourse with the clerk dissipated like it had never been. Head held high, I turned and walked to the door, admittedly not as gracefully as I would have liked. I could hear scurrying behind me as they gathered the rolls of toilet paper that had toppled when my elbow accidentally connected with the tower in my path.

Shortly thereafter a squad car pulled up beside me. The policeman asked me for identification. I patted my pockets but seemed to have misplaced my wallet. I waited for the next question. Instead, he took my arm and guided me into the back seat of his patrol car. It felt good to sit down. I hoped he wouldn't make the siren go; my head hurt, and the noise would be terribly loud this close to its source.

Soon, he pulled into a parking lot and escorted me to a waiting room. I knew it was a waiting room but not exactly what all the people were waiting for. None of them looked injured. I waved my fingers in a little goodbye to the nice policeman. He gave me the same look as the store clerk had. What was it?

37

Did I have something gross on my face? I scrubbed at it and stared at my hands. They were filthy. I must have forgotten to wash this morning. I wondered what time it was. I looked around with the vague hope that maybe a clock would be on one of the walls. No clock but there was one of those calendars with a picture on the top and the dates on the bottom. I could just make out the name of the month. June? How could it be June?

I experienced a vague sense of alarm. I should get back to my campsite. Everything would be all right if I could get back to Harvey. I was a bit unsteady but made it through the door and into the unbearably bright light. There were steps. I didn't remember climbing steps. I fell in slow-motion. It was kind of nice. When I hit my head on the sidewalk, it bounced a bit. Who knew that your head could bounce? Little silver stars were everywhere. *Pretty*, I thought.

***

I needed to pee. I didn't need to open my eyes to find my way to the tiny toilet in Harvey. My legs didn't work! Alarmed, I opened my eyes and tried to sit up. My body refused to obey me other than— and I could have been mistaken about this—my eyes seemed to be open. There was a terrible greenish light that flickered and made my head hurt even more. But I really needed to pee and tried to get up again.

"Just pee," said an exasperated voice somewhere to my right. "There's a tube plugged into you. You know. Down there."

I turned my head toward the voice, which was a very bad mistake. Bile surged up my throat. Endless

38

heaves wrenched my body into spasms. At some point in what must be the hell that my mother always warned me about, a second voice said, "What a mess!! God, I hate these ones."

Rough hands manipulated me. When I realised they were taking my clothes off, I flailed about. Unbelievably, the second bout of nausea was worse than the first. Weak, sweat-soaked, shaking, and defeated, I let them do anything they wanted.

A laser stabbed me in the eyeball. A part of me accepted this as something I must deserve. Another, very small part, somehow knew that I was in a hospital and that someone was checking the contraction and dilation of my pupils.

Gentle hands probed my skull. I clenched my entire body.

"Relax."

Easy for him to say; he wouldn't be puking himself inside out any second.

"You banged your head and have a minor concussion. You'll feel better in a few days. Now, try to follow my finger."

I squeezed my eyes shut and imagined that finger jabbing me in the eye.

Two cold thumbs pried my right eyelids apart and I stared into a man's face, looking slightly impatient, and with an impressive five o'clock shadow.

"You were reported as being under the influence of unknown drugs and possibly dangerous to yourself and others. The police brought you here and, when you tried to leave, you fell down the steps. You're in the Psychiatric Ward of St. Mary's Hospital. You with me so far?"

I couldn't simply blink my eye with his thumbs holding it firmly opened and doubted if opening my left eye would constitute a sort of reverse blink. I resigned myself to a slight nod, expecting to vomit some internal organ—that's all there was left—directly into his face, I hoped. He seemed to realise this and removed his thumbs from my person.

"My name is Doctor Peters. A nurse will be in shortly to help you bathe and dress, and then she will give you something to help you rest. Of course, she will also be in to wake you periodically," he wrote a note on his clipboard then looked at me again, "because of the concussion."

I tried to clear my aching throat. He reached for a cup with a bendy-straw and put it in my hand. I sipped.

"Thanks," I whispered.

The next half hour was humiliating in the extreme. The nurse was very thorough, and every inch of my skin felt like it had been rung between an abrasive pair of rollers. She made me put on one of those hospital shirts that tied in the back and left your bum out. When she was done, she propped me up, stuck a can of something in my hand and said, "Drink this. All of it."

It was revolting. She knew exactly how revolting. Strong arms folded across her chest; she scowled until I was sucking air. She took the empty can from my hand, indicated that I should lie down, and turned the light out. "Go to sleep," she ordered.

My eyes snapped shut and, with no strength left in me to keep it at bay, I slept.

The aroma of toast made me smile a little. I was starving, and it was exactly what I wanted to eat. I stretched my arms over my head. Every muscle involved with that simple move hurt. I opened my eyes and, very carefully and slowly, surveyed the room. My mind was functioning a bit and I remembered the Doctor's words. This was not just any room—it was a room in the Psychiatric Ward of a hospital. There were two beds separated by a flimsy curtain on a rail, which was open at the moment. I had a nightstand on my left with a matching cupboard at a ninety-degree angle to it.

An orderly wheeled a cart into the room and put a small tray on my nightstand. Behind him, a tiny, ancient man scuttled in, stole my breakfast, and scuttled out. The orderly didn't even look around, he simply placed a second tray on my table. I brought it towards me before anybody else could take it.

What kind of a place was this? How sick were the patients? How do I get out of here?

"He does that with all the new ones," snickered the girl in the bed beside me.

I recognised the voice as the one who had told me about the catheter. I looked over. "Um… thanks for your help. Earlier." My face was hot with embarrassment.

She shrugged. "Name's Harriet. I'm schizophrenic, and I recently had an encounter with something sharp." She raised her leg and showed me the broad bandage covering her calf. She looked at me expectantly.

"Flotsy," I began. What do I tell her? Keep it simple, I thought. "I see bad things and fell and hit my head."

"Oh." She returned to her breakfast, ripping her

41

bread into tiny pieces before rolling each piece into an even tinier ball.

I stared at her as a sense of refreshing insignificance washed over me. When you're just one crazy person among many crazy people, you didn't stand out. And whatever was in the medication had let me sleep unmolested by visions. This could be the best thing that had ever happened to me.

On the third day by my, albeit unreliable, reckoning, a nurse brought me a small pile of material consisting of an outfit of loose trousers with an elastic waistband, a tunic, and a pair of one-size-fits-all open-backed slippers, all in a faded shade of puce. "Put them on," she said and closed the curtain a couple of feet giving me some privacy and at the same time allowing her to keep an eye on me.

I swung my feet over the side of the bed and sat for a few seconds to make sure my head would remain affixed to my shoulders. The whirling stopped and, still sitting, I took off my night shirt and dragged the tunic over my head. I rested for a minute, slightly breathless, and pulled the trousers on as high as they would go before sliding off the bed until my feet touched the cold tile. I stood. So far, so good. I finished pulling up the pants, dropped the slippers to the floor, and toed my feet into them. I opened the drawer in the small cabinet near my bed, thinking my glasses would be there. It was empty.

"Have you seen my glasses?" I asked the nurse.

"What glasses? Your eyesight is fine. Follow me," she said.

I guess in here strange eyes were not strange at all.

I shuffled along, which was the only way to keep these too-big slippers on. She told me that I was about to undergo a psychiatric evaluation. Even though I knew that this was bound to happen, given where I was, I was terrified. I was definitely not at my sharpest and only hoped that I could be vague yet relatively normal-sounding. The story of my life was unusual, but I had never hurt anyone or stolen anything, and I certainly wasn't the only person in the world who lived like a gypsy, under the radar. Still, who hadn't read stories about what can happen in the loony bin?

Doctor Reynolds was a woman of about fifty with muddy brown eyes and a tight mouth. Her hair hung straight to her shoulders and she continuously pushed it back behind her ears. Had she not heard of scrunchies or hair clips?

"Flotsy, is it?"

She peered at me for the first time and I felt a little sullied. She asked me basic information—date of birth, address, employment, family, friends—all of which I had answered a number of times already. I doubted if anyone working here communicated with anyone else who worked here and, if that was the case, there was precious little chance of them communicating with the patients.

"Tell me about these... visions of yours." The left side of her upper lip lifted in a sneer as she spoke. "When was the first time you had one? How old were you?"

My mind froze. Where had she heard about my visions? Harriet? But, for all I knew, in the state I'd

43

been in, I could have been screaming out my hard-kept secrets to all and sundry.

I glanced up at Doctor Reynolds and quickly looked back at my clenched hands. I desperately wanted help, but I even more desperately wanted help from someone who would listen with an open mind. My true story was not for this cynical, burned-out woman in front of me. It would be easy to bluff my way out of here: I could tell her I had terrible insomnia and took too many over-the-counter drugs—it happens—and fell and bumped my head. But I was back to myself now and didn't have much practice lying to anyone let alone a supposed mind doctor. On the other hand, I was safe in here and fairly certain that, if I was released, it would only be a matter of days before the visions returned and I would be right back on the seemingly never-ending wheel of self-destruction. The magic blue pill distributed at bedtime had given me blessedly dreamless sleep and, for this, I was prepared to compromise my principles, at least until I could talk to someone who would sympathise and give me a bottomless prescription. I could then gladly begin a brand-new life, one where I could live in a community, get a job, meet people, make friends—even have a boyfriend. Who knew? It was a worthy goal.

"Well. You do speak English, don't you?" Dr. Reynolds was getting impatient.

I'd keep in simple and close to the truth.

"I'm thirty-two and had my first vision when I was thirteen years old. It was of an accident at the dock where I saw my father killed." This painful memory never failed to hurt, and, to my dismay, I

44

burst into tears. Racking sobs shook my entire body. What was the matter with me?

I was whisked out of Doctor Reynolds's office and escorted back to my room.

"Swallow this, dearie, it'll make you feel better." The ward's nurse put one of the blue pills in my hand and held out a paper cup filled with water. I reached for it and stared at how my hand shook, like it belonged to someone else.

"Never you mind," she tutted, and brought the cup to my lips so I could drink. "There. All better." She helped me lay down on the bed and brought the covers up to my shoulders.

"Thanks," I murmured as the blackness descended.

My next session was with a different doctor, this time a young man named Campbell. He looked like a graduate, which could mean he was not jaded or that he had fresh new ideas as yet untried or, worst case, had no idea what he was doing. As least it was not Doctor Reynolds.

"So. How are we today?"

Oh, no. Not an auspicious opening question. "Fine," I replied.

He spent a few minutes reading my chart—if that's what they called it in a psych ward.

"So. I see that the wound on your head is healing nicely." He smiled at me. Nice smile. "So," he repeated

This could take a while.

He chewed on the end of his pen.

"So," he began again, "how do you feel about these visions?"

How do I feel? How do I feel? The tears started

to burn at the back of my eyes and my throat hurt.

"I feel scared and helpless," I whispered. "I feel bewildered and useless. I can't sleep, I can't work, I don't have any friends, and I can't go home to my family. I'm alone." Tears poured silently down my cheeks; I felt them drip off my chin and plop onto the backs of my forearms which were tightly crossed at my chest. What was happening to me?

It was about then that the orderly brought me back to my room and the nice nurse gave me a little blue pill and put me to bed.

Man, I gotta get a grip.

***

"Good. You're awake. It's time for a play-date!" Harriet was hovering over me, her myriad braids swaying an inch from my eyes. She plucked at the covers on my bed, limped out the doorway, and turned left.

Over the last few days, I had met my fellow 'residents,' as the staff called us. It turned out that I was in a ward with minimum-risk mental patients. That meant patients with little or no violent behaviour, just behaviour that was in some way unacceptable for normal social interaction. The mission on the wall at the nurses' station said that they were supposed to encourage a normal routine—a routine that would sustain us in the real world.

I had been given two changes of clothing and was expected to be up and dressed, and in the dining hall by 7:30. We helped prepare the food, loaded it into serving bowls and platters, and sat down to eat like one big happy family. I zeroed in on the residents who worked the most efficiently and insinuated myself into their small group. Harriet, not surprisingly, limped around the kitchen, giving advice, sampling food, and generally making a noisy nuisance of herself. You couldn't help smiling at her, though, with her braids swinging and her mouth in a wide grin.

Harriet popped back into the doorway of our room. "Come on sleepy-head. Play-date! You'll miss all the fun!"

I put on my slippers and followed. This would be another group-therapy attempt by the psychiatrists; the previous three that I had attended didn't get much further than all of us gathered in the same room. The doctors were trying to get not-so-sane people to participate in sane activities. So far, their success rate was a smidgen above zero.

There were a few other late-comers wandering down the hall toward the multi-function room at the far end. This was a room filled with natural light from tall windows facing south and was about the size of a small auditorium. There were chairs set up around card tables, an assortment of couches, a big television screen installed high up on one wall and protected by fine mesh, and a few large, boardroom-style tables. These last had been positioned to form a rectangle with chairs placed around the outside perimeter. It looked like we were going to have a business meeting. Ha.

Harriet was waving madly at me from the far end. She had saved me a seat.

Doctor Campbell stood at the door. He kept glancing down at his clipboard as if it held all the answers. The residents were getting restless, and the orderlies were kept busy herding strays back to their seats.

Suddenly decisive, Doctor Campbell strode into the room and squeezed through a gap between the tables to stand in the open space they made. We quieted as he turned slowly in a circle to study each of us. When he looked at me, his eyes softened. Did he like me? I had never seen it before, not so surprising when you consider that, until very recently, nobody looked me in the eyes at all.

When he had completed his scrutiny, he glanced at the clipboard. "Okay. Here's what we're going to do. First," he pointed to a big black guy with a bald head, "Jeffrey, please give one of these to each person." Doctor Campbell took an envelope from one of the pockets of his white lab coat and handed it to Jeffrey. Inside was a selection of glittery stars, the kind that you can lick and stick to a flat surface.

As Jeffrey did this, I noticed that the stars came in four colours. Sheesh, the Doc's going to divide us into matching colour groups—how original. What will he do next? Ask us to gather matching colour residents together into sub-groups and brainstorm ways to help ourselves become normal citizens?

Yup. That's just what he did. It took about ten minutes for everyone to get back on their feet, separate the tables, and put the chairs around them in this new configuration. "See how well we work together, doc," I muttered under my breath, "just like good little children." The next step, theoretically, was for the people with the same colour star to sit together at the same table. The good doctor hadn't counted on Harriet who, while the rest of us did as we were told and moved tables and chairs, 'borrowed' stars from bewildered patients and stuck them to her forehead. In a few minutes, she had quite a collection and hobbled over to a reflective surface—one of the windows—to admire her handiwork. She clapped her hands and ooooh'd and aaaaah'd at her latest work of art.

All the moving about had re-opened Harriet's leg wound. Happy that this drew even more attention to her, she swung her leg about, making it bleed freely. The orderlies wheeled in a bed, strapped her to it, raised her leg, and applied compression. The wide grin on her face was only slightly marred by a wince of pain as they rolled her out of the room. The de-starred residents shuffled to their favourite spots in the room, the session over.

Doctor Campbell was quite red in the face. I almost felt sorry for him.

***

There was a definite pecking order among the residents, especially among those who had been here longest. The same squabbles and protective stances were as evident here as in any—albeit somewhat more functional—home. There were the mother types who tried to scold and feed and groom everyone; the youngest-children types who expected attention every minute of the day; the middle children who remained on the fringes; and the oldest children who were weary from the burden of being responsible for everyone else. The father types were the worst: they gave orders and expected to be obeyed. Their actions required the most frequent interventions by the orderlies and nurses. I sometimes wondered why they were even in this ward, but I guess the reality was that we would encounter bullying types and had to learn to either deal with them or avoid them. I chose to keep well off their radar.

Lastly, were the black sheep—my favourites. These were usually the manic-depressives who were wildly creative in their manic phase. Sometimes it got out of hand, like when John gathered as many people as he could into a single bathroom cubicle in order to submit a new entry into the Guinness Book of World Records for 'most loonies in a loo.' He thought this was hilarious and even had the orderlies chuckling. It was all the weight on the toilet that snapped the pipe from the wall and flooded not only the bathroom but the floor below which was, unfortunately, an administrative office. The records in the filing cabinets were ruined. John quickly slid into a deep depression, but I could see the glint of amusement in his eye that lasted well into the meds that he humbly swallowed.

For my part, most people ignored me. I had cast myself as a middle child, content to observe. All the reading I had done to figure out my own situation gave me insight into the behaviour of the people around me, including the staff and doctors. I knew how to act to keep myself here without drawing undue attention. I happily took my meds, slept without visions, and, for now, that was enough.

One day, there was a new guy. He was tall and gangly. The skin on his hands and arms was leathery like it had been baked for years in the hot sun. I didn't get a good look at his face.

Harriet immediately stood in his path, hands on her hips, and introduced herself. He sidled by her, took up position at one of the tall windows, and stared at the sun. Amazingly, Harriet did not pursue him. She had a puzzled look on her face and returned to the sketch pad she doodled on, designing something or other. Her work was quite lovely when the mood struck.

The air in the room seemed to thicken and dust began to swirl in a lazy dance. Alarmed, I looked around to see if anyone else had noticed. No one had. Now, even more alarmed, I wondered if this could be a new type of vision. The inside of my head began to expand, pushing against my skull. I must have passed out for a moment because the next thing I knew the new guy was gripping my arm and guiding me through the multi-function room and down the hallway. Harriet didn't even look up. No one looked up. It was as if they were in another world. Or maybe I was. I couldn't seem to focus my eyes very well and couldn't get a look at the face of the man towing me along. Maybe he was a new doctor or a new staff person I hadn't seen yet. Whoever he was, I couldn't resist going with him and I couldn't think. He was probably taking me to my room to fix this weird new head thing.

We did stop in my room but only long enough for him to gather my few things into a pillowcase. We continued down the hallway. An orderly waited at the locked door that led out of the ward and opened it for us. He seemed dazed, but I couldn't trust my own senses, everything was off and blurry. I sneezed from the dust that whirled around us and the guy handed me a tissue. We took an elevator down to the main floor and walked out of the building. I wasn't even surprised to see Harvey parked at the curb. He settled me into the passenger seat, buckled my seatbelt, and slid behind the wheel. I leaned my head back and had a nap.

***

The smell of wood smoke tickled my nose. It was familiar and welcome. I stretched my arms over my head, safe in the camper's cozy cocoon, and rested for a few minutes, content.

A tendril of alarm was trying to worm its way into my consciousness, but I easily pushed it back into the dark where it belonged. There was nothing I could do about it anyway and this tiny world was where I wanted to stay. The smoke drifted past again, like incense, and I slept.

If it wasn't for my great need to pee, I would never have moved again. I squirmed out of my blankets and opened the side door to breathe in the fresh morning air. Like any number of campgrounds, a well-trodden path led to the washrooms. I always used campground facilities when I could; emptying my own black water was not my favourite activity. On the way back to my site, and not in such a hurry this time, I looked around. The birch trees had lost most of their leaves. Must be fall. That was about all the detail I needed right now. Nothing else seemed important.

My RV was parked in a choice spot overlooking a small lake surrounded by dense forest comprised not only of birch and maple but also of evergreens like pine, fir, and spruce. Being so late in the year, I had few neighbours. I extracted a fold-out chair from the innards of the camper and brought it to the lakeside. Sighing, I sat and gazed at the water. Peace and quiet was just what the doctor ordered.

52

As soon as I thought it, I tried to shove it back. Just that one word, doctor, had triggered an avalanche. I gripped the arms of my chair and held on until it was over.

The first part of the inundation—the days before I was admitted to the hospital—was disjointed. I had lost all sense of time in my battle to stay awake. Fleeting images of blood on my forearms, coffee dregs and sour milk spattered about, the sweet-sick smell of rotting food, and an overwhelming sense of defeat were not even the worst of it. I had been a menace to the innocent clerks at department and drug stores, demanding amphetamines. I had haunted the streets where, if there were any drug dealers around, that was where they would be. People had given me a wide berth; I looked bad and I smelled bad. It was unbearable to remember what I had become, and I fervently wished that the police had picked me up earlier.

In the hospital, I remembered puking my guts out and the shame I felt when someone else had to scrub the dirt from my body. I remembered Harriet's braids and the in-your-face mask that she wore. I remembered the other residents, and the nurses and doctors and orderlies. But most of all, I remembered that there had been no visions, no visions at all, while I had been confined in the psych unit.

I sat in the camp chair with the cool breeze on my face and began to sweat. They would return. I had to get back to the ward. I had to get the little blue pills that took the visions away.

I lurched to my feet and stumbled into Harvey. The keys should be in the glove box where I always kept them. Tissue, maps, flashlight, mini first-aid kit, but no keys. Frantic, I threw the contents out the door and spread them out on the ground to search through again, ripping the maps apart in case the keys had wedged themselves into one of the creases. Soon, the contents of my home were strewn about, and the light was fading. I sat on the ground, put my head in my hands, and wept.

"You okay?"

I covered my ears.

"Missus? You okay?"

The voice was young and high. A little girl. God. I did not want to deal with anyone let alone a little girl.

"I'm fine," I said, not looking up. At least I had my glasses on. I vaguely recalled that they had been lost and apparently found.

"You don't sound fine, and your campsite's a big mess," she observed. "My mom would make you put your things away right now. She always makes me put my things away."

Keeping my voice under tight control, I said, "I'm fine thanks. Now please go back to your mother."

Her shoes scuffed the gravel, hesitating. "I'm going now, but you really should put your things away." I listened hard until the sound of her footsteps faded.

Torn from my misery, I looked around at the chaos. I forced myself to my feet and shoved my stuff into a pile in case the neatness gestapo should return. A campfire would distract me, and I busied myself with the kindling conveniently stashed beside the pit and soon had it started. It didn't take

54

long to find the communal shed with the larger wood and, as the last light of the day disappeared, I huddled beside the fire intent on the flames.

My eyelids grew heavy. I floundered to my feet and splashed water on my face. The thought of coffee made me gag. I staggered back to my camp chair by the fire. My body cried for rest, and even the horror of repeating that inexorable slide into madness could not keep sleep at bay.

Cold and uncomfortable, I started awake. It was still dark. My neck ached, and I rolled it from shoulder to shoulder. I smiled. It had been a mostly natural sleep, although there had to be meds still swirling about in my system. But I couldn't help comforting myself just a little with the hope that maybe, just maybe, the visions were gone forever. Maybe all the little blue pills I'd had had at the hospital had eradicated them altogether.

A second night passed in the same manner. The following day, I continued to search for the keys and wondered how I could have possibly driven here without them. In fact, I couldn't remember driving here at all. I walked to the entrance of the campground and studied the map pinpointing its location. As I understood what I was seeing and where I was, I had to grip the side of the signboard: I was in the north-central states, a three-day drive from the hospital. How could I not remember a three-day drive?

Logic told me that someone else must have done it—either that or I had developed a split personality, and I really did not want to pursue that line of thought. Okay. Continuing on with the logic: if someone else had driven me, then that someone else had the keys. God. First of all, why? Why would someone spirit me away? Why would someone go to all that trouble? Why would I be of any interest to anyone? Why had he or she disappeared, taking my keys with him or her? Second... I guess there was no second; I had covered it all with the whys.

About the fifth day, my tendency to cleanliness and organisation returned with a vengeance. By the end of the morning, Harvey gleamed inside and out, and the only thing that could be still sullied was my guitar. I hadn't intentionally saved it for last; I just did not want to see the collateral damage my instrument had suffered from how badly I had abused myself at its expense. The hard carrying-case looked intact and the clasps were securely fastened. I flicked them open and, after a deep breath to prepare myself for what lied within, I opened the case. The hardwood had been polished to a satin sheen, and new strings glittered like jewels. A sudden spurt of tears filled my eyes as I lifted it from its velvety nest. I strummed the strings gently with my thumb and adjusted the tuning. I played. I closed my eyes and let the music fill me with peace.

Refreshed, I returned my guitar to its case and continued with the few remaining chores that would bring my small world back to as normal as it got. I gathered my laundry into a pillowcase and, with a pocket full of change, headed to the facilities. While the washing machines did their job, I went to the next building and took a shower in a significantly larger stall than the very convenient but very small one in my camper. Nothing like clean everything to set the world right. Ha.

There was a small grocery store next to the now closed in-ground pool. Whoever had parked me here had made sure that I would have every convenience, if you discount the part about not being able to go anywhere else even if I wanted to. The man behind the counter was reading a newspaper and glanced up when I walked in.

"Ah, good," he said, "the lady in 42." He bent to dig a parcel out from beneath the counter. "Miss Ducharme?" he asked.

I nodded.

"This was left for you." I reached for the package. "Good thing you came by today," he continued. "You see, the campground closes for the season tomorrow." He shrugged his shoulders. "But you're paid up til then, so just be sure to vacate your site by 11:00 am. Everything been satisfactory?"

I nodded.

He smiled and returned to his paper.

I picked up a few essentials, paid the man, and hurried back to the camper. I studied the package. It was a wrapped box about the size of a ream of paper with my name and site number on it. I shook it a bit. Eureka! The muffled, yet distinctive, sound of what could very well be keys was music to my ears. I ripped the brown paper off, opened the cover, and looked inside. The keys were indeed there as well as about two hundred dollars in cash. These were atop a soft, woven material. I shook it out. It was a shawl of the most beautiful swirling shades of blue and red and cream. It smelled like a gentle rain on hot sand with maybe sage mixed in.

I knew the smell of hot sand; I had grown up on

57

Prince Edward Island, after all, with its many excellent, sandy beaches. The hot sand there did not smell like this, though, but there was something compelling about this *mélange*. I gathered the shawl in my hands and held it to my face. The aroma filled my head as I breathed deeply. It was wonderful.

After a few minutes, I set the shawl aside and studied every detail of the package more closely. But there was nothing to tell me who had done this.

That evening, I lit another campfire and cooked myself something more healthful than the canned food I had been subsisting on. I kept busy folding my laundry and packing everything just so for heading out the following morning. The Sleepy-Time tea did no more than make me need to pee and I endured the long night, dozing off for a few minutes now and then. Ironically, as I felt physically better and better, the dread of a vision would just not allow me to rest.

***

As I'd feared, the nightmare visions soon returned to torment me and pushed me from place to place seeking some small relief, even if only for a few days.

It was cowardly of me, but I had given up trying to find a medical or psychiatric explanation for the visions, let alone a solution. The blue pills, I had learned, were extremely addictive and had harsh side-effects over even medium-term use. Anything remotely like it had the same prognosis. I was worn out and unwilling to find myself at yet another dead end.

I zigzagged across the continent and, with winter coming, headed generally southwards. I studied maps and chose uninhabited areas as destinations and soon reached the southwestern desert. It was here, in this seemingly bleak landscape, where I found a modicum of peace. The harsh land offered little in the way of subsistence and only a few prospectors or archaeologists or hikers ventured here. Of course, there were the natives I glimpsed occasionally, but they left me alone, as if they knew that this was what I wanted. I would occasionally be plagued by dreams of distant atrocities, but they were misty and soon dissipated. Except for the loneliness, it was as close to perfect as I allowed myself to expect.

When I needed money for supplies or to exchange my latest batch of books and music for a new set, I fired up Harvey and visited one of the glittering casinos that dotted the desert towns like jewels. I had never questioned the uncanny luck I had at the tables, and I tried to be smart about it. I was careful not to win too much in any one place and lost occasionally to add verisimilitude to my forays. I lived comfortably and worked hard to maintain invisibility.

I frequently changed where I parked my Recreational Vehicle—a misnomer for me if ever there was one, I did not recreate—so as to not unduly tax the fragile landscape, and always left the area in the pristine condition in which I had found it. This also spread my casino visits out more equitably and safely.

I had my favourite spots, though. If I parked near the edge of one of the numerous escarpments, the setting sun transformed my otherwise bland and forbidding 'front yard' into brilliant ribbons of colour. Other favourites were the places where the wind had sculpted the bones of Earth into fantastical shapes. I could entertain myself for hours with the stories that these inspired. I had even taken to writing some of them down to fill the long nights.

Best of all, during the precious few hours at the beginning and end of the day when the heat was bearable, I worked the small gardens I had planted at various locations. These were a great source of enjoyment for me and I was constantly amazed at the bounty that even this arid land provided, if you knew what to plant and where to plant it, that is. At first, my strategy was trial and error until one day I noticed a tiny patch of greenery tucked into the shelter of an overhanging rock. A little moisture sometimes accumulated at dawn and the shade of the overhang kept it from evaporating too quickly. Once I knew what to look for, I found a number of similar mini-oases and cultivated hardy shoots into the dry, desert air.

Occasionally, a breeze would carry that magic combination of hot sand and water and sage, and I would breathe deeply of its bouquet, always gone before I had had my fill.

It was almost enough to make me forget the sea, but, when the heat shimmered above the land, it sometimes caught me off guard. On a summer day, the Gulf could look just like that. It twisted my heart into a knot with the missing of it and I would seek the refuge of Harvey's dark interior.

Time passed, and I seemed to have found, if not my niche in the world, at least a place where I could sleep most nights and not cause anyone discomfort with my presence. No one had to look at my spooky eyes, and I didn't have to see them recoil and retreat as fast as they could. My life was likely as good as it would get, and I had resigned myself to this with a calmness that surprised me. It could be that the various philosophies I had read over time had given me a certain stoicism to accept my fate.

I would have liked to visit home but knew better than to inflict myself upon my family. According to the exceedingly rare letters from Jacinthe, I knew that they were still alive. My brothers had both married and I was an aunt to three nephews and one niece. My mother had been unwell and been in the hospital. Should I go see her? Would she be glad to see me? Would it help in any way? I brooded over this news for many weeks. It would likely make things worse—at least that's what I told myself—and I stayed away. Jacinthe had said nothing to encourage a visit and this reinforced my decision to leave things be. I hadn't heard anything for a while now, even though I still diligently penned a short, weekly missive. It had become a habit and, early on, I had taken to making a copy of them as a kind of record of my life, such as it was.

One morning, I found a small packet of seeds on my doorstep. Turning in a circle and voicing my thanks to whoever might have given it to me, I hurried to my latest patch of worked earth and gently pressed them into the soil. I didn't know exactly what kind of corn they were, but I looked very much forward to seeing what they would become. After all, I surmised, why would someone go to the trouble of giving them to me if they were not extraordinary or at least viable? It would take time to see just exactly what they were, though, and I had other gardens to tend, but would return often to nurture them along.

It was a lot of time and effort to produce what was, it turned out, a tough kind of maize that barely softened even after a good long soak and a good long while in the hot embers of my fire. I shook my head. That's when I heard a soft snicker on the gentle night breeze. Someone had been toying with me with the so-called donation of seeds, and that someone had returned to laugh at his stupid prank. Since my experience with this kind of situation was minimal to none, I became immediately angry. If only my curse could send visions out instead of only receiving them, I would give this miscreant a piece of my mind. Ha. Maybe my time in the dry desert air had desiccated bits of my brain and I could actually give him or her a piece of it.

"You've had your little joke, now leave me alone." I heard the distant scrape of what could have been a boot on stone, then silence.

Why couldn't my so-called gift benefit me once in a while? Why couldn't it display an image of who was annoying me? It was frustrating in the extreme. Who had given me the bogus seeds? More importantly, why would anyone bother to do such a thing? It had been a long time between the planting and the harvest; rather lame for a practical joke, but I fervently hoped that it was all this was.

I did not want to be the target of some crazy kind of stalker. A stalker who gave his victims seeds? Didn't seem likely, but there were all kinds of people out there. I should know. My visions when I had lived in cities were often of the gut-wrenching stalking type. The tension would fray my nerves until there was nothing left, and I became a numb, rag doll, tossed about on a sea of anguish. I wanted to do something, anything, to help the victim, but a dearth of details and total uncontrollability were two of my visions' greatest burdens. On the rare occasion when I had recognised some landmark, I haunted the location hoping to spot the person that drove the stalker's obsession. Either I had the location wrong or gave up too soon, but I had never been able to warn a single victim. It didn't matter that they likely wouldn't believe me, even if they listened to me in the first place, but I would have been able to assuage a tiny fraction of my mountain of guilt. I had eventually resigned myself to the fact that I wasn't meant to interfere, but rather only be tortured by witnessing what happened to others. A fitting castigation for I know not what.

I barely slept that night, planning where I would go next. I poured over maps and wondered if I could stand the far north. Maybe the seed-stalker hated the cold. It was worth a try.

The motorhome was readied for a road trip before the sun had risen. I would make some coffee and be on my way. I would definitely miss my gardens and cursed the stalker long and with feeling. I opened the door for one last look around the area for anything I might have left behind.

A bouquet of the most aromatic flowers that my olfactory lobes had ever had the privilege of sniffing was on display in an old pot.

"You had better decide to show yourself," I said into the crystal desert air, "if you think I will

63

stay here for one more minute with you lurking about out there." I gathered the garden tools I had also spotted and stowed them in Harvey, all the while breathing the intoxicating smell of the floral arrangement. Wait. I looked down at the flowers. Maybe they were poisonous. Maybe they would make me pass out or go into convulsions. I had to get out of here right now! I turned for the door.

The coyote sat very still. Even seated, I could tell he was a big one. He gently panted, displaying very white teeth, and turned his head to look to the side. I followed his gaze. There was a man standing there.

The man doffed his cowboy-style hat and opened his mouth to speak; his white teeth alarmingly like the coyote's.

"Name's Joe," he said. "Sorry about the cattle corn." He gestured to the flowers, by way of apology. "Just wondered what would happen. If you could change it."

"Change it?"

He nodded.

"Into what?"

He shrugged his shoulders.

A man of few words. We looked at each other. There was something trustworthy yet alarming in his gaze. My instincts told me that he was not dangerous, at least to me.

"Mind if I sit?" he asked.

I tossed my instincts into the nether region from which it had come. Why would I even consider such a request? This was the person who conceived and implemented the stupid stunt—the stupid, time-consuming, embarrassing stunt—of the corn! What did that say about his stability? Nothing good, and I had had personal experience with people of unstable mind. There was no telling what this man would do. And he had a coyote with him! Abruptly remembering this threat, I glanced sideways at the beast. He seemed to smile. I must be suffering from heat stroke. No—the poisonous flowers were exacting their toll! I swayed a bit.

The man rushed towards me, catching me before my legs gave way, and set me gently on the ground. He turned and rummaged around in Harvey, invading my space, and retrieved the two camp chairs.

This was the first time that the spare was brought outside. It had been one of those just-in-case-my-other-one-broke purchases, but I couldn't help feeling that a line was being crossed, a line I didn't want to have crossed.

He helped me into one of the chairs—my usual chair—and paced while I recovered from my swoon. Gods, I had swooned, just like in the old movies. At least I hadn't pressed the back of my hand to my forehead.

The coyote had sprawled in the cool shade beneath the Winnebago looking quite content. The man continued to pace.

My jitters had calmed enough to allow me to think. I had read about a strategy that suggested going along with the problem-person until a safe exit revealed itself. One thing was certain: if I was to get out of this alive, I had to do something. I took a slow, deep, calming breath, and threw myself into the role.

"Coffee?" I offered.

He nodded.

"Would your… dog like a drink?" I knew he wasn't a dog, but I couldn't quite bring myself to consider the concept of a tame coyote.

"Yes. And he isn't anybody's 'dog.'" He put his hat back on, shading his eyes from the rays of the rising sun. "Thank you," he added.

While the coffee cycled, I poured a generous bowl of water for the coyote and gingerly placed it where I thought it would be convenient for him. He approached it cautiously and sniffed it in several places before lapping the bowl dry. He looked up at me and smiled again—who knew a coyote could smile? —turned in a circle two or three times, and lay down. In moments, he was sound asleep.

"I wish I could do that," I sighed, as I poured steaming coffee into mugs. The familiar aroma wafted into the air and blended with the flowers in an intoxicating combination. I inhaled deeply, momentarily forgetting my earlier paranoia.

I passed a cup of joe to Joe, smiling at my own internal witticism, and remembered to offer my own name. "I'm Flotsy, by the way."

"Ah, but Olivia is so much prettier."

I could feel the flush creep up my neck and into my face. "How do you know that name? Who are you? What do you want?" Hot coffee splashed onto my hand; I barely noticed. The flowers. This time I was hallucinating and could no longer feel pain. What was it about this guy that had made me drop my long-held shields, that made me forget the many gambits I had perfected over time to deal with any intrusion into my life? I was in deep trouble.

Joe took his time replying. "I know you

because I need to know you. That's how it works."

"That's how what works?" My mind whirled; maybe I could still save myself. If I could get inside and lock the door behind me, I could lock the other door before Joe had time to run around to the driver's side. I stood.

He narrowed his eyes at me. Dark eyes, I noticed, almost black like his hair.

"I have a… gift… too," he said before I could take my first step. "It made me find you a while ago and liberate you from the psych ward. It made me drive your rig," he jerked a thumb toward my RV, "and set you up in a campground. It made me find you down here and made me leave that corn so you would plant it and come back to this spot to see what grew—I had to be elsewhere for a while—and, well, here we are."

I felt the chair behind my knees and carefully sat down again, cooling coffee intact. I stared at him. He had continued speaking but I hadn't heard much after the words *gift* and *psych ward*.

I had read studies and experiments done on people purporting to have telepathy and telekinesis and other unusual abilities. Then there were Tarot cards, dream analysis, previous incarnations, angels, and so on and so on. I had investigated them all. But I had never actually gone to speak with any of the specialists or attended any of the myriad group sessions. I tried to talk myself into it; I had even arrived at the doorstep of a meeting or two. But the shunning of my friends and neighbours, of my entire village, way-back-when had left a deep mistrust of revealing myself and my gift to anyone, and I just couldn't do it. I thought of it as anything but a 'gift.' It had ruined my life. What kind of a 'gift' was that?

This was the first time I was face-to-face with someone else who may have some sort of ability. Or not. But I found I was intrigued enough—or lonely enough, I admitted to myself—to learn more.

"We should talk," I said.

Joe nodded. I would learn that he did that a lot.

Chapter 4

We exchanged bits and pieces of our life stories, and I told him a little about my visions and my frustrations. He, too, felt removed from everything and everyone. Joe had learned the frustration of getting to know people and places early on, and then be forced to leave without warning, to perform yet another commission for the thing that controlled his life. He was in the desert because he had to be.

"But what, exactly, is your gift?" We had been dancing around this question, Joe obviously reluctant to elaborate, but I was determined to find out if this was just another hoax, an elaborate hoax to be sure, but a hoax, nevertheless.

Joe looked down at his hands, which were clenched tightly together. "I'm pushed in a certain direction, to do a certain thing. If I fight it…, well, it's better not to fight it." He unclenched his hands and rubbed at a diagonal scar on his right palm that was visible even from where I sat. "What I am made to do can be mystifying and sometimes seem stupid," he nodded in the direction of my garden, "but I'm also beginning to see a weird sort of connection."

"What do you mean by pushed? Do you think someone is controlling you?"

He thought for a moment, and then shrugged, completely uninformative.

Notwithstanding Joe's paucity of words, this was the most interesting conversation I had ever had, and I did not want it to end. "If you could tell me about your incidents, or even about just one or two of them," I hastily modified my request as Joe's eyes widened, "perhaps I can help. Perhaps my," I hesitated, "experience could shed light on this connection you mentioned. Worst case is that it might help clarify your thinking."

Joe abruptly rose and walked away, the coyote in his wake.

I was not given the chance to fling a comment at Joe's receding back about his rather rude behaviour, as inside my head, there erupted a full-blown vision. This was no flimsy, spectral scene like my previous one-time awake-in-the-day episode. The bright, desert day simply vanished, and I was plunged into darkness. I could feel my heart thump faster and faster. I tried to lift my hands to my chest, to my head; I tried to squeeze the arms of the camp chair. Nothing worked. Was I having a heat stroke for real this time? I smiled. A stroke could be a good thing. My soul strained to free itself from this life of meaninglessness, from this life reduced to the lowly goal of getting through each day. I sighed, gave in to the enormous pressure, and let go.

Slowly, details began to emerge in the inkiness. I was in a cave. I was looking at a big rock, a big rock in dark place. The rock opened its mouth.

***

It was night when I came back to myself and I shivered with cold. Hours had passed. I must have been in some sort of vision-trance, not the tragic, beautiful death I had hoped it would be. Oh, well. I couldn't even die right. Teeth chattering, I clambered into Harvey, lay down on my bed, and wrapped the thick duvet around me. Suddenly exhausted, I slept.

The next morning, when I emerged somewhat later than my usual time, Joe was sitting in one of my camp chairs. He looked terrible. About as terrible as I felt. Neither of us spoke as I made strong coffee and searched the cupboard for my secret stash of indestructible ginger cookies. If you let them melt in your mouth, they scoured away the residue of a bad night.

We ate and drank in silence, the coyote nowhere about.

"Where's your friend?"

Joe looked up at me. His eyes were bloodshot and haunted, and he took a few seconds to focus on what I had asked.

"Bob?"

I burst out laughing. "Bob?" I spluttered. "You call your coyote Bob?" I had to put my cup down before I dropped it and laughed some more. I was clearly sleep-deprived and perhaps more than a wee bit over the edge.

"What's wrong with 'Bob?'" A slight curl formed on one side of Joe's mouth—possibly the beginning of a smile. "I named him after a university acquaintance."

I grinned at him, suddenly feeling much better, hysterical or not.

"What happened to his ear? Why does it flop forward like that?

Joe shrugged. "It was like that when we met."

He tried to smother a huge yawn. "Mind if I have a short nap? I had a hard night." He put up a hand to forestall my questions. "I'll tell you all about it later."

He would have crawled under the motorhome just like Bob had done but I insisted he stretch out on the bed that filled the back section of Harvey. If he either curled up or lay diagonally across it, he would fit, sort of; he was somewhat taller than my five-foot-three. Too tired to argue, he lay down and was asleep before I had pulled the curtain across the bedroom opening. I went back outside.

Bob waited for me. He was sitting, his feet neatly together and his bushy tail wrapped around them, in the exact same spot as when I had first seen him yesterday. I went back inside the motorhome to fetch a bowl of water. Hey, wasn't it supposed to be the dog who fetched? I also dug into my tiny cooler for a bit of leftover meat. Bob's nose twitched. He padded over to me, gently took it from my outstretched fingers, and gobbled it down without taking his eyes from mine. I then placed the bowl of water on the ground and he followed his apparent routine of approach, sniff, and lap it dry.

I had work to do and not much time before the desert sun made it impossible. I inserted tools into my gardening belt, grabbed a bottle of water, and began the hike to my little garden a few hundred yards down a nearby arroyo. Bob watched me for a few seconds and decided that his master had the right of it. He curled up in the shade under the vehicle. I hummed to myself, happy that both of my boys were comfortable.

Wait. What was happening? Was I so starved for companionship that I would leave everything I owned in the control of a man I barely knew? And what I did know was more than a little weird. And

72

there was always the very real possibility that this was all a well-planned scam, or some other more insidious plot. Ha. As if I warranted more than a passing glance. I gotta stop reading so many novels.

Still, I turned back and quietly approached the motorhome from a different direction, expecting I don't know what. Bob opened one eye and followed my movements. I eased open Harvey's door and listened. There was no sound of furtive rustling, no sound of drawers being searched—only Joe's soft snore. I went back outside and sat in Joe's chair. Huh. Joe's chair. Should I trust him, or at least consider the possibility of trusting him? Knowing me, I would ponder this all day, tie myself in knots, and be no closer to an answer. Sometimes, you just had to jump in.

I resumed my hike to the arroyo. The garden looked good. Another useful trick I had learned was to plant things that I could eat but that the local fauna found distasteful. It didn't leave much variety, but it was fresh. After a little weeding and bolstering of the tiny dykes I made to help trap the least amount of moisture, I returned to my campsite.

Except for the circle of stones outlining the cook fire, the area was empty. No Bob, no Joe, no Winnebago. Too devastated to cry, I sat on the hard ground and stared at where Harvey used to be.

The sun began to set, and the cold desert night descended. I continued to sit. What I was waiting for I couldn't say but, if I didn't move, the world might also stand still and not move forward into the bleakness that was left. The brick wall that had nearly enclosed my heart began to mix another layer of mortar. When it had achieved the right consistency—not too long now—it would trowel on a thick layer of goo and carefully place the final few bricks that would protect me from the vagaries of the world, from the hurt that lurked around every corner, from my own *naïveté*.

It was at times like this that I really wondered why I kept on going, not that I was feeling sorry for myself; well, not too sorry anyway. The brief idea of death as a way out skittered across my mind, but it was just not something I could make happen; it would have to happen on its own.

The next place would be the same as the last one, the next person would be the same as the last one (well, maybe not exactly like Joe), and the next vision would be something that I was helpless to do anything about. Maybe the lesson I was supposed to take away from this latest disappointment was to accept the futility of it all and somehow find peace in that revelation. Seemed rather dismal, but there it was.

Soon, I would stand, brush the dust from my pants, and head towards the highway. I would likely reach the nearest town by dawn and the walk would keep me warm. Vague plan in place, I stood, gardening tools clinking at my waist, and began the trudge toward the next episode in my life.

My mind flitted here and there throughout the night. From the very, I had maintained an open line of communication with my family and rented post office boxes in cities and towns that were central to where I was at the time so that they could correspond with me. My mother had replied once, about two years ago, to my hundreds of weekly missives. She had written that my brothers barely remembered me and that she did her best to correct the gossip they heard about me from the villagers, about how their sister had killed their father. I could only imagine how not-very convincing she was. Both of my brothers had married and given her beautiful grandchildren. She herself had remarried and was content. They all lived happily within walking distance of each other, and she felt it would be best for everyone if I remained on my travels. Message received loud and clear.

My friend, Jacinthe, had written a couple of letters in the first few months, telling me how the other kids envied my big break to freedom. Funny how when I wasn't around, they could speak of me as though I were normal. Soon after she started seeing Louis Gallant from the next village over, the letters became more erratic. My mother had been sure to mention in her letter that Jacinthe was expecting her third child and that she and Louis were the perfect couple.

I picked away at all the hurtful things that had happened in my life because of something I couldn't understand and couldn't control. Just like picking at a scab, it only made me bleed again, but I couldn't help it. It was a night for beating myself up.

Roughly ten years ago, when I was maybe twenty-five, I had tried yet again to use the foreknowledge of my visions to help in some way. This was on one of my attempts to live in a city, stubbornly hoping that a city's inherent anonymity would diffuse the visions. I approached my neighbour who was a detective stumped by a particularly difficult case. I knew a bit about what he was looking for and how stumped he was and offered my mostly unpredictable assistance. He took me up on my offer. I must have caught him in a weak moment when he thought that he had nothing to lose, except possibly his credibility.

This was one of those extremely rare occasions when I recognised the location in a vision. I posited that it may have been because, in the interests of helping with the case, I had actually studied the town and cruised all of its streets over the past week. I led him to the house I had 'seen.' The door was ajar. I stepped in when the detective announced the all-clear and looked upon the miscellany of a life gone bad. A dusty hookah in the corner spoke of earlier drug habits. The rusty spoon and discarded needles eloquently explained what had emaciated the corpse at my feet. The detective had found three other bodies huddled together on a filthy mattress. In the mundane way that extreme shock can sometimes take one, I thought that the air was surprisingly fresh for so many dead people.

My detective-neighbour gently turned me around and guided me back to the squad car. He made me sit inside, opened a bottle of water, and handed it to me. I sipped automatically. He said he would be back in five minutes to take me home.

A few days later, I gave away everything I owned, bought a not-so-new car, and drove until I couldn't see straight.

At one time, I had considered some type of psychosurgery, perhaps a lobotomy. The downside was that, from the many books and articles I had read, no one knew for certain that special psychic abilities resided there; the upside was that I wouldn't care one way or the other. This unfathomable ability was soul-destroying and downright terrifying. It wouldn't be so terrifying if I knew not only that a thing was going to happen, but also something practical about it, like who or where or when. I was always too late to do anything about anything.

That was the trouble with prescience, as least the trouble with my kind of prescience.

I paused in my long walk to the highway to stretch my legs and sip from my dwindling supply of water. I had debated leaving my garden tools behind, but they were a link, a link to something I loved to do and, even though they made noise and weighed me down, I kept them with me. I felt pathetic, holding on to such a useless gesture.

In the clear air, I could see the glow of a town's lights. I would make it to some roadside diner in time for breakfast, and the cook would likely be happy for someone to wash dishes in exchange for an egg and a cup of coffee.

He was indeed happy for some help once he was certain that the things hanging from my belt were fancy garden tools and not weapons. I grudgingly sold them to him for a twenty-dollar bill; it wouldn't do to have someone not quite so affable decide that I was packing.

I hitched a ride with one of the truckers at the diner. He was a non-stop talker which suited me just fine; no need to think and I was heartily sick of thinking. He hailed from Missouri—or Mizurah—as he called it and would be happy to take me all the way to meet the missus. I then heard all there was to know about Helen and his wonderful chillen. He was entertaining and a gentleman, but with nothing other than twenty dollars and the clothes on my back, I needed to begin rebuilding my stake.

About mid-afternoon we neared a medium-sized town complete with three casinos on the main strip. Tom the trucker bought me a meal, gave me a hug, and pulled out of the truck stop. I watched him go. Seemed like people were always leaving. *Stop it*. I mentally slapped myself. Time to win a little cash.

I was dressed in gardening clothes and my boots were a mess; I chose the most disreputable-looking casino. On that first visit, I stayed just long enough to win the money for essentials, but I'd be back.

Three days later, the town behind me, I eased the accelerator closer to the floor. The midnight-black Monte Carlo shot forward. Wow, what a dream car—well, a dream car to me anyway. I cruised through the cool evening air of the open desert, feeling good about the day. Time for some music. I pressed the on button, but with the first bar of an old hippy song, I felt a jolt that had nothing to do with the beat. Damn. A flat.

The second jolt took me by surprise and I made the rookie mistake of yanking the steering wheel hard in a vain attempt to compensate for the sickening fish-tailing. The car was moving way too fast and began a stately 360-degree spin.

The rear passenger tire bit the soft shoulder and dragged the rest of my beautiful car backwards off the asphalt and began the seemingly slow-motion descent, bouncing and jouncing down a long and not-so-gentle slope. Thank the gods for seatbelts, but I wish they had designed one for the forehead too or had had the decency to pad the steering wheel. At last, the car came to a stop.

A car accident in the middle of the night, in the middle of nowhere, with a lump on my forehead the size of a walnut. It doesn't get much worse. And then the first coyote howled, soon joined by a chorus of its buddies. I hoped it was Bob on the lead vocal. No, that was the singer in Supertramp—what was his name? —telling me something about quiet moments... quiet moments.

I was stiff and sore, and my headache was bad. The door opened easily enough, and I leaned sideways to get out, but something was holding me back. I threw up; at least it landed outside of the car. The seatbelt which likely saved my life dug into my midriff and when I finally found the release catch the relief was intense. I carefully stepped over my mess and tried to assess the damage in the starlight. Didn't look good. I would need a tow to get back to level ground to change the tire or tires; I couldn't see for certain if one or two had blown, but probably two. I would definitely not recommend that car dealership. The rest of the car seemed okay, nothing I couldn't handle, only I needed a short rest first.

I crawled into the back seat, careful not to jar my head, and slept. Somewhere, a small voice said that I probably had a concussion again and that I should try to stay awake. I told the small voice to shut up.

"You're not an easy lady to catch up with," a different small voice said. I told it to shut up too.

"Sip a little of this." A trickle of tepid water touched my lips and my parched body lapped it up. "That's it. Just a little more."

I wanted a whole lot more, but he took it away. I feebly grabbed for the cup.

"You can have more later." An arm reached under my shoulders. "Okay. I'm going to help you sit up."

I immediately threw up on whoever it was trying to move me. I didn't dare open my eyes just yet. "Sorry," I whispered.

"My fault."

How could it be his fault? Oh, yeah. It was Joe's voice. "Bastard," I hissed. At least I tried to hiss; I wanted to hiss.

"I know. I'm sorry."

I tried to push him away; he stank of puke. Instead, he began to slide me out of the car. I retched a little.

"I'm going to carry you up the slope to Harvey and take you to the hospital. Here we go."

The only thing I could do was hold on during the interminable climb and the never-ending drive.

The doctor was gentle and soon the pain disappeared, though a most annoying nurse kept waking me up. I knew she had to, but she was still a most annoying nurse.

The next morning, I felt almost human. My head and a few other parts hurt, but on the whole, I would say I was a lucky woman. Except for the bastard, of course. I opened my eyes to slits and when that didn't bother me too much, I opened them all the way to look at the pristine hospital room I was in. Some merciful soul, probably that annoying nurse, had closed the venetian blinds so that only dim light penetrated the room. I would try to remember to thank her for that. Maybe. If she stopped waking me up all the time.

A card was propped on my night table. 'Olivia' it said. Must be from the bastard. I ignored it and instead reached beyond it for the glass of water complete with bendy straw. I quite liked bendy-straws; I hardly had to move my head to have a satisfying drink. My poor head; second concussion in three years. I'd have to check how many times a person can get bonked hard on the head without something becoming too squishy or too broken to put it back together again, like Humpty Dumpty. This harmless simile brought on the image of a gooey, dinosaur-sized egg splattered on the ground, with my torso and legs sticking out from it. Great. I reached for the convenient puke tray.

A clipboard preceded the doctor into the room. "Good afternoon. How are you feeling?"

I reached past the puke tray, grabbed my water glass instead, and took a few sips. After a shallow breath or two, I answered. "Sore, but mostly okay."

He poked and prodded, had a look in my eyes, lifted the bandage on my head and had a look there too, and pronounced me fit. "Speak with the duty nurse on your way out. She'll set you up with painkillers and process your payment. You should rest for at least three days and that means laying-down rest." He turned to the next page on his clipboard and walked out.

"Thanks," I said to the empty room.

While I pondered where to start, the annoying nurse came in and watched as I got out of bed. She nodded. "You'll do. Your clothes are over there in the cupboard. Here are enough pills to get you through the next few days. Call me when you're ready to leave and I'll bring a wheelchair around to take you to that nice man who already paid your bill and is waiting outside."

"It's the least he can do," I muttered under my breath.

Bob was in the motorhome happily smearing the passenger-side window with his slobber. Great. Then I was face-to-face with the latest person to disappoint the hell out of me.

"I'm sorry," Joe said.

"You keep saying that as though it fixes something." Hurt and rage boiled up inside me and made my head hurt. "If you would please drive my house to someplace safe and quiet, you and Bob can take yourselves back to wherever it is you came from." I opened the door, and one look had the coyote scurrying into the rear of the vehicle. Bob was no dummy. My excellent moment of defiance was ruined when I got a bit dizzy and Joe had to help me step into the RV.

We drove in silence to a full-amenity campground. I had to admit that the easy access to a store and washroom with running water was welcome. Joe pulled into a site with a shady area created by cleverly hung canvas beneath which he had placed a self-standing hammock complete with pillows and a light throw blanket. My, my. The boy wasn't half stupid either.

He came around to open the door for me and help me out of the vehicle. I wobbled a little. He steadied me with a hand under my elbow and guided me to the hammock. Bob trotted over, did his triple twirl, and lay down. Good idea. The light breeze smelled wonderful and I soon slept.

I woke to a tantalising aroma. My belly grumbled, loudly. I heard a familiar snicker as Joe brought over a bowlful of something. The savoury broth was at just the right temperature and the bread just a bit chewy.

"I must admit: your apologies are pretty good."

Joe smiled. This was the first time I had seen him smile. The taciturn face became different. Not handsome—it was too long and craggy to ever be called handsome—but it was alive and interesting.

"I really am sorry."

The moment was gone. "If you say that again without any explanation of why you stole Harvey and left me stranded in the middle of the desert...," I stopped and closed my eyes tightly until the worst of the pain subsided.

Joe was instantly at my side with a pill and a glass of water. I took them from him, swallowed, and lay back on the pillows, drained.

"I've never talked about this before, so please bear with me if I fumble a bit."

He arranged his chair so that he was facing me. Bob sat by his side. It looked as though this was going to be a team effort.

"The first time he came into my mind, I was about twelve," Joe began.

"Wait a minute," I interrupted, "who's 'he?'"

"It's a bit complicated."

I closed my eyes and turned my head, slowly, to the side facing away from them.

"Can I continue?" He waited until I waved my hand in a gesture for him to go on.

"He doesn't use words, exactly, but I know what he wants me to do. I say 'he,' but I don't know

83

if it's even a who or a what that's manipulating me.

"The first time it happened, I thought it was just a vivid dream. I remember telling my sister about it. She's three years older and, at the time, it seemed to me that she knew everything. Her reaction was less than illuminating. She thought it was unbelievable that I would bother her with my stupid dreams.

"I had the same dream about a week later and again a week after that. Then it became more frequent. I thought I was going crazy and my mother made me speak to the school counsellor who knew about colleges and jobs but knew nothing about this kind of thing. She, in turn, referred me to a psychiatric clinic where the doctor prescribed relaxants. All they did was make me sleep longer so the dream could repeat itself several times a night instead of just once or twice.

"You should understand that I come from a middle-class family and lived in a middle-class neighbourhood. Everyone had a station wagon. The boys played baseball and hockey, and the girls took ballet and music lessons. A typical Canadian town. You didn't have many crazy kids in a typical Canadian town. More drugs were prescribed. My parents were getting scared and my sister thought it was cool to have a real psycho for a kid brother.

"Eventually, I did what the dream person wanted me to do, and the dream stopped. Just like that."

I stared at him. "What did you do?" I didn't know what to expect but I cringed just a little anyway.

He looked as though he would cry, but I've since learned that this look was his prelude to a good laugh. "I had my hair cut."

My jaw dropped. I must have looked as dumbfounded as I felt, and he slapped his thighs and let out a bellow of laughter. I threw a pillow at him. Bob jumped up, grabbed it out of the air, and raced around the hammock. Joe caught him, no doubt because Bob let him, and they wrestled with the pillow until it was quite beyond salvation. I had to smile; how could I not?

I shook my finger at him. "There had better be more to this story, Joe, or I'll throw something more substantial."

A startling thought occurred to me. There was something in the way he pronounced certain words. "What's your surname anyway?"

He looked at me over his shoulder, still intent on the solid belly rub that he was administering to an ecstatic Bob. "Gallant."

I was stunned. "Hey, Joe." Something in my voice made him turn fully towards me. "What's the name of this mid-sized Canadian town you come from?"

"Just a small place on the east coast. Charlottetown. Ever heard of it?"

"Oh, yeah," I breathed. What were the odds of two Islanders meeting up in the middle of the Arizona desert? "I'm from North Rustico. Last name's 'Ducharme,' in case you didn't know already."

We stared at each other for a minute. "Finish your story," I suggested. "We'll talk about this… coincidence later."

***

Two full years went by before a second dream

85

had come to Joe. But he recognised its clarity and feel immediately. At fourteen, he felt only a tiny bit better equipped to handle it. One thing he had learned was that, this time, he would keep it to himself. He was just beginning to be looked upon as normal after the first incident and he did not want to jeopardise this.

His second 'assigned' task was as mundane as the first one: obtain a specific model of camera. His birthday was coming up and the camera was not too expensive. He was actually kind of interested in trying it out. Like the first time, the dream stopped when he had the camera in his hand. Other tasks inserted themselves into his dreams over the next few years until he had quite a collection of electronic equipment. His parents were content that he seemed to be headed for technological geekdom and never questioned his accumulation of gear. Joe still had no idea why this was happening to him, but as long as he acquiesced, nothing else in his life was affected.

He wondered if he could possibly be doing this to himself, and that was a scary thought. On the plus side, he became reasonably adept at taking apart and putting back together all sorts of gadgets. But what he would rather be doing was reading books, all sorts of books. His sister rolled her eyes at him whenever they chanced to meet, usually when she was coming into or going out of the house. Her opinion that he was cool had only lasted while he was officially psycho. After that, she looked upon him as her nerd-and-geek-infested younger brother, to be avoided at all costs.

When he decided to attend the University of

Toronto, it had as much to do with their excellent faculty as it had with the multitude of libraries he could access. At the airport, his family waved goodbye and hurried back to their interrupted, busy lives. They loved him, surely, but he was not the outgoing, social type like everyone else. He would never fit in and he knew it. Better to be in a big city, where no one knew anyone.

Of particular personal interest to Joe were books on aberrations of the mind, so much so that he really should have changed his major from English to Psychology. There were books on the paranormal, of course, and on the many manifestations of behavioural disorders. But nothing quite fit his experiences and all the extra-curricular reading he was doing was affecting the courses he was supposed to be studying. Surely, his professor of Shakespeare had said to him, you can come up with another angle in your analyses besides the aberrant behaviour angle.

After similar comments from other professors, he shoved his personal research aside, along with the large box of notes he had taken, and concentrated on getting his degree. He had no specific plans for what he would do when he did graduate. He was getting a BA, which during a sloppy debate at the local pub, he and a buddy decided that it stood for Be Anything. It turned out that that was exactly what would be required of him.

The day after graduation, a very powerful dream began, not only at night when he slept, but also superimposed on his view of the world during the day. At first, he was terrified of leaving his small apartment. What if the dream came upon him when he was crossing the street? Or boarding the subway? He could be killed. Then the dream shifted, and he somehow knew that it would be safe for him to go out.

The worst of it was the knowledge that something was not working quite right in his head, and he began to despair for his sanity. He was all of twenty-three years old, fresh out of university with a degree in English, and the thing inside his head insisted that he apply for work at a daycare centre nearby. He wasn't sure what he wanted to do with his life, but changing dirty diapers was most definitely not on the list.

He tried to fight it, but after a few days, dishevelled and frustrated, he stomped into the Just for Kids daycare. It was as bad as he had imagined: there were kids everywhere, smelling bad and squealing in their supersonic voices. In their midst was a young woman who looked up when the Tinker Bell door chime played its merry tune. The welcoming smile beginning on her face was quickly replaced a look of dismay as she took in his appearance. She handed the little person she had been holding to a second adult and came towards him. As soon as their eyes met, he knew what he had to do.

He turned, raced outside, and clutched the well-dressed man approaching the daycare's door. The muffled explosion that came a second later toppled both men to the ground. Joe felt an irresistible urge to get up and run, and run he did. No one came after him or seemed to even notice him.

Back at his apartment, he turned on the shower

and began to discard his clothes. It was then that he discovered the state of his T-shirt. Or what was left of his T-shirt. It was charred and torn like a blow-torch had been applied to it.

The evening papers carried the story on the front page: 'Attempted Mass Murder at Local Daycare.' 'The Clumsy Criminal,' the paper dubbed him, had had explosives taped to his abdomen. When he tripped and fell on his face a few yards from the daycare door, they ignited, instantly killing him. There was minor damage to a nearby vehicle. It seemed that 'Clumsy' had been stalking one of the young women who worked there. She was terrified of him but never imagined he would do something like this. 'You can never tell about people and what they are capable of doing,' she was quoted as saying.

Joe stared. It would seem the stakes had changed; collecting electronic equipment for no apparent reason had turned into surviving bombs and saving lives. He was like Superman, only completely invisible.

That had been the start of his new career.

In between saving people from bad guys, he took on odd jobs. The entity that used him had powers Joe could not understand and a benevolence that was astounding. The assignments had him travelling out of Toronto so often that he finally gave up the expense of an apartment and bought a used VW van.

And, so, for the past twenty years, he had been travelling all over North America saving people, buying equipment for an as yet-to-be-assigned task, and doing whatever else the entity required of him.

In his off-time, he read, went to movies, and worked-out, just like a normal guy, if a loner.

***

Bob had curled up and was fast asleep. By the angle of the sun, it was nearing mid-afternoon; three hours had passed in the telling of his story. I looked at Joe, at this tall man with the craggy face and tired eyes. I believed him, and I did not need any kind of supernatural power to tell me that he was a man of integrity.

"So, when you sto... borrowed Harvey, you were on a mission?"

Joe nodded. "I left you a message. In the dirt."

I could feel my eyebrows rise nearly to my hairline.

"Maybe not the best plan. Please believe me when I tell you that I did not take your house and abandon you on purpose." At her skeptical look, he backtracked. "Okay, it was on purpose, but for a really good purpose."

I was suddenly very tired. "I understand, and you are completely forgiven, especially if you let me join Bob in a pre-supper nap."

For the next few days, I recovered while Joe and I got to know each other better. He entertained me with some of his more humorous rescues and I described some of my visions, trying not to dwell too often on my frustration that what I 'saw' almost never gave me sufficient details to actually do anything. I glossed over my luck as the gambling tables, something which I never understood but didn't want to examine too closely in case I jinxed myself.

The more we talked, the more I toyed with the

idea of an interesting partnership developing. If my indiscriminate visions and his very specific missions should ever overlap... No, he was doing very well all on his own. He could take action and affect the outcome. Why would he want the details of my useless nightmares to bog him down and depress him? I discarded the possibility as a bit of wishful thinking.

Our domestic arrangements were quite simple. Harvey housed my bedroom, small emergency lavatory with shower, and communal storage for clothes and food and my constant, yet ever-changing supply of books and music. Joe and Bob were happier sleeping outside; the motorhome, although quite comfortable, made them claustrophobic. I also suspected that he was setting himself up to be able to leave at a moment's notice if he got a 'call' and, as far as Bob was concerned, the whole of the outside was his bedroom.

"Bob is getting fat," Joe stated one morning about a week into my convalescence, and in typical Joe fashion, they were off, trotting into the wilderness just beyond the campground.

While they were gone, I dug into my stash of money and went shopping. I bought a motorcycle that came with a small, easily-removable side-car. The man at the motorcycle store fitted Harvey with a hitch and trailer and loaded the equipment onto it. If Joe didn't know how to ride a bike, he could learn. Having never bought many thank-you gifts in my life—and I was pretty certain that Joe had never received many—I was well pleased with myself. Anyway, I could always return everything if the idea bombed.

My energy was returning but it didn't take much to tire me out and I went to bed as soon as I returned to the campsite.

A vision came to me as I slept, and it was a doozy.

Chapter 5

Every ounce of my being screamed for release from the oppressive onslaught that crushed me. Shrieks from hell shredded my brain. Ripping, wrenching, tearing. I couldn't breathe. I couldn't see.

I woke gasping for air. Sweat soaked my tank top and shorts and plastered my hair to my head. I groped for my water bottle and shakily brought it to my lips. I felt about as bad as when the Monte Carlo had gone off the road; it was like I'd been beaten by a thug after he'd throttled me. Would the nasty permutations of these visions never end? I feebly pounded the thin mattress as hot tears mingled with the sweat on my face.

Sometime later, I put on a long shirt and grabbed some clean clothes. The showers at the campground had plenty of hot water and I planned on using a lot of it. Still tired but clean and dry, I heated soup out of a can—Joe would be horrified—followed by a mug of hot chocolate.

Feeling better, I chose a totally escapist novel and appropriated Joe's hammock to read. I had barely begun when a picture thrust its way into my sight, blotting out the words on the page and everything else around me. I dropped the book and groped about for the notepad I always had nearby to jot down lists of things to do or ideas or whatever. The picture before my eyes was at first a snapshot of a landscape from the air and I frantically sketched what I was seeing. The picture, as if I suddenly hit the 'play' button on a disc player, began to move downwards, descending in a dizzying spiral. I tried to close my eyes before impact, as the scene plunged into Earth.

My pen froze. I felt the same sense of darkness I had had in that very peculiar and scary daytime vision in the desert, the vision of the rock in a dark place, the rock that had opened its mouth. A new level of dread gripped me, and I tried to wrench myself from this assault. But it was the second one in as many hours and my resources were worn thin. I gave up the battle. I couldn't escape. I wanted it all to stop.

The vision suddenly eased its grip on my mind, and a measure of light was cast upon the now-motionless scene. A calm, underground sea stretched into the distance, its surface glinting with reflected minerals. It was quite lovely and remarkably refreshing. Perhaps this was what dying looked like. I knew I was not dead, but even just the thought that my torment might be over was a balm.

Too soon, my meditative contemplation was distracted by a shiny point emerging from the highest point of the stone ceiling. Unlike all my other visions, there was no accompanying sound, but I didn't mind since I never had any control over anything anyway. In slow motion, cracks spread from that central point of extrusion, looking similar to when the windshield of a vehicle is struck by a rock.

Huge pieces of ceiling began to break away and, as they struck the water, turned its mirror-like surface into a battle zone. The focus of this silent vision zoomed in on a particular piece of rocky debris as it descended from the ceiling. It had a jagged sword-like shape and arrowed into the water with barely a ripple. Seconds later, a tower of water shot up into the cavern dwarfing all else. I could see nothing but the dazzling sheets of it rising to the ceiling and arcing back to the surface.

A new form began to take shape. Not unlike my spiral descent at the onset of this vision, the water of the underground sea began a slow, circular dance. The stately swirl moved faster and faster, sucking the water into the depths of Earth. The sword-rock must have ruptured the bowl in which the sea had been contained.

I was instantly back in the hammock, shaking and breathing fast. The meaning of this vision was crystal clear: the rock-creature was showing me a future attack on its home—for lack of a better word. I stared at the crude drawing I had made, and the notes scribbled alongside it. Okay. Here were details that I had so often craved from my visions. Now what? Fix a broken rock?

I was still sitting outside when Joe returned. It was dark, and I was in the deep shadow beside the motorhome, but he came directly to me.

"You must have eyes like a cat," I said.

"It's your hair."

I kept my hair short to differentiate myself even more from the girl I used to be, with long brunette hair down to my waist. It had turned completely white a few years after I had left home, and with the tinted glasses, most people thought I was a lot older than thirty-five, and no one from the Island could possibly recognise me. I figured Joe was about forty-three and, as far as I could tell, didn't have a white hair on his head, but he, too, looked a lot older. Our lives had not been easy.

"Tell me about your vision."

He pulled up a chair and listened carefully to my halting description, at the end of which, I felt limp and drained, but I soldiered on and passed him my notebook with my picture and scribbles, further elaborating as I recalled additional details. Joe jotted these down and studied the drawing, turning it this way and that.

"This is bad," he finally said.

I waited for him to go on, which he finally did. I was learning to be patient, though I hoped he wouldn't tax my newfound virtue too often.

"I had a 'call' while we ran. It led me to a canyon ten kilometres west of here, in the foothills. There was infrastructure where there shouldn't be any and it was well hidden from the ground and, I'd guess, also from the air. We waited. Two hours later, a silent-running caterpillar-like jeep came into view. A camouflaged door in the wall of the canyon opened and the vehicle drove in. We were too far away to see inside. We waited another two hours but nothing else happened. I came back. Bob stayed."

I wondered briefly if he had listened at all to me describe my vision, so completely had he ignored it. Then the pieces came together, and I understood. "You can tell from my chicken scratches that the place you went to is the same as this?" I pointed to the notepad on his lap.

He nodded.

"Are you thinking that the entity pushing you around and wherever my visions come from are on the same page?" This sounded too much like my

96

earlier wishful thinking and I immediately regretted voicing it. "What do we do now?" I hoped he would not want any answers or even conjectures from me. I was in the dark much deeper than from any other vision I had ever had, and that's saying something. But this one didn't even have humans in it; it went beyond impossible.

"Sleep. I'm worn out." He slouched over to the hammock and sat to take off his boots. In another few seconds he was down to his underwear and asleep.

I sighed, went in the motorhome, and crawled into bed. I stared at the ceiling for a while and tried to stop my mind from whirling with speculation. But sleep came whether I wanted it to or not.

The next morning, Joe insisted that we wait before talking about the events of the day before. After food and coffee, he said, we would go for a walk. "You need to move before your muscles become flaccid."

Nice way to put it, I thought. *He notices that my muscles need toning but not the motorcycle and side-car.* I wasn't about to point them out since he seemed to be either too blind to see or didn't care. My patience-o-meter was approaching the red line.

I sighed. My practical side overcame my sulk and I thought that, if I had to walk, it would be where *I* wanted to go. We needed information, and a Library was just the place to find it.

Librarians have always been my friends. We shared the same love of books—from their beautiful bindings, to the worlds between their covers, to the ranks and ranks of them in perfect Dewey Decimal order. We sensed this about each other and consequently treated each other with respect. This Librarian was a stocky young man whose pudgy fingers delicately turned the page of the illuminated manuscript that he studied. From my vantage point, I could see his eyes caress the page, willing it to become a part of his very being. I know I get a little carried away, but I love books, and a Library is their most sacred repository.

When he had closed the book and his vision cleared, I approached him. He listened to my request for information regarding a certain tract of land north and west of the community. I had barely finished my request when he hurried off into the current events' section and retrieved the newspapers and magazine articles that had covered the big story of last summer. He placed them on an empty table and waved me to a seat, a veritable *maître d'* of food for the mind. I smiled at him and, like the gourmet he knew that I was, immediately applied myself to the cornucopia in front of me.

An outdoor adventure consortium, DoItNow!, with the support of the town council, wanted to buy a large piece of land west of town which was owned by the environmental group, One World. It would have meant money and jobs for the town and, together with the adventure consortium, they applied considerable pressure on the environmental group to sell. Some of the tactics used were despicable, and exactly what the consortium would do with the land was never clear—only hints about an innovative and exclusive sporting experience for the wealthy. I silently applauded the head of One World, Larry Fulman, for not giving in an inch. Something prompted me to look him up. He had contracted an unusual disease while on a trek in Guatemala and had died recently. The new Chief Executive Officer was one Jeremiah Hughes who, as far as my research could unearth, had moved up through the ranks.

In last week's local paper, a small article in the business section announced that the town council and DoItNow! were gearing up to make a second offer to buy the land.

Maybe my short stint with my neighbour-detective had taught me more than I thought. Of course, it could also be the myriad mystery novels I had read over the years, but it seemed to me that there were too many connections for this to be unimportant.

I presented my findings to Joe. I waited. I waited some more. Maybe his entity was giving him a new mission that would take him off on a completely different tangent and I would be on my own. This distressed me. I'd had someone in my life for ten days and I already counted on him. This made me angry.

"I'm out of here."

Joe nodded.

I grabbed my things and stormed out of the Library. I strode to the corner and waited for the light to change. What was the matter with me? Had I been so out of touch with people that I no longer knew how to just be with someone? Probably. When would I have learned to interact with a friend? Certainly not on the Island, except for Jacinthe, and in the years after I had left, most of the people I met were passing acquaintances, nothing more; I moved too frequently for anything deeper to develop. What if one of my visions badly affected someone I had grown close to? It would devastate me, and I couldn't risk it, not again. That's what I had been telling myself. But what if I was just plain scared to let anyone in? The light changed, and I was glad to move on.

Joe joined me in the little *café* I had found tucked away on a dead-end side street.

"So, were you a tracker in another life?" I asked, trying to lighten my own mood.

Joe cocked his head to the side. "Is something bothering you?"

I never knew if this guy was being told something by his entity or if he was just plain perceptive. "Why? Do I look bothered?"

He sighed.

"Okay, I'm sorry. Yes, something is bothering me. You."

He sat, waiting. He was very good at waiting. I hated that.

"It's just that…," I began.

He waited some more.

I struggled to find the words, not something I normally had to struggle with since so much of my self-imposed solitude had been filled with words, thousands of words, maybe even millions of words, but they were words on paper. I shrugged. "I'm better with plants."

Joe did that rare thing again—he smiled.

I smiled back. "You should do that more often," I said, and he lowered his head, face sober once more. *Rats*, I thought, *leave it to me to never know the right thing to say or the right thing to not say.*

100

He must have sensed my withdrawal. "We can work through it, Flotsy. Neither one of us is good at this, but we can work through it."

He reached across the table and laid a large hand on top of mine, the hand with the scar. I could feel the ridged line of it. He had never told me the story of the scar and I wondered if this was a good time to ask. Was he sensitive about it? Would he get up and leave? Gods, this friend business was hard.

Gently turning over his hand, I ran a finger along the white puckered skin. He didn't so much as twitch.

"I can't feel a thing through the scar tissue but sometimes the palm around it aches." He gently retrieved his hand from mine and massaged it.

"Can you talk about it?" I asked. Then quickly added, "It's okay if you don't want to."

He rummaged in the pocket of his jacket and squeezed a bit of cream onto his palm and continued to massage it. "Arnica. Good for easing a little pain."

I waited for him to continue; I'm learning.

"One of my assignments went a little off the rails," he paused, "or rather, I went off script. This time the bad guy was a woman, which doesn't often happen. She seemed so fragile and lost that I thought, and not for the first time, that my Handler had got it wrong."

"Handler?"

He looked up. "Oh. I have all sorts of names for him: Dip-Shit, Weirdo, Boss Man, Crazy-Ass, Your Eminence—I think he likes that one. Stupid Head for when I'm feeling pouty; Sir for when I'm feeling juvenile and sarcastic; Bastard for when I'm tired. Sometimes I put a few together, like Dip-Shit Crazy-Ass Bastard. I have lots more, but you get the idea."

I smiled and nodded.

"As I was saying," he fingered the scar, "this particular time involved a woman bad-guy. I just couldn't get it through my head that she was going to do what she was going to do. I mean, how could anyone, let alone a pretty, petite blond, do something like that?"

Pretty, petite blond? If that was Joe's type, I was out of the running. Us Maritime girls were brought up on meat and potatoes, and bread and sugar, and tended towards a certain... roundness. My mother had already topped two hundred pounds before I had left the Island. I was a long way from that, but petite would never be an adjective that described me. Wait. Was I a little bit jealous? Couldn't be; must have been some kind of a knee-jerk girl-boy reaction.

"Something like what?" I asked, not only because I wanted to know but because I wanted to shake off that brief touch of the green monster.

"My assignment was to stop her from murdering an entire ward of residents in the long-term care facility where she worked as a geriatric nurse. Over time, the Boss Man had given me a certain amount of latitude in how I accomplished my missions, and I decided to take a little time to study the person. Sandra, the nurse, practised on herself with the knife she planned to use to kill her patients. She kept the blade well-honed so that when she practiced along her own arms and legs, the wounds closed cleanly. She wore long sleeves and

102

long pants to hide the bandages.

"My dilemma was that she also cared deeply about the people she cared for. I saw how she treated them, and you can't fake that kind of compassion. I just didn't get it. So instead of simply grabbing her on her way into work on the designated night and letting His Eminence protect me from harm in his usual way, I told her that I knew what she was about to do. She began to cry and couldn't stop. I didn't know what else to do so I put my arms around her, thinking... well I don't really remember what I was thinking or if I was even thinking at all. She clung to me, and while she went on sobbing, took her knife out, said she had to cut me loose too, and stabbed me in the side, thankfully right into the leather wallet in my pocket. She yanked the knife out and came at me with it; I tried to take it away from her." He stretched open his scarred hand. "She sliced my palm open, and in my split second of shock, she flipped the knife around, and rammed the pommel into my temple. I was a long time coming to and I couldn't remember at first where I was or why I had a bandage around my hand. It seemed she had wrapped it before she left me lying there unconscious." He examined the wood grain of the *café* table for a time, rubbing his thumb along it.

"Later, the police came. They counted thirty-four patients in their beds with their throats sliced open, and one young woman who had bled to death in the chapel's confessional with approximately one hundred and sixty slashes up and down her arms and legs.

"For a while, I took up drinking. It made me

103

quite sick, but at least I couldn't think about what I had let happen. The Boss Man was silent for a long time and when he returned, it was to make me clean up and cut my hair." Joe smiled, but just a little. "Of course, he pestered me until I did it and that's when I started calling him The Nuisance."

I offered to get us another cup of coffee and a little something sweet to eat.

Joe nodded.

I waited at the counter for our order, emptied by what I had heard. I vowed that I would never feel sorry for myself again and that I would use some of my own hard-learned lessons to lend a hand instead of avoiding contact at all costs. I would take small steps and fine-tune my approach to each situation. Buoyed by my resolve, I returned to our table.

Joe was gone. I don't think I'll ever get used to that.

I looked down at the two lemon-cranberry muffins on the plate in my hand and smiled. His loss.

Chapter 6

To my surprise and the surprise of everyone else in the *café*, Bob trotted in, came over to my table, gently gripped my sleeve with his bright white teeth, and tugged on it. I rose and went with him through the complete silence of the coffee shop and into the bright sunshine. He looked up at me and smiled.

We skirted the main streets—very smart idea considering a coyote was in the lead—and met up with Joe, who sat on a crate in an alleyway with his back to us. I increased my pace.

Three scruffy little boys, or maybe one of them was a girl, leapt up from where they were sprawled on the filthy pavement when Bob appeared. He waded into their midst and was hugged, scratched, and kissed with vigour. He smiled. Bob smiled a lot. The four of them raced to the end of the alley and disappeared around the corner, three of them shrieking in delight.

Joe watched them go, a rather happy expression on his face. "That coyote is such a ham."

"What was that all about?" I asked.

"Everyone underestimates kids," he stated. "They can go places and see and hear things that no adult ever could. And, because of Bob, I'm an okay adult, so they're not afraid to tell me things. Like what little Ben heard from his hiding place in the ducting at the in-camera town council meeting yesterday."

"Is there a big Ben?" I interrupted.

Joe smiled.

Maybe I should voice more of my—so far strictly internal—comments. Joe had a very nice smile.

"With money received in some legal but likely sideways manner from DoItNow!, the town has acquired, the land from One World. Ben didn't know what a lot of the words meant, but he understood enough to know that heavy equipment and construction was talked about. Being six, he's very excited about the big trucks coming to town."

"You risked Bob retrieving me from the *café* and trotting through town to tell me this?"

"No. And I would never put Bob at risk. He," Joe touched his index finger to his own head, indicating The Nuisance, "did it. The head of DoItNow! arrives shortly to personally meet with the council."

He got up and started walking. I caught up to him in a few strides. "Did your Handler tell you that too?"

"No. The talk."

I counted to ten.

"The talk at the *café*."

Oh. "Is that why you pulled your disappearing act."

"Yes. I thought I could find out exactly what time he arrives, and I did, and, thanks to little Ben, we know why he's here."

***

Maximillian Wendall Richardson exited the limousine. I disliked him at first sight, and not just because he would very likely ruin a beautiful piece of Earth, but also because of his manifestly arrogant demeanour. It oozed from him.

106

His complexion was fair, and his blond hair was cut so short that it looked white like mine. He was tall, about six feet but not quite as tall as Joe, and he looked fit. His thin lips turned down at the corners. I could not imagine that a smile would have the audacity to make an appearance on that sour face.

He marched toward the main entrance of the town office, his minions scurrying ahead to open the door for him before he reached it.

Joe tapped me on the shoulder and gestured for us to leave. All we could do for the moment was have a look at Maximillian Richardson and glean our first impressions.

He led the way to the Library and we spent the rest of the afternoon pouring over newspapers, magazines, and internet websites. The pieces we found on Richardson told us little about the man as a person but a great deal about the man as a business mogul. He owned an array of companies that ranged from adventure consortiums—he had twelve of them—to marketing, construction, waste systems, pharmaceutical research, banking and investment-related companies, and these were just the ones he was directly linked to. Who knew how many more he manipulated through others? This man had the power and resources to do anything he wanted.

"I know this company," Joe said and pointed to a convenience-store chain. "A friend of mine manages one of them." He got up and made to leave the Library.

Except for when his Handler called, I was getting tired of him leaving when it suited him.

"Wait a minute," I stage-whispered at him.

He turned back and seemed surprised to see that I had remained seated at the table. He stood there. I was determined to finish the article in front of me and not let him bully me into rushing out before I was done.

He sat down and looked off into the distance: a man waiting.

I finished the article, made a few notes, and packed up my things. When I stood, so did Joe and we left the Library together. Once outside, he stopped.

"I'm not used to having to think of anyone besides myself. I'll try harder."

I felt ashamed; guilt and me go way back. "Me too," I muttered. We hurried to the campsite to plan our next step.

Bob, exhausted and happy, waited by the motorhome door, his tongue lolling out. I filled a bowl with water which he drained and I refilled. He took a cursory lap to declare that it was his, stretched front and back legs, and sprawled beneath the hammock. He was to be envied.

Meanwhile, Joe had finally noticed the motorcycle/side-car and was examining it closely. I handed him the key. Bob sprang up at the sound of the engine starting and retreated to a safe distance from this loud and smelly thing. Joe turned it off.

"He doesn't like it." I was disappointed.

"You got this for Bob?"

"Well, yes. For you and Bob. But if Bob doesn't like it, it won't work. He would have trouble keeping up with you." I hesitated. "Assuming *you* like it?" I was definitely not an

108

expert at gift-giving.

"You got this for us?"

"Yeah." Was the boy dense?

Joe came over with the obvious intention of giving me a hug. We did that awkward dance of whose-arms-go-where, finally gave each other a cursory squeeze, and stepped apart.

"So, can you drive one of those things?" I asked to break the moment of discomfort; at least I felt discomfited.

"Since I was a kid." Joe smiled. "Want to go for a ride?"

Interesting how Bob perked up his ears at that question; maybe he had some domestic dog in his genetic makeup, or perhaps somewhere in his spirit. He ventured closer to the bike and gave it and the side-car a good sniffing over. Satisfied, he lifted a leg and peed on the rear tire.

"Get in, boy," Joe invited, and Bob gracefully sprang into the side-car, did a couple of circle-turns, and sat down on the leather seat, tongue lolling out, and smiling.

Joe opened the panier and brought out the two helmets nestled there. He handed one to me and made sure it was secure before putting his own on. He gracefully straddled the bike, started the engine, and gestured for me to climb up behind him.

My palms began to sweat, and I felt like a school kid with a crush. It was just a ride on a motorcycle, not sex, for gods' sake. I would have to think about that crush and sex thing later. Hiding my nervousness, I lifted my leg, squeezing my eyes shut at the correlation that sprang to mind of Bob's leg-lifting, and got myself aboard. It was surprisingly comfortable, and Joe seemed confident. He put it in gear and we began to move. I grabbed on to the first thing available, which was Joe, and held on tight. He patted my hands that held each other with a vice-like grip around his waist.

"Relax," he shouted over the sound of the motor.

Right. I looked over at Bob who sniffed the air as hard as he could. After a while, the sound and vibration of the bike lulled me into numbness and I gazed at the scenery flashing by. Joe took us southeast, out of town, and in the opposite direction of the suspicious canyon.

A roadside diner was visible up ahead and Joe pulled in at the far side of its dusty parking lot. Bob leaped out and disappeared into the surrounding desert. I was not a graceful woman at the best of times. My dismount would have ended in a bruised posterior had Joe not reached around to steady me.

"You'll get your bike legs. Don't worry," he said.

Right. We ordered some burritos and beer and ate outside at a picnic table shaded by a faded umbrella.

Joe pointed to the motorcycle with the neck of his bottle. "Thanks."

"You're welcome, and it's not only for saving my life." I hated thinking about that accident because my pretty car had had to be junked; the bottom bits had all been torn off. "My idea was that when The Nuisance called, you and Bob wouldn't have to steal someone's motorhome to respond." If that stung a little, I was okay with it.

Bob appeared out of the scrub with something

hanging from his jaws. Thankfully he turned around and disappeared from view once again.

"We won't see him again until tomorrow," Joe said.

"How did you two meet anyway?"

Joe sipped his beer. "I haven't known him long, maybe six months...

＊

He had been camping on a mesa south of Las Cruces in New Mexico. He had just finished a task in Albuquerque and needed a break from the city. It was likely his small campfire had attracted them— he didn't usually light one for that very reason—but he was tired and sore and had let his guard slip.

Some of the desert gangs are ruthless and he was pretty sure that if His Eminence didn't intervene soon, it would be very bad for him. They had already beaten him and tied him up, and were scattering his belongings everywhere, some of them into the fire which was now a large one. The blaze was quite beautiful, his stuff adding a kaleidoscope of colours to the flames. He thought if that was the last thing he was going to see in his life, he was going to damn well enjoy it.

Like wisps of smoke, coyotes moved sinuously in among them, nipped here and there, and disappeared again. One of the gang members charged after the coyote that had tripped him, and the snarling of a great many more coyotes nearly drowned out his scream. His comrades formed a phalanx of sorts and, guns blazing, piled into Joe's van and gunned the engine, abandoning the horses that they must have staked somewhere nearby.

Joe would have much preferred to be shot in the

111

head than be savaged by coyotes; he was not at all pleased by the turn of the night's events. There was a snuffling behind him and he struggled uselessly against the ropes that had him trussed like a pig ready for the spit. He felt hot breath on his wrists and rolled as hard as he could in the opposite direction. They did this manoeuvre until Joe had exhausted himself. The next time he felt the breath, he wasn't fast enough, and the coyote got a grip on the rope. The animal proceeded to pull and gnaw on it, its sharp teeth grazing Joe's arms.

It finally dawned on Joe that he should be dead already—there had been at least a dozen coyotes. He stopped struggling and tried to help the beast working on his bonds. Once he co-operated, the job was done in a few minutes. He finished untying himself and crawled over to what he hoped was an intact water bottle. It was battered but not punctured. He drank all of it. He searched for and found another.

The coyote sat about ten feet away and watched him, panting and licking his chops. The adrenaline that had sustained Joe was draining out of his system, leaving him weak and shaking, but Joe felt a surge of gratitude towards the coyote that had saved him. The only thing he could find that would hold water was a cast iron fry pan that was pretty much indestructible. He put some water in it and dragged himself away a few feet, leaving the decision to drink it or not up to the coyote. He knew he needed to tend to his injuries but needed to rest more. He sprawled on the hard ground and slept.

When he woke to the sun blazing down on him, Joe felt about as bad as he had ever felt in his life—

112

body cut, bruised, and aching, and a thirst that was urgent. After a couple of attempts, he got to his feet, holding his gut which had taken the worst of the pummelling. Kicking a few things about, he found a sweater only somewhat singed, and a pair of pants with $3.27 in the pockets. The nearest gas station was about seven kilometres; he had to make it that.

Joe limped to the road but had not gone much farther when he spotted a coyote paralleling him about a hundred yards inside the scrub. It made him nervous; coyotes can be devious creatures. He tried hard to believe that this was the same coyote that had helped him, but he couldn't tell—it was too far away, and Joe wasn't at his best. In fact, he wished he hadn't seen the damn coyote at all because he now wasted precious energy keeping track of the animal and peering about looking for others who might be in on the hunt.

It disappeared altogether before Joe reached the crossroads with the gas station. The attendant was not sympathetic but, after Joe spent two dollars on a pepperoni stick, gave him the key to the public washroom as long as he promised to leave it in the same condition that he had found it. That wouldn't be hard; it was a filthy mess. But it had water. Joe bathed his wounds and drank as much as he could.

Of course, his Handler chose that moment to hurry him on his way. Joe was mostly okay with that because the Boss Man usually made sure he got to where he was supposed to be in one piece.

The king-cab of the pick-up truck at the pumps was crowded with people but the box was nearly empty, and for his last dollar and twenty-seven cents, the driver agreed to take him to the nearest town; he'd be going past it anyway. As they pulled out of the station, Joe saw a blur of motion streak across the parking lot. The coyote leaped into the box with him and immediately hunkered down, ears flat. The people in the cab, intent on their beers and tamales, hadn't even noticed.

Joe and the coyote stared at each other for a few seconds. To say he was uneasy with this arrangement was a laughable understatement. The coyote, however, yawned displaying very white, very sharp-looking teeth, rested its, no his, chin on his front paws, and slept. This was Joe's first hint of the coyote's practical side. That's when he named him Bob, after a classmate of his who was also practical and somewhat hirsute. Coyote Bob. It had a nice ring to it.

At the outskirts of the town, the truck slowed for a stop sign. Bob jumped out and trotted away. Joe watched him go and wondered if he would ever see him again. He was pretty certain he'd be able to recognise him by the way his right ear flopped forward—sort of like a salute.

Joe hopped off in the middle of town and waved his thanks to the driver. His mission was at a ladies' hair salon a few blocks away. He gave the Dip-Shit the mental finger for sending him into such a place, but he had learned some time ago the futility of arguing. The door chimed when he opened it and twelve pairs of eyes immediately focused on him like they were controlled by the same gunner operator. He smiled, which he hoped would make him look less threatening, but it seemed to scare them rather than charm them. He supposed he looked down on his luck; well, he *was* down on his luck.

It was then that he saw the tendril of smoke snaking its way between the slats of the bifold door behind which the washer and drier were kept. His Handler had visualised for him what would happen if the heat should reach the industrial-sized containers of volatile hair supplies that were also kept there.

One of the hairdressers was approaching him with a pair of scissors in one hand and a comb in the other. He dodged past her, grabbed the fire extinguisher from the wall behind the counter, and raced to the back of the salon. The patrons were too alarmed by the sudden appearance of Bob scratching and howling at the door to extend a leg to trip him.

When he yanked apart the doors, the smoke gagged him and made his eyes water. 'Get out!' he tried to yell. Bad idea. He had taken in a lungful of the toxic fumes and coughed for a few seconds. Joe could hear the distant sirens, but they would be too late to stop the explosion that would rip the building apart and kill or maim pretty much everyone within a hundred feet.

This was the part of so many of his missions that Joe tried to block out: the actual putting-himself-in-harm's-way part. He wrapped a hair towel around his hand, prepped the fire extinguisher, opened the dryer door, and sprayed for all he was worth. The flames licked at him for a moment, singeing his face and arms, and then sputtered out, filling the small room with acrid smoke. It was all over. He left through the service door at the back.

He staggered out into the blessedly cool, clear air. Bob was there, waited while he gasped a few breaths of clean air, and led him away from the area.

He would heal quickly but not immediately, which was a major flaw in the Handler's plan for which Joe harangued him over and over. If the Asshole can protect him from close encounters with bombs and bullets, he could surely come up with some magic potion to instantly heal these more superficial wounds—though they never felt superficial at the time. It was likely some stupid rule that required him to suffer for all the good he did. How fair was that?

Bob brought him to a tiny park complete with shade and a drinking-water fountain. He was getting to like this coyote…

***

"After that, Bob hung around a lot. I think he likes the hero business. I read up on coyotes to try to understand why they appear in so many legends. Bob's smart, but I wouldn't say he has any kind of a sacred power except for how The Nuisance might be using him. But who am I to doubt anything? Regardless of why Bob does what Bob does, I'm glad for his help and companionship."

Our beers were empty. "That is a great story," I said. "Thanks."

We walked back to the bike and this time I got on with a little less awkwardness, not smooth by any means, but not without some dexterity. As we rode down the highway, my eyes wandered to the vacant side-car, not as certain as Joe that we would see the coyote again anytime soon. I missed him

116

already.

Chapter 7

Maximillian Wendall Richardson examined his manicure while Councillor Something-or-Other droned on about their partnership and how excited the whole town was to be working on a joint project with such an internationally acclaimed and prestigious organisation. Richardson let his lips form a smile, though he in no way felt any kind of pleasure. This tedious ritual must be endured, however, to ensure that all documents were duly signed. It would not be long before this little piss-ant of a town would regret the day they had welcomed him with open arms. His smile widened.

He stood when his name was called. Applause thundered through the chamber. He waved and smiled some more, and strode to the microphone, shaking hands as he went. He would have to get another manicure.

At last the platitudes were done, the documents signed, and the copies made. He spoke once more with the mayor before excusing himself, citing urgent business that he must attend to, just as he would attend to any urgent business that should arise on this new project they were embarking upon today.

As soon as the limousine door closed and the darkened glass obscured him, Richardson made the telephone call that would begin changing the shape of the land. The caverns to the northwest of the town that he now owned—the town's lawyers should have taken more time to thoroughly research who owned the land around the subject property—

would be connected to a series of caverns beneath the adjacent land he had purchased a few years ago under another of his companies.

Maximillian Wendall Richardson now controlled a vast reservoir of underground water and would sell it for obscene amounts of money to whoever paid his price. He felt a spurt of satisfaction.

Chapter 8

I woke to the annoying sound of someone knocking on the small window behind my head. Even more than a week after the accident, I still had a little trouble waking up and had the occasional headache.

The knocking came again. It had to be Joe and he'd better have a very good reason for waking me. I came completely awake. Joe would never bother me unless it was urgent. I banged back on the window to let him know I was up and felt around for some clothes. We met in the kitchen part of the motorhome where Joe was preparing coffee for us. Good man. I sat and waited for him to speak. I was getting really quite good at this patience thing.

He finished making us coffee and produced a couple of muffins to go with it. This was beginning to look a lot like breakfast and it was only—I squinted at the clock above the tiny stovetop—3:30 in the morning. He sat diagonally across from me, extending his long legs into the aisle.

"He wants you to work with me."

No need to ask who 'he' was. I nodded.

"I don't like it much but no sense in arguing with the Boss Man."

I nodded again. If Joe didn't get to the point soon, all the coffee and muffins in the world would not stop me from strangling him. So much for my recently touted well of patience.

"It seems the town's new best friend does not have their best interests at heart and we are supposed to find a way to stop him."

120

It was not surprising that Richardson had an ulterior motive, but usually the Boss Man just said, 'do this' and Joe did it. "What do you mean about us finding a way to stop him? Don't we just do what whatever His Eminence decrees?"

"That's the way it has always worked before. This time it's different." Joe shrugged. "If he wants it this way, there is no other choice."

I wasn't so sure. "You know my vision about the rock?" Joe nodded and looked at me more closely. "You know that the rock is where DoItNow! is planning to begin whatever it is about to begin. And you also know that that is where you and Bob saw work already underway. It's all tied together." We nodded at each other.

We drank our coffee and Joe made more. We discussed how we could possibly thwart the workings of such a huge organisation. It seemed an impossible task to me. Joe disagreed.

"He would never give us something unless we could do it."

I considered this. Because Joe had always succeeded at the Boss Man's tasks in the past, we should be able to succeed at this one too. Reasonable deduction, but it seemed to me to be also a very good way of instilling a false sense of security. This time, everything was different; this time perhaps the Boss Man wasn't as sure of himself as before, or maybe just didn't know what had to be done. I said as much to Joe.

He sat silent, thinking. I waited.

"It doesn't matter either way," he declared at last, "because we have to try."

"Okay. But let us not forget that this mission is

different and that we may not be able to count on anyone else besides ourselves. Can we agree on this and proceed as though it were true?"

Joe nodded.

We also agreed that we needed more information and arrived at the Library just as it opened for the day.

"How about you have a look at that convenience-store chain your friend manages, and I'll see what I can find on Richardson's staff. We'll meet for lunch and review what we have."

Joe nodded.

Most of what I found was what I expected to find: men and women with impeccable backgrounds on the Boards of his companies, brilliant marketing, generous hiring practices encouraging staff to stay longer than normal, and no hint of accounting hanky-panky. Sounded too good to be true. I would have to dig deeper and, happily, the open philosophy of Richardson's companies allowed me to gather names and contact information for many of his staff.

Starting with the top executives, I began wading through pages of information available on the Internet about their various histories, looking for I didn't know what exactly, but I hoped I would recognise it when I saw it.

I sensed a presence looming over me—Joe— and pushed my chair back.

"Wait." He was looking at a picture of the latest employee I had been researching. A pretty girl, blond I noticed, was pictured in the head-shot that the company's website provided.

"I've read some of her articles," Joe said. "It

seems a bit off that she would be working for Richardson."

Interesting. I ran a search on her writing credits prior to joining Richardson and printed a selection. My eyes had had enough screen time and I would read these in hard copy over lunch. I also printed some of the current articles she had written for Richardson; she was a relatively new employee in his Environmental Relations department.

We exited the Library and walked across the street to the diner that advertised quick service, but I especially liked that it had booths with large tables so that we could spread out our paper booty. We ordered and ate as we read our own and each other's print-outs.

With fresh coffee steaming in our mugs and our table cleared of the lunch dishes, I took out a fresh sheet of paper, put Richardson's name in the middle of it, and drew a circle around it.

"Nice," Joe said and smirked. I had never seen him smirk before; it was not attractive.

"Moron."

I drew a line extending from Richardson and drew a second circle at the end of it and inserted the word Companies. From this I drew several more lines with circles at the ends of them and began to insert the names of Richardson's various companies. Joe came around to my side of the booth so that he could better see what I was doing.

"It's a way to organise your thoughts to see if links exist among a multitude of items. Or it can be used to come up with new ideas sparked from what you already know."

Joe picked up a different coloured pen and

began adding to the mind-map I had begun. We stopped for a minute while I taped additional pages around the central one to give us more room to expand into new categories.

I loved stationery supplies. Various coloured pens and markers, post-it notes in all their permutations, glue sticks, tape, scissors, stapler: I loved them all. Soon, our paper was festooned, ready for us to decant.

"Where did you learn this?"

"Offhand, I can't remember, but journalists use it, analysts use it, and, really, it can be applied to any problem you're trying to solve. It's a way to bundle information and generate ideas," I explained.

Joe sat back and admired our large and colourful diagram. "You're smart, you know."

High praise coming from the man of few words. I think I blushed a little—at least my face felt warm. On the other hand, I had had a few unexplainable sensations of warmth lately and not all of them had to do with Joe's proximity. Ah…, must be the not-so-subtle signs of that fun time in a woman's life. I had hoped for a while that I would have side-stepped these inevitable symptoms, as a sort of redress for the anguish that my curse brought me. No such luck. It seemed I had yet another topic to research, one that likely would not include Joe's active assistance.

I wiped the dew from my brow and turned my attention back to the collage before us. It required further scrutiny and perhaps some culling. I needed a break to clear my mind. Joe and I looked at each other and simultaneously said, "Walk?" This was getting weird.

Chapter 9

Robyn McMaster didn't much like her supervisor but that was a small price to pay for the chance to make a difference. He could harangue her all he wanted about some grammatical disagreement; he was too focused on arguing the finer points of tenses and points of view to ever really look at what she was saying. In fact, she had become quite clever in focusing his attention on myriad unimportant aspects of her articles—the parts he liked. She wasn't proud of this; she was, however, unwilling to sacrifice an opportunity of getting important messages to their readers for the sake of a man who felt the need to control every comma and semicolon.

What she wrote was exactly what they had hired her for, which was to demonstrate to the world that Richardson had the well-being of the environment uppermost in his mind at all times. She had visited a number of his sites and could state with conviction that, when an environmental assessment was required, he had never compromised its terms in any way. This was an amazing accomplishment from a man who could and did buy and sell anything he wished.

She glanced at her in-box. A message from the man himself. The hairs on the back of her neck prickled. She had never received anything directly from Richardson before. What could it mean? Had he somehow discovered how she manipulated her supervisor? Would she get the sack? He had left the subject line blank—that couldn't be good. She was tempted to accidentally press the delete key and claim it had never arrived. But what if his tech goons could trace her action? She was driving herself into a state and had no reason to be nervous. She would just open it.

A quick click of her mouse and there it was: The Desert Project. The office was full of rumours about Richardson's latest venture. That it was big was the only description that was consistent. She gave her full attention to the content of the email. He wanted her on site to document the project from start to finish. There would be a handsome bonus and a chance to make a name for herself. He would, of course, provide guidance, but with her exceptional record, he had no doubt that she could handle this. It started in a week and would likely last a full year. The Human Resources staff would be happy to help her with any arrangements she had to make.

She read it through again. There was nowhere in it that gave her a choice or asked if she even wanted to do this thing. She sat back, nonplussed, trying to grasp the entirety of what it meant. It meant that she would have to uproot herself from her home and live in the middle of the Arizona desert. She supposed that she could say no. No one was forcing her. She smiled. Who was she fooling? This was the chance of a lifetime. She had even taken a few courses on fragile desert landscapes simply because it interested her. She printed off the email and the attachment that came with it, signing the form to confirm her acceptance to work on the project and to maintain its confidentiality until otherwise notified. She faxed it to the number at the bottom of the form. Her supervisor was going to be livid.

The next few days went by in a whirlwind of preparation. Finally, Robyn disembarked from the company jet and into a wall of savage heat. She would get used to it—it was just the extreme contrast from her moist, cool home on the west coast. She and several other recruits were bussed to the hotel that would be their home for the duration of the project. She unpacked and neatly stowed her things in the suite, which had a small kitchenette, and headed to the hotel's ballroom for the welcome meeting and reception. There must have been at least a hundred people gathered there, mingling in small groups. She nodded to the few people she recognised, but most were new to her. Richardson mounted the steps at one end of the stage and stood behind the microphone stationed there. The conversational buzz quieted.

"Welcome. You are the privileged few chosen to be part of what will be the pinnacle venture of the Richardson Corporation. I am confident that you have the skills and abilities to transform my concept into the glorious enterprise that it is destined to be. I give you now the Manager of the Desert Project, Julius Bell, who will go over a few items." Richardson shook hands with Bell, clapped him on the shoulder, walked off the stage and out of the room. Robyn guessed that he didn't want to cramp anyone's style at the reception to follow. She had noted that bars were set up in all four corners of the room and the buffet smelled delicious.

Bell's comments were vague and mercifully short. He concluded by reminding everyone that work would begin the next morning. He smiled when he said this, but Robyn decided that two glasses of wine would be her limit.

She wandered from group to group to try to learn more about who they were and what they did, and perhaps deduce what this project was about. There were geologists, architects, landscape designers, all manner of engineers, explosive experts—she raised her eyebrows at that one—and administrative staff. She learned that there was a second set of accommodations a bit closer to the site that housed the heavy machinery operators, electricians, plumbers, carpenters, and general labourers. This 'glorious enterprise' had a serious price tag well before it had even begun.

Robyn returned to her room, no closer to understanding the goal of the Desert Project.

Chapter 10

I floated down a stone passageway which gradually descended deeper into Earth. I wasn't afraid. The air was fresh and sweet and smelled a little like the ocean. The crystals in the rock walls glinted and twinkled; I was delighted by them. It felt like this was exactly what I should be doing.

The passageway widened and the ceiling above my head rose until I was in a spacious dome filled with crystal stalactites reflected in still pools of water. I rested on a smooth outcropping, content.

Softly at first, a murmur began. I could discern cadences and thought it might be a prayer or incantation. I listened harder and words began to emerge.

***

Something cold shocked my system and my eyes snapped open. Why was Joe shaking the life out of me? Why had he flung the contents of his water bottle into my face? I was getting mad.

"Stop it!"

Joe put the empty bottle down and gripped my shoulders once again. He looked as though he'd been through hell; he looked like that a lot. The boy should take better care of himself. Wait a minute. "What happened?"

Instead of replying, Joe helped me to my feet. Onlookers had gathered. "She's okay. Too much sun," he told them. He put an arm around my waist and walked me to a side street at the end of which was a little park with a shady gazebo in the middle. He helped me to sit.

"Joe. Are you going to tell me what happened, or do I have to…"

He opened his mouth to speak, so I shut mine.

"We were walking."

I nodded.

"You stopped."

This could take some time.

"I waited for you to continue."

A really long time.

"You crumpled to the sidewalk."

I yawned. I couldn't help it even though the thought of crumpling to the sidewalk horrified me.

"You were smiling. You looked ecstatic. It was very strange, so I tried to shake you awake. When that didn't work, I poured a bit of water on your face."

Bit of water! My hair and shirt were soaked.

"You woke up."

He kept looking at me.

I yawned again. "I don't know what happened, but I'm pretty sure it was a vision of some kind. I need a nap." I stretched out on the hard bench, unable to stay awake, and confident that Joe would watch over me.

***

Bob had bad breath and I wish he would stop panting in my face. "Okay, okay. I'm awake."

The coyote stood, looking at me; Joe was nowhere to be seen. I sat up and rubbed my sore shoulder and neck, regretting the lack of any cushioning on the bench. Bob trotted down the gazebo's steps. He looked back and waited. I got the message and wrenched myself to my feet. After of few seconds to be sure I was steady, I followed.

130

Joe was at the outskirts of town, a newspaper tucked under his arm.

"It's begun." He opened the paper and on the front page was Richardson waving from the front of a hotel. Work was scheduled to begin on the new project within the month.

Deep in our own thoughts, we quick-stepped back to Harvey.

Bob was there when we arrived, curled up in his favourite spot under Joe's hammock. We had been given permission to commandeer a second picnic table; the campground was not busy, and the owner liked that we paid in cash. On it we spread our collage of facts and speculations and studied it. We needed a plan and we needed it soon.

"We could look at this forever and still not know what we're supposed to do. I say we get closer to the action."

Joe's idea had merit, and I couldn't blame him for needing to take action, especially considering how the Boss Man had always used him in the past. I did not want to act prematurely, though. My sidewalk vision must be relevant to what was going on and I was reluctant to proceed without more clarity. The vision was in a rocky place and a rock had tried to speak to me twice. I believed that the rock was now trying to communicate with me in a more genteel fashion so that my system could accept its message without the extreme overload it caused. This sounded pretty crazy, even to me. I said as much to Joe.

He pondered for a while. For Joe, this meant just shy of five minutes.

"Let's try this: lie down and open yourself to

131

the rock. Be the instigator for a change, to see what happens."

It said a great deal about our strange and wonderful relationship that I nodded, went into Harvey, and made myself comfortable on the bed. How does one prepare oneself for communion with a rock? There is likely no Idiot's Guide on the Library shelf, so I used the simple meditation practice of relaxing my body, starting with my toes and working my way up to my head while slowly breathing in and out.

I let my relaxed mind skitter where it would, gently pulling it back when it tried to concentrate on some detail. I considered the butterfly, only in slow motion, fluttering from place to place, never staying very long. It was pleasant and when my body changed into the butterfly's form and my wings fluttered, it felt natural to continue into the sunlit grotto. Delicate ferns floated above beds of soft moss. Still pools of water reflected the glittering crystals embedded in the rough walls. This was a very nice place.

A welcoming outcropping of stone was the perfect place to rest and I sat, once again in my own body, to admire the beauty around me. Music began, softly at first. I wanted to listen to the music and my attention focused on it. It was sad and hopeful at the same time. It was a song of need and a song of plenty. It was a song of asking and a song of giving. I think I understood.

Joe sat on the side of the bed with his head in his hands. I think his shoulders were shaking. Was he crying?

"You okay?" I whispered. My throat was very

dry.

Joe started. He turned, gathered me up, and crushed me into a hug. Pleasant though this was, I couldn't breathe very well.

"Water," I croaked.

He let go and made sure I was steady. The glass of water with a bright red bendy-straw was at my lips in two seconds. Ambrosia. I would buy shares in bendy-straw stock, they were that wonderful.

Bob shoved his wet muzzle under my hand, forcing me to pat him. That coyote was definitely part dog. I scratched him behind his ears, just where he liked it. His smile was wide and happy. It was good to be with my boys.

"How long was I out?" I asked without looking up from my ministrations.

"Two days."

Shock stunned me. Two days? The look on Joe's face said it all. He had been worried, really worried.

"The Arrogant Asshole wouldn't let me do anything. It was the most difficult mission he ever gave me." He scrubbed his hands over his face. "Did you learn anything?"

It would take me days to piece it together, and the request asked of us was not worded in such a way as to be easily translated into how it could be accomplished. "In a nutshell, Richardson's project has to be stopped."

Joe nodded.

"Not just because it would destroy a very beautiful piece of the desert but mostly because it would destroy the nexus of a being—although I'm not sure that's the right word—that lives there, sort of. We'll call it a 'she' because she sounded like a woman, in the way the music floated. She tried to explain her purpose but lost me somewhere in the three-billion-year story. Yep, she's old. It has to do with the formation of life on Earth and how the stars and gravity are involved and how it all works together." I sipped more water. "Can you imagine? This is big, really big." I yawned. This business was wearing me out.

I stretched and swung my legs over the side of the bed. "Bathroom and something to eat, then we'll get to work… if I can stay awake."

Joe nodded. I had my first good look at him.

"Did you watch over me the whole time?" *Stupid question*, I thought. The lines on his face had deepened and he looked exhausted.

"Change of plan. All three of us eat and rest. No sense trying to sort through this in the state we're in."

"It's good to have you back," Joe said as he went outside to make us food that would be no doubt filling and nutritious. Bob trotted behind him, drooling ever so slightly on my floor.

We gathered again ten hours later. The food and long sleep had done us the world of good and we were ready to go to work. The first step was for me to try to elaborate on my… I couldn't call it a vision like my earlier visions, it was too all-encompassing for that. It was more like a revelation. I walked Joe through it as best I could but when it came to the details of the 'conversation,' my vocabulary could not possibly have the right words because, rather than words, she—and we would have to come up with some sort of name to avoid confusion—projected impressions with multiple aspects.

"Try the mind-map way," Joe suggested.

We spent a few minutes taping paper together. I added big sheets of construction paper to my mental list of things to buy when next we were in town.

I wrote 'She-rock' in the middle and proceeded to draw lines with a word at the end of each one. Joe looked on in silence. When I ran out of initial thoughts, we looked at each other.

Words like 'protect' and 'survival' and 'fix' and 'help' were just not that useful. The others I had written were also of minimal use. There was nothing on the page that told us what we should do. If this was the entity that had given me visions most of my life, it seemed to me that it had taken a left turn somewhere. Why would such a gentle creature have given me the horrors that I had seen? I went back a step. Just how many of these entities were there anyway? Joe had one and I one, and now maybe a second one. I said as much to Joe.

"We may never know why we see these visions and hear these voices. Maybe we're both crazy and, in our case, like attracted like. Maybe we're both in some mental institution right now, dreaming this whole thing with the help of friendly pharmaceuticals." He raised his hands in frustration. "Regardless of what the reality of our situation is, we have a job to do and I, for one, want to get on with it."

When I opened my mouth to protest that we didn't know our first step yet, he raised his hands again.

"I know, I know. We need a plan." He rose and

135

began to pace back and forth beside Harvey.

Bob sprang to his feet and growled deep in his throat. It was the first time I had ever heard him do that or seen him in what I can only describe as his protective mode. It made me shiver. He was a formidable ally.

Joe came over to the picnic table and turned our working papers face down.

The young woman who approached our campsite was petite and blond. Figures. She stopped at the edge of our site and stared wide-eyed at Bob; I had to give her credit for not pointing out the obvious—that Bob looked a lot like a coyote.

"I'm Robyn McMaster."

"We know who you are," Joe said in a low voice, "but not why you are standing at the edge of our campsite." He was not pleased; Bob's hackles rose even higher. Joe put a hand on the coyote's head.

"Please give me a chance to explain," Robyn pleaded. "I know how this must look, but I need your help."

I sensed her sincerity and stepped beside Joe to put a hand on his arm. He relaxed, but just a bit.

"Come in and have a seat." I pointed to the second picnic table that was relatively uncluttered. "Joe will make some of his excellent coffee and you can tell us everything." Joe harrumphed and went into the RV to get the coffee going. Bob remained on alert, unconvinced.

We knew nothing about this woman except for what we had read in the Library. The articles she had published were very good and both Joe and I agreed with many of her views on environmental

136

protection. But she worked for Richardson now and the timing of this unexpected visit was disquieting, to say the least.

The aroma of coffee preceded Joe out of the motorhome. I rose to help him carry mugs and milk and our hoard of cookies. Bob sat on his haunches and kept his eyes steadily on the newcomer, panting a little to show his marvellous teeth. Robyn squirmed under his gaze. I didn't call him off. I shouldn't be enjoying myself at her expense, but, well, she was blond and petite.

"I was in the Library," she began in a low, sexy voice.

Of course, I thought.

"In the reference section." She had a sip of coffee and made a face.

"A bit strong for you?" I asked in my sweetest voice. Joe looked at me and went into Harvey for hot water and poured some into her cup.

"Much better." She smiled up at Joe.

My belly clenched. Was I jealous? Had I even thought about Joe in that way? I hid my consternation by dipping a ginger snap into the brew. Joe was my friend—my only friend. Could I share him? The question made me want to scream. My mind said that, surely, I didn't expect him to remain solely at *my* beck and call, but my heart said that he was mine, mine, mine and anyone wanting a piece of him would have to fight me for it. The gods only knew what I would do if forced to make a decision right at that very moment.

It's no wonder I had avoided this type of intimacy all my life: it was scary at first, and, at least for me, seemed to be desperate and clingy once the friendship had begun to take shape. Was it worth all this? I watched Joe watching Robyn as she spoke. Watched how he admired her sleek hair, her beautiful skin, her gorgeous shape. Her husky voice was just plain sinful. My brain finally took charge and interrupted these juvenile thoughts. Robyn was inside the organisation; she could help us. How could my petty jealousy compete with that trump card? Gods, I had to get over myself.

Robyn continued. "You had books open and papers spread over an entire table and I couldn't help but notice what the topic was. I was researching the same thing." She shrugged in apology. "You were both totally engrossed, reading and making notes. I thought that maybe we could help each other, so I followed you." She looked at me, concerned. "I hope you're feeling better; I saw you faint on the sidewalk." I nodded, and she continued. "I waited while you rested in the gazebo and then followed the three of you back here to the campground, so I would know where you were staying. And, when I could get away again… well, here I am."

"Patient woman," Joe said, "Flotsy rested there for three hours."

Robyn's chin stiffened. "I am a patient woman," she retorted, "when it's for something important."

She looked at me again. "Flotsy? That's an unusual name."

I tried to smile but, from the look on her face, I did not succeed very well.

"As I'm sure you know, I work for Richardson. He personally assigned me to his Desert Project,

138

just as he personally chose everyone for the Project. From what I can gather, this is the first time that he has taken such a hands-on interest in any of his projects. He usually steps back as soon as the initial idea is passed on to his management team; they look after implementation. Oh, I'm sure he gets reports and such, but he never actively participates, doesn't directly contact the people on the team, and he most certainly never remains on site. There is something very different about this project and I'm beginning to suspect that there is something very wrong about this project and I want to know what it is." She looked expectantly at us.

We stared back at her.

"Oh," she said. "You don't know what he's up to either. I suppose I could just talk to the Project Manager; he looks like a reasonable guy and must know the big picture. But if he does, then he must be in on it—whatever it is—and I run the risk of compromising my position. You see, my job is to document the project, so I have access to and have spoken with members of each team. They know what their separate teams are expected to do but the teams are kept apart from one another and told only what they need to know for their component of the job. I can't piece it together. I'm a writer not a general contractor." She sighed. "But I have an uneasy feeling about it."

Having just had a lengthy conversation with She-rock, I was surprised to feel myself tilt sideways in the chair. I remember thinking from some faraway place that I was glad I didn't have my coffee cup in my hand—it would have made a mess. Robyn softly shrieked. Huh. I didn't know a person could shriek softly.

I gently floated to a shelf in the grotto. There was no butterfly escort this time.

Joe was fast and had mostly cradled my fall to the ground. I knew this because that's where I was when I returned to myself with Joe squatting next to me protecting my head. I say 'mostly' cradled my fall because my elbow hurt like crazy; it must have hit the ground first. Next time, I would have to have a word with She-rock about taking a bit more care of my physical person.

In his usual careful way, Joe helped me to my feet and made me sit while he examined the arm I obviously favoured. Gentle though he was, I hissed at the least pressure near my elbow.

"Hard to say if it's broken," Joe declared. "Have to have it X-Rayed."

He looked at Robyn. "There's ice in the freezer, plastic bags to the left as you go in the door, and a towel in the bathroom." Assuming that she would know what to do, he busied himself unhitching the motorcycle/side-car trailer from the back of Harvey.

Bob put his head in my lap. It was a great comfort to stroke his soft head and feel the heat of his body. A tear slid down my cheek and I wiped it away. He licked my hand. It was as if he understood completely what I needed just then. We watched the bustle around us, content to be still.

With the bag of ice numbing my arm, we piled into Harvey for the drive to Emergency. The wait there was mercifully short. My elbow was bruised and swollen but not broken. The sling and ice helped, but the pills helped more. We picked up a quick dinner—something Joe does only in extreme

140

conditions; he says the food in restaurants will kill you—and returned to the campsite.

Only when Joe was satisfied that I was as comfortable as possible, did he allow the first question. I quite liked this protective part of our friendship. Robyn had remained on the sidelines for the entire duration of this little crisis.

"She-rock?" Joe wondered.

I nodded.

"Something urgent?"

I nodded and looked at Robyn.

"She in?"

"Yup."

I smiled. Robyn's head swivelling back and forth during this cryptic conversation was entertaining. I sighed. It was time to open my heart a wee bit wider and let someone else in.

***

The telling of our three stories took time, but we agreed at the outset that it had to be done. Bob came and went, slept, paced, came and went again, and sat panting at us. His was a simpler life.

You don't hear stories like Joe's and mine every day, but Robyn's expression remained attentive and neutral. It occurred to me, as I fumbled with descriptive phrases while I spoke, that I would have to create a whole new vocabulary to portray the snatching of my consciousness. Her questions, when they came, assumed that what we had said was factual. I had to admire her for that.

She, on the other hand, had led an ordinary life: ordinary parents, ordinary siblings, ordinary friends and neighbours and boyfriends, ordinary ambitions, and ordinary jobs. She liked pizza (who didn't?),

141

not-too-spicy Mexican food, the occasional beer or glass of wine, classic rock, and comfortable yet fashionable clothes. I might have nodded off a time or two and hoped she couldn't tell through my tinted lenses.

I became more attentive when her sultry voice grew excited, which, of course, only added to its allure. As a beauty queen contestant (what a surprise), she had very seriously considered the answers to the questions posed to her by the panel of judges. In this particular contest, the participants had two days to compose their replies and submit them in writing.

"Wait a minute," I interrupted. "You could go home before you answered? You could ask people for their opinions, look for information in books and on the internet?"

"But it had to be your own, personal answer," she said, and then stiffened. "Did you think one of us would cheat? Did you think *I* would cheat?" Her face reddened, and her voice had taken on a screechy quality.

Joe stepped in. "I'm sure that Flotsy's comment," he glanced my way, "was based on the more predominant and sensationalistic opinion of beauty contests that one sees in tabloids and movies."

"Oh. Of course."

To my dismay, she apologised. I had much to learn about people and what made them tick.

She continued her story. "The question was 'If you could, how would you change the world?' It was a huge surprise to me, and to everyone who knew me, that this question was the pinnacle upon

142

which I based the direction of my education and career goals. To answer the question, I first needed to know what state the world was in. Sure, I had read the headline stories about food shortages and over-population and natural disasters, but a little deeper research opened my eyes to the vast number of ways in which humans abused the planet. It was that one beauty-contest question," she smiled at me, "that opened my eyes beyond the comfortable bubble I had been living in, that showed me how I had never done anything truly important, and that pointed me in a direction where I could, maybe, make a small difference.

"My strength throughout school had always been writing, so I earned a master's degree in investigative journalism, did volunteer work at every save-the-whatever organisation in the northwest, and was published in journals and magazines. And here I am, very keen to let the world know if someone as powerful as Richardson is indeed on the up-and-up when it comes to the pristine desert in which he proposes to do," she shrugged her shoulders, "I-don't-know-what." She sipped her doubtless cold coffee.

My arm had started to ache somewhere in the middle of her story and I had trouble concentrating. Joe, with an uncanny sixth sense, shook out a couple of the painkillers from the bottle on the table and passed them to me. I grimaced back at him.

"I shouldn't have tired you. I'm sorry." Robyn rung her hands and looked distressed.

I was too tired and sore to do more than wave a hand in dismissal, which was a bad idea since I used my bad arm and it jarred my elbow.

"Time to rest," Joe declared. He helped me up and into Harvey. When I was as comfortable as possible on the bed, he said, "I'll go over our mind-maps with Robyn. Maybe she can add things we've missed or had no way of knowing."

I nodded.

"And, don't worry," he added, his face in its usual bland expression, "this is strictly business."

I wanted to punch him, just a little, but the meds had kicked in and I gratefully slipped into a pain-free and healing sleep.

Robyn returned to our campsite the next morning.

Joe paced while I looked at the mind-map spread out on the table; they had made considerable progress in filling all the remaining blank space. It seemed to have taken on a life of its own and grown beyond anyone's capacity to grasp the whole of it, let alone decide what to do about it.

"You've been busy," I commented. One item caught my eye. "What's this one: 'aquifer'?"

"The studies on the size of the aquifer, some of which is beneath the general location of the Desert Project, are inconclusive. It's difficult to measure accurately," Robyn said, "but some experts believe that it covers a much larger area and is far deeper than generally thought."

It didn't take a rocket scientist to connect to the need for water in the desert, especially for the more populated areas. "When you say 'larger' and 'deeper' what, exactly, have these experts postulated?"

Joe sat down beside me to hear the answer

Robyn looked at us. "Some say that, for want of

a better term, it's the mother-lode of aquifers, and could supply water to a city the size of Los Angeles for many years. But at that level of use, it wouldn't be able to renew itself and would eventually go dry. In one article, it was speculated that if it were depleted, the enormous and empty space that once held the water would collapse on itself."

She rubbed her hands together—the subject an obvious trigger for her enthusiasm—and continued. "The whole underground system in this area is an intricate matrix of checks and balances. Changing this rather large part of the equation, could cause a domino effect resulting in a cataclysm the like of which we've never seen before."

I interjected. "Okay. So. Richardson could tap into this aquifer, sell all the water for unbelievable amounts of money, and for the grand finale, watch as several square miles are destroyed when the land caves in?" My disbelief was fairly clear in the tone of my voice.

"It would be more like the entire southwest as well as most of the west coast that would be decimated. This area is riddled with fault lines and old rhyolite volcanoes," Joe added.

Robyn nodded.

Another nodder. Sheesh.

Robyn smiled at Joe and he smiled back.

They were having a moment. I bent my head and bit my tongue to hold its acerbic remark at bay and concentrated on forcing my heart to stay open to this new friend. A smile was just a smile. It was not a declaration of undying love. Exclusive, undying love. I had to remember that there were all kinds of love, and that you could love all kinds of people. Somehow, it just didn't feel that way.

"Rhyolite?" I asked, steering them away from the smiling-at-each-other moment.

Joe tore his eyes away from Robyn's, or perhaps I just imagined that he did, and looked at me. "The important thing to know about rhyolite volcanoes," he explained, "is that they explode violently, like Mount St. Helens. Volcanoes made of basalt—the black rock—don't usually explode."

Joe and Robyn did that smiling thing again. Instead of making myself crazy, I concentrated on the mind-map and noticed another of Robyn's additions—you could tell that it was hers: the ink was pink. This one read 'roller-coaster.' It surprised a laugh out of me.

"Roller-coaster? Is Richardson planning some kind of extreme ride for when this part of the planet explodes?" I put on my version of a carny's voice. "Be the first to experience the ultimate force of nature! Get your million-dollar ticket and ride the volcano!" I snorted with laughter and, in that most embarrassing kind of moment, noticed that I was the only one laughing.

I sobered. "Okay. What about the roller-coaster?"

"It was just something I overheard. One of the engineers was asking about installing rails and, Bell, the Project Manager, said that the rails were meant to hold a light load. So, it could be something to transport people into and out of whatever Richardson is building, and, who knows?, maybe he's building an amusement park. Hence, roller-coaster." She huffed. "It was just a way to remind myself that Richardson could be up to anything."

I hated to admit it, but Robyn was right. We had to keep our minds wide open.

"Sorry. You're right, of course. I blame my untoward reaction on the meds and the fact that I'm starving. Sorry," I repeated, to make certain I had actually said it, not just contemplated saying it.

Bob eased his head under my hand. I stroked his soft ears and gave him a smacking kiss on the nose. He sneezed. The tension around the table dissipated as though it had never been. That Bob.

We ate Joe's delicious meal and spent a couple of hours chatting about anything but the project. We had decided that we were getting nowhere and that our minds needed to be distracted for a while.

Bob dropped a stick onto Robyn's foot and, before she could think through what she was doing, she picked it up and threw it. Bob raced off and brought it back, dancing sideways, back and forth. A little dismayed at her own courage, she jogged into the field next to the campground and spent a good half hour trying to wear out the coyote. Joe and I could have told her that thirty minutes was barely a warm-up for Bob.

Winded, Robyn returned to the campsite and announced that she had better get back to her hotel before she was missed. We agreed to meet again in two days, during which time, she would do her best to learn what she could.

Joe insisted on giving Robyn a ride to town on the motorcycle. I watched them leave feeling that somehow a part of me had been severed. What if he never came back? What if they decided to put all this intrigue behind them and ride off into the sunset? What if they were innocently stopped at a light and a transport truck veered out of control and flattened them?

I didn't have to wonder why I always had these thoughts of impending doom. It was an instinctive reaction burned into me that day when I couldn't save my father; he had left for work one morning and never came back, and I had known it would happen. Afterwards, my mother would step out for a quart of milk and I was certain that she would be robbed and beaten and left for dead in some dark, smelly alley. My friend, Jacinthe, would go skating on the barachois pond and I knew that she would plunge through the thin ice and into the frigid water below and drown in the darkness.

It was always like this, vision or no vision. I always expected the worst to happen and, when it didn't, I felt no relief. All this meant was that the disaster was around the next corner or at the next stop light or even in the freezer section at the convenience store. The sense that something bad was about to happen followed me like my own personal black cloud. It's a wonder I left Harvey at all. But then bad things could happen inside Harvey, too, couldn't they? I was getting very tired of myself.

Sometimes I believed I was just trying to fool myself. If I expected to be disappointed, it was bound to happen because that's what I expected, but when something turned out right, I remained uneasy, not convinced. I would be cautiously pleased when something good happened, but not *too* pleased because things could take an about-face in an instant. With a mind that worked like this, it was no wonder that I was never truly happy, that I never

148

truly believed what anyone said, and that I never truly thought that anyone could consider me a worthy friend or, and I barely whispered this to myself, worthy of romantic love.

I sighed, heaved myself to my feet, and, with Bob dogging (no insult intended to Bob) my steps, set about cleaning up our campsite and preparing something simple for dinner. With one good arm, this took me the whole time Joe was gone.

He rumbled into the parking spot behind Harvey and cut the engine. Bob raced over to inspect his sidecar and delicately jumped in and out, careful not to crush the paper bags sitting on the floor—good things came out of paper bags. With the flair of a magician, from one of the bags Joe pulled out a bone that could have come from a brontosaurus and, with reverential care, Bob opened wide his jaws and accepted his tribute. He hurried out of the campsite; he liked to feast in private.

Joe had also picked up ingredients for salad that he promptly began to assemble. It would be a welcome addition to the sandwiches I had managed. We ate in companionable silence. My dark thoughts while Joe had been gone seemed to have, ironically, purged my dark mood.

"We're a little closer to understanding what we must do," Joe said as we sipped after-dinner coffee, "and now we have someone on the inside, someone who has access to much of what is going on."

"Has The Nuisance given you any clues?" I wondered.

Joe shrugged. "This is the longest time in a very long time that I haven't been pressed into a mission. It tells me that The Nuisance wants me to

149

focus on fixing this one, whatever that might mean. I've got to say that it's unsettling to not be thrust immediately into action. It's making me jittery." He drummed his fingers on the table top. "I think Bob and I will do a little reconnoitering at the project site."

It was a good idea. I knew this. But, of course, I couldn't help thinking that Robyn had everything to do with Joe's urge to be closer to where she might be. I straightened my arm and felt a twinge in my elbow, but only a little one. It was definitely on the mend but could not be counted on if I needed it.

"When do you think you'll go?" I asked.

"Soon."

He rose and began gathering a few useful items for his stakeout. I watched and wondered what I could do to assist.

"These mind-maps are getting a little out of control. I think I'll work on eliminating duplications and combining obviously related items. It might spark a new idea. Anyway," I continued, "if I rest my elbow for another day or so, it should be as good as new."

Joe nodded and mounted the bike. Bob materialised and hopped in the sidecar.

I watched them ride into the twilight and quashed the image of the fiery crash that instantly sprang to mind.

I reviewed the material we had gathered thus far and studied our mind-maps. Frustrated that no new ideas leapt off the pages, I extinguished the lantern and, in its place, lit a small campfire and let my mind wander where it would.

Chapter 11

Joe, silent from many years of being alone, and Bob, silent by nature, watched the activity in the valley below. There hadn't been much need for a stealthy approach, though. Gone was any attempt at subterfuge. The place was floodlit like a night-time major league baseball game, and the noise from earthmoving and other heavy equipment funnelled up into the sky like the roar of some great beast.

The previously hidden entrance had been enlarged to accommodate the construction equipment. A steady stream of trucks filled with debris lumbered away from the site to empty their loads and return for more. A grouping of trailers had been installed beyond the entrance; satellite dishes and antennae bristled from their rooftops.

Bob stiffened, and Joe followed his gaze with high-powered binoculars. Robyn exited one of the buildings in the company of three men. They were in animated conversation and Joe could just make out the recording device in Robyn's hand. A summons to the site must have been waiting for her at the hotel; this could mean a new development.

When the ground shook, it was difficult to tell if it came from the activity at the project site or from some other source. One of the men with Robyn grabbed her by the arm and frantically gestured towards the parked vehicles. They ran to one of the HUMMERs and, before the doors were closed, the driver had the wheels digging into the dirt and the vehicle racing away. Workmen abandoned whatever they were doing and left the site in the fastest people-mover they could find. In minutes, the place was empty, the echo of the retreating vehicles reverberating in the air until only the white noise of the still-functioning electrical equipment remained.

Joe knew an opportunity when he saw one. He slithered down a deep crack in the hillside, hidden in a deep shadow courtesy of the bright floodlights. He reached the bottom; he would be visible with his next step, but there was no other choice if he was to see first-hand what was going on inside the cliff. There were likely security cameras, but he hadn't spotted any. Bob nudged him with his nose and trotted over to the entrance. When there was no reaction, Joe followed. Maybe the security guards had also vacated their posts.

His first impression was of a gigantic meteor strike like he'd seen in the movies, only this one was inside. What once might have been a natural cavern had been enlarged; the machines that had done this had left erratic gouges in the walls. The floor, too, had been scraped and flattened into the semblance of a road that descended before curving to the right into blackness. Hugging the rock wall behind a structure that doubtless held offices by the way thick wiring ran into to it, Joe and Bob descended into Earth.

They walked down the gigantic corkscrew road that had been carved into the sides of a seemingly bottomless hole in Earth. They had been walking for more than an hour when Joe noticed how completely quiet it had become. It was like being inside one of those sensory deprivation machines where all sound and light and weight are artificially suppressed.

Bob had ceased examining every puddle and crevice and stayed close to his human's side. Joe put a hand on his head; it was a great comfort to have him there. The heavy-duty flashlight was also a great comfort.

At last, they reached the end of the constructed road. Joe crept to the edge and shone his light into the depths. Its pitiful power could not reveal what might be at the bottom of the abyss.

Joe was suddenly aware of the unimaginably massive amount of rock all around him and especially above his head. The quiet became eerie. Bob fidgeted. It was then that he heard it. A sigh—a sigh so profound that tears filled his eyes.

***

I was alone for the first time in weeks and was surprised to feel good about it. The solitary life I had led before Joe had been comfortable. I knew where I stood at all times—so very easy when you only had yourself to consider. I had been in control of my life. Sort of. If you didn't count the visions.

The flames of the campfire danced and played with each other and I was amazed by the infinite variety of their movement. The ancients had the right of it by naming fire an element for it was certainly elemental.

The ancients also named earth an element. My experiences with She-rock certainly spoke of her elemental nature. It occurred to me that it was impossible to describe something when you had no point of reference and no possible comparison. Metaphors and similes did little more than provide a whiff of the forces that were at play.

153

***

She-rock sighed. I saw Joe in a deep, dark place, Bob at his side. Tears ran down his face and I felt them on my own cheeks. No. I felt exactly what Joe felt because I was inside Joe's head. Joe looked up and I saw the terrible gashes on She-rock's body, pieces of her in discarded piles along the twisting path. Joe bowed his head, turned, and trudged back towards the entrance; Bob, tail between his legs, followed.

***

After a time, I heard the motorcycle entering the campground. Joe pulled his chair over, sat next to me, and reached for my hand; Bob jammed himself between us.

"You were there," Joe said.

I squeezed his hand by way of response.

"That was She-rock." His voice held a hint of the same awe I always felt when she communicated with me. "The tremor was her trying to help us help her, and I think I know what to do."

I closed my eyes; I had seen it too. She-rock had shown the precise locations for explosives that would disable Richardson's project, and at the same time, protect She-rock.

"But it will be very dangerous. Someone could get hurt."

I squeezed his hand again, afraid that, if I spoke, the tightness in my throat would be apparent. I knew who would get hurt and maybe even killed. This time, it was not my propensity for always dwelling on the worst-case scenarios, but rather the vision that She-rock had shown to me, and only to me. She was running out of time and if we didn't do

154

this thing, so much more than her existence would be ended.

Joe gently removed his hand from mine. I heard him rummage around inside Harvey and, shortly, the scent of onions frying in butter wafted out to where I sat. Leave it to Joe to consider the practical things and, I must admit, I was glad that he often thought of food. Bob sat patiently nearby, his eyes a little duller than usual. The day had been hard on all of us.

Replete, I added a few pieces of wood to the fire, mostly so that I had something to do while the coffee brewed. I stepped beyond the reach of the fire's light to look around for the moon; she should be rising soon. Of course, she did no such thing—it was us rising to meet her as was appropriate from my point of view. Interesting how semantics got it wrong so often. It made me wonder about how many other things we got wrong so often and so easily, without thinking.

Take Robyn, for example. Here was an intelligent woman of reasonably good looks (okay, great looks) who was willing to sacrifice her career and maybe more for something she believed in, and not because she had some entity pushing her around but because she believed in what she was doing. Maybe I had never given humanity much credit for doing the right thing. On the other hand, between being shunned by my family and an entire village, as well as by nearly everyone who had had the misfortune of making eye contact with me, I didn't have much to go on. Reading books about people had never given me the gut feeling that I knew them and could trust them. I had such a minimal amount of experience to call upon to connect their body language to the way they spoke and to the look in *their* eyes. All this made it difficult to believe in my own instincts. I had observed people's behaviour, of course, but that was too superficial to give me any real sense of them. I could ask Joe what his thoughts were on this; after all, he said that he had made friends at University.

His timing, impeccable when he wasn't on a call, was perfect as he joined me at the edge of the firelight and handed coffee to me. We stood there for a time, silent, sipping our drinks, content for the moment.

"Do you want to talk about it?" I asked.

Joe sighed. "You ever feel something that you've never felt before? How do you talk about that? How do you know what words to use?"

My stomach dropped. I knew this was coming; I should have been ready. It should have had no effect on me. My mind just didn't get the message. Why was that, anyway, when your body knows your feelings better than you? I forced myself to rally.

"She's a nice girl," I began. "Smart, pre…"

"What are you talking about?" Joe interrupted. "You were there, weren't you? You saw what they did." He turned to face me. "You think I meant Robyn?"

Even in the mostly-dark, I could see the disbelief on his face. Even in the mostly-dark, I fervently hoped that he could not see me. Futile hope. He took the empty cup from my hand. I couldn't meet his gaze. He turned, deposited the cups on the picnic table, and strode from the

156

campsite. He'd be back, I told myself. He had to be.

The long night had begun with a healthy dose of self-depredation. A good cry followed by plenty of nose-blowing and another, shorter, session of beating myself up finally exhausted me. It was then that I had my first epiphany. I realised that I was human. This might be obvious to most people, but most people are not me. Accept it, let it go, and get on with it. What else was there to do?

Joe still had not returned. Bob trotted over to me and I performed my morning ritual of greeting him with rubs, scratches, pats, and generally saying hello. I filled his dishes and gathered my washing-up things to prepare for the day.

When I got back to the campsite, freshly showered, Robyn and Joe were there. *Accept it, let it go, get on with it. Accept it, let it go, get on with it.*

"Joe, I'm sorry," I blurted. *Apologise.*

He waved a hand, beckoning me to join them. "Forget it. Like I said before, we're both new at this." He looked up. "Robyn has uncovered some interesting information."

I noticed that his eyes were bloodshot; he hadn't slept much either. I would not even think that he might have been up all night with Robyn; they probably just met this morning. *Accept it, let it go, get on with it. Apologise.* I figured if I repeated it often enough, it would become my new, automatic reaction. Seemed like a plan.

"They had to close the project down to allow for further study," Robyn said. "The tremor was unexpected." She looked at Joe, eyes wide. "Joe tells me that the tremor had nothing to do with the excavation, but rather was caused by your... friend." She stumbled to a halt.

"She-rock," I said. "Friend? I think we'd have to expand the definition of the word. She's herself and not like anyone or anything. Regardless, She-rock needs our help and, believe me, we want to give it to her."

"Yes," Robyn agreed, "and the tremor may have bought us a little time to come up with and implement a strategy to stop Richardson while his project is on hold."

Joe and I looked at each other. We knew one way to stop him: bury the project with well-placed explosives that would not affect She-rock or the aquifer. But it wasn't the best of ways for a very good reason. Joe could be killed and maybe Bob, too. I didn't like it one bit. Joe, on the other hand, seemed resigned to his fate. This would not do at all.

"I know what you're thinking, Joe, and you can just forget about it. The Boss Man hasn't been in touch with you, so you don't have an..." I waved my arms around, searching for the right words— what was it that Superman had? It eluded me; I'd just have to make something up. "You don't have an impervious force-field to protect you. We will come up with an alternative. She-rock is desperate and fighting for her life here. I understand that. We," and I looked directly at Robyn for the first time that morning, "are going to fight." Bob in his usual I-know-what-you-just-said-style, licked my hand.

Chapter 12

Harder." There was no denying that Richardson was not happy.

His masseuse dared not wipe the sweat from her brow. He would know that the rhythm had changed, and she would be fired. She needed this job. She set her jaw and pushed.

***

Freshly showered and shaved, the CEO of one of the largest corporations in the free world struggled with a recalcitrant cufflink. *Where was that valet?* He would have to be dealt with; he would be re-assigned to some menial position in some poisonous factory in some third-world toilet. He would not survive long—just long enough to learn that mistakes are not tolerated.

The pieces of the diamond-encrusted cufflink pinged when they struck the marble floor. He stared at the broken *objet d'art*, for that was what it was. He had had the cufflinks designed and handmade by the most talented craftsman in the world. He ground his teeth together. Perhaps the valet would first have to watch his family suffer.

Seismologists and geophysicists worked frantically to find the source of yesterday's tremor. All manner of engineers prepared designs to prevent any damage to the work already in place.

He poured scotch into crystal and took his drink out to the balcony that overlooked the landscape he would transform. Setback after setback plagued this project, like when his first offer to buy the land had been refused. He, Maximillian Wendall Richardson, had been refused! And now the explosives were not doing the job as quickly as predicted and may even have caused a tremor.

Richardson swirled the golden liquid in his glass. This glitch was nothing more than an opportunity to flex his not-inconsiderable muscles. He had not had a worthy challenge in a long time.

It puzzled him, though. Preliminary studies had shown a high percentage of certainty that his scheme would succeed. He pressed a button on his watch. His personal assistant appeared. "Who signed off on the surveys?" He didn't have to explain himself; his assistant would know what he meant. Less than five seconds later, he learned who had embarrassed him.

Chapter 13

Joe took the motorcycle to town to buy food, with Bob in the side-car, of course.

Even though neither Joe nor I had slept, we had already begun to plan our strategy. It was kind of funny, actually. Four of us against all of them.

I retrieved paper and marking paraphernalia from Harvey and Robyn laid our tools out on one of the picnic tables. Coffee brewed. All was in readiness for our brilliant ideas to flow forth.

For the moment, Robyn and I were alone. She looked a little nervous and I quite liked that. I wondered what Joe had told her about me. Mmmm. Maybe I could find out. Our eyes met and, in the manner of awkward conversations everywhere, we both began talking at the same time.

"How long have you and..." Robyn said.

"What did you and Joe..." I said.

We laughed. Well, not exactly laughed. More like tittered. I flushed, having never tittered before.

"You first," I said, gracious hostess that I am.

Robyn studied her hands. Hands, I noticed, with long elegant fingers ending in light-pink, perfect nails. I looked at my own: short and strong-looking. Best not to compare hands. She cleared her throat.

"Umm...," she cleared her throat again.

I made her very nervous. Maybe that was not a good thing after all.

"Are you and Joe..." she stalled. "Umm, you know, going out?"

I let the silence drag on for a bit.

"As in, are we sleeping together?" I don't know why I was being so cruel. *Accept it, let it go, get on with it. Apologise.* Oh, yeah. I'd forgotten that. "No. We're just friends."

"Oh." The relief on her face said it all. She was going to make a move on Joe. *Accept it, let it go, get on with it. Apologise.* This was going to be hard.

Joe pulled in. We busied ourselves preparing the breakfast ingredients he had purchased, ate, and quickly cleaned up.

"Okay," I began. "Tell us what you found."

Robyn pulled a tattered piece of paper from her purse. Cute purse, I noted. She put the paper on the table and flattened it with her cute hands. *Stop it!* It was company letterhead.

"The janitor likes to talk, and I like to listen. He told me about the tedious rounds he makes and how everything had to be handled just so. The boss's orders. I distracted him yesterday with a little bathroom problem that he had to deal with right away and, while he was busy, I rummaged through his trash can and found this."

Joe had already read it. I picked it up. The letter was to one Godfrey Smythe. Wait a minute, I knew that name. Parapsychologist. Of course, I had read about him during my 'search for an answer to the universe' phase. Richardson was demanding his presence immediately. I could understand why the letter had been scrunched into a ball and thrown out. I imagined a much more genteel request had been sent and, likely, by private jet and hand-delivered to Smythe at his home in England.

"This is unexpected." I continued to study the letter, particularly Richardson's signature. It was

162

peculiar. Handwriting was a curious thing and—it embarrasses me a little to know this factoid—there was such a thing as Graphotherapy, which is when a person changes his or her handwriting to disguise something in their personality. I was certainly not an expert, but my instincts told me that something wasn't quite right with Richardson's signature. I looked up.

"Was there any indication in all the material that we found on him that Richardson would even consider anything like parapsychology?"

Joe and Robyn both shook their heads. I told them about the psychological possibilities related to handwriting and asked if they knew anything about that. They shook some more. I gave them a précis of what I knew, and suggested we do some research in case there was new information that might help.

Bob stood, alert, looking at Joe. They left.

"Man, I hate it when they do that."

Robyn looked confused. "What's going on? What happened?"

Ah, a virgin. "That is what happens when the boys get a call."

Her look of confusion intensified.

"You know. The Big Guy, the Boss Man, The Nuisance? He just sent Joe on a mission."

Her face immediately filled with worry.

"Yeah, I know. And I don't think it will ever get any easier to see them go."

We gathered a few pertinent pieces of information and some extra paper. We decided it would not be a good idea for us to be seen together. We would walk to town, leaving ten minutes apart. I would go to the Library while Robyn visited the trio

163

of bookstores in town. Our clever 'cloak and dagger' game would culminate by arriving at the gazebo in two hours from two different directions. We were possibly a little over the top with our attempt at subterfuge, but it made things more fun. And who knew how paranoid Richardson was, especially considering the new information we had?

There was little updated information under Parapsychology and I did not find anything recent on Godfrey Smythe. I expanded my search for data on him and it was like he had disappeared from the planet. There were none of those convenient little links that gave you clues to a person, especially a person like Smythe who was, at one time, a well-known research Parapsychologist. I wondered if he had had a falling out with the Society of which he had been a prominent member. This would fit. Richardson would pick a rogue.

The important question was, what could Smythe possibly discover? Would he be able to detect She-rock? It didn't take any thinking at all to know that this would be a bad thing. Not only would he dissect and study her, if this was even possible, but he would reveal her to Richardson. I swallowed, my mouth dry. *Don't panic*, I told myself. *Panic just makes you stupid, and when you're stupid, you do stupid things*.

We rendezvoused at the appointed time. Robyn had a plastic shopping bag as well as a good-sized paper bag looking remarkably like it had a small grease stain on it. Baking? Maybe I could get to like this girl; it seemed I was a sucker for people who fed me.

We sat and distributed the food between us.

164

When the first croissant had satisfyingly melted in my mouth, I bought us coffee at the little take-out across the street.

"Did you find anything good?" I asked.

She wiped her fingers on a napkin and opened the bag from one of the bookstores. "This one has a good overview of the current parapsychological world and who is in it, and this one is..., well, see for yourself." She displayed the bizarre cover of the latest Beyond, wherein any and all stories about the fantastical things people had seen or heard—or what the staff of the magazine fabricated in a slow month—are made available to the rest of the world. Lucky us.

Robyn saw the sour look on my face. "Wait. Before you discount it, take a look at this." She opened the magazine to a story about spelunking into the face of darkness. She had circled in pink highlighter the following excerpt: *So, me and my buddy tied off our lines and crawled into the tunnel on our hands and knees. Our helmet lamps were all we had for light. Andy, in front of me, stopped and I ploughed into him. Jeez. "Hear that?" Andy whispered. I listened hard. There was nothing. "Come on, man. We gotta keep...," And then I heard it. It was like the rock around us was one big woofer, only turned down way low with the bass way up. It made my whole chest cavity vibrate, kind of made me feel a bit like puking. I shoved at Andy's boot and started backing out. After a minute, he did too. The weird sound kept on going the whole time and I swear it was saying something. Andy and me, we retraced our route as fast as we could and didn't stop til we were in the truck and headed for the cantina down the road. The guy there had told us not to go in, but did we listen? I went back to the cantina later, when I was, like, calmer, to see if he would tell me more. I had to spend a LOT of money on beer, but he started talking. Seems there's a legend about that cave system, about how it was alive and lured cavers into itself. It had to be true; too many cavers had gone missing. No one and nothing was ever found: no clothes, no equipment, no bones. The locals call it La Boca—The Mouth.*

The hand-drawn map below the article was in Coconino County, north of Flagstaff, Arizona.

I looked up at Robyn, huge grin on my face. "That's not far from here."

"It's better than that. Coconino County is on top of some of the aquifer. I've already sent an email to the publisher requesting the contact information for the guy," she checked the article, "Sam Maguire, who wrote it. Maybe he'd be willing to give us more details. I already searched for him on the net, but no luck there."

This was promising, but I tried not to expect too much. I couldn't help but think that, even if it gave us another access point to She-rock, what could we do about it?

"If we can find another way in, maybe we could sabotage some critical part of Richardson's project without getting caught."

Or without anyone getting hurt, I added to myself. "This is great, Robyn, really great. While we're waiting for the contact information on Sam, maybe you could find something out about critical systems, or, better yet, steal a copy of their engineering plans. I'll bet we can find an engineer

166

to have a look at them for us, and maybe find a weak spot." It was Robyn's turn to smile.

"I know just where to find such plans."

***

Joe spotted the guard before Bob. Of course, Bob was scouting in the other direction, but it made Joe feel good just the same. That coyote was always ahead of him. He smiled. Bob. Bob was a ham and a protector, and had a nose like a, well like a coyote. He would never dream of saying such things out loud—Bob's head was big enough already. Those two ladies doted on him. It worried Joe, a little, that maybe the wildness Bob needed to survive was being compromised. They'd have to sit down and have a serious talk. Joe did an internal double-take at this. That's what being alone for so long does to a man. But with Bob, you never quite knew...

The guard moved, continuing his patrol. This was a new level of security added some time in the last day or two. There were at least two dozen guards, and they were armed; in addition, the patrol patterns and timing were unpredictable, changing randomly. Their mission from Clueless—Joe's latest nickname ever since Robyn had been brought into this dangerous situation with Richardson—had been no more complicated than observing this change and incorporating it into whatever plan they devised. The journalist was a big help, certainly, but she had no special gift. She wasn't... exceptional, which wasn't the right word, but he and Flotsy had known about the unusual and unexplainable nearly all their lives. This was all new to Robyn and, somehow, it didn't seem fair that she might suffer their fate.

Bob tugged on the lace of his boots. Ever since the coyote discovered that it annoyed Joe to have to re-tie his laces, Bob took every opportunity to undo them. Bob tugged harder. Joe smiled. He had remembered to double-knot them today.

A scrape of boot on stone, and they were flat on their bellies. They waited, vigilant.

When the sun had baked them to the point of medium-well, they inched away. No more fooling around.

***

It was late in the day. I bought some food and hiked back to Harvey. Robyn had left earlier; she had some writing to do before her return to the site tomorrow; Richardson expected regular reports.

I puttered around the campsite, cleaning and organising, which always relaxed me and helped clear my head. She-rock had been uncommunicative for a few days and I worried about what this might mean. Had the gashes done irreparable damage to her... umm, communication system? Was she dead? I sat abruptly. Even if She-rock were dead, I would continue to try to stop this despicable project. She-rock had made the outcome very clear. Maybe that was why she now left me alone. Her message had been delivered and received, even if it had caused some damage to the recipient along the way. I flexed my arm. My elbow was pretty much back to normal and my headaches were gone. Small price to pay.

My laptop was fully charged and the books I found at the Library were in a neat stack beside it. The world of parapsychology awaited my scrutiny. There had to be some reason for Richardson to bring in Smythe and I was the best equipped to find out what that was, if, of course, it existed on paper or online. I wondered if on paper would ever become *onpaper*? No more procrastinating—Hi-Ho, Hi-Ho.

I emerged later with a sore back and aching eyes. The notes I had jotted down were scant. Aside from myriad Earth-worshipping sects and theories of creation, there wasn't much study done, outside of fiction, on Earth as a sentient being or beings, or on Earth as a repository of sentience in any form. Every geologist knew that rocks could be tapped in ways that elicited sound, but nowhere was it written that rock made sound of its own volition. What kind of gizmo could Smythe possibly have to test rocks, if that was even what Richardson had in mind? We could have easily jumped to the wrong conclusion because of our own unique, I hoped, knowledge. Even as I thought this, it came to me. What if Joe and I were not the only *gifted* people around? The 'what ifs' in our strategy-planning were growing like some kind of alien bacteria.

Joe and Bob drove in just as the chili was done. Nice timing. One look at Joe and I pointed to the showers; he must have been crawling around in the dirt. Bob's coat, on the other hand, looked the same as always. Lucky Bob.

We were catching each other up over supper when my laptop beeped. Robyn had heard from the magazine publisher who had given her Sam's telephone number. I immediately worried that Richardson had his staff's communication with the outside world monitored, scribbled Sam's number down, and deleted the message. We had to come up with a better way to exchange information, especially given Joe's update. This was not only getting more difficult, it was getting even more dangerous.

Chapter 14

Smythe was a disappointment, but most people were.

Maximillian Wendall Richardson never allowed anyone to impress him. 'Good first impressions' were for the unwashed masses who knew nothing about excellence. His father had taught him well. It still gave Richardson a jolt of satisfaction that he had had to eliminate him. But he had been a weakness, and his father had taught him to rid himself of all weakness. He smiled. The look of shock and pain mingled with pride on his father's face was a moment he recalled whenever he felt the least uncertain about what his instincts told him to do.

Earlier, Smythe had told him a preposterous story about inanimate objects capable of speech. The proof was a chunk of basalt in a hermetically sealed container on his desk. Smythe had placed detection devices on the outside of the box using hardware-store suction cups. Wires from the devices were connected to a control box, which in turn was connected to Smythe's custom computer. He had written a program to interpret the subtle frequencies emanating from various types of rock and discovered repeating patterns, patterns which resembled those of human speech. In his excitement, he had made the grievous error of announcing his discovery at a World Parapsychology conference. His colleagues, who by the very definition of their profession, ought to have minds open to endless possibilities, unceremoniously shunned him from the entire parapsychological world. No one would speak to him, no one would publish him, and, certainly, no one would continue to fund his research.

But Richardson's team was thorough and had unearthed Smythe in the squalor of his basement apartment. The man had been whisked from his pathetic life and delivered to the Project staff hotel. Richardson was determined to leave no stone unturned. He smiled at his own clever witticism.

Richardson noticed a fine line of perspiration spring out at Smythe's hairline. A disappointment indeed. "Tell me why I should listen to you."

"Well, sir," Smythe swallowed, his Adam's apple, grotesquely large, bounced up and down, "you asked me to use my research to discover if there was sabotage at your excavation site."

"I know what I asked you."

"Yes, sir. Sorry, sir. The basalt in the box is from your site. Its patterns are most complex. With your permission," Smythe loosened his tie, Richardson frowned, "I would like to place my equipment at the cut-face and have your men remove a slab of rock."

"I see." Richardson sneered. "You want to hear if the rock cries."

Smythe reddened; sweat began to bead more densely and run down his gaunt cheeks. Richardson turned away; the man sickened him. But what was the harm? If nothing came of it, this so-called scientist could be flattened beneath the next slab to come crashing down.

Chapter 15

The Chief Engineer came out of his office leaving the door open and sauntered in the direction of the cafeteria for his usual afternoon break. Robyn smiled as she passed him. A few steps later, she stopped, reached into her bag for her compact and opened it to help her adjust an earring and, as soon as the scanning camera had swiveled to point in the opposite direction, slipped inside his office. She had interviewed Jeff a couple of times while he sat at this very desk and thought she could guess where he kept his password.

She wiped her palms, slick with nervous sweat, on her jeans. Robyn opened the computer. In a few seconds she had access and found what she wanted. She inserted the memory storage drive and pressed the download button.

It was taking too long. She glanced at her watch for the hundredth time. There were three minutes left in Jeff's break and the download was only 87% done. She was not cut out for this kind of work. Journalism? Yes. Investigative journalism? Never.

The instant the 100% done flashed on the screen, she extracted the drive, and was careful to leave everything exactly as she had found it. She used her compact again angling it in the doorway to check that the hallway was empty. The little, round mirror was not a great reflector, but she worried that the overhead lights might make it glint. She shoved that worry away—it was no time to dither. The corridor was empty, and the camera pointed away from her. Robyn tried very hard not to rush. The storage drive in her pocket felt large and heavy. Her skin crawled; she felt she had fooled no one and was being watched at this very moment.

When she finally reached her own office, she opened her computer at the document she had been editing, finding some comfort in the familiar task. She reviewed and typed for several minutes and suddenly stopped. She had had an idea and didn't want to give herself away, and immediately shuffled through some papers on her desk.

Robyn kept files and a few envelopes in the side drawer of her desk. She opened the drawer, searching through the files with her fingers and pulled one out from the end nearest her, and, at the same time, thumbed an envelope against it. She let the envelope drop into her purse, which sat open on the floor beside her chair. Placing the retrieved file on her desk, she leafed through the documents within, extracting a clipping. After a few minutes, she returned the document to the folder and slid it back into the drawer, closing it.

The end of the workday approached. She went through her usual routine of saving her work and straightening her desk. With her purse under her arm, she headed for the washroom. She scrawled the name of Flotsy's campground and site number on the envelope, applied a few stamps, and put the drive inside it. She folded the envelope and stuffed it into the front pocket of her jeans.

The employees' bus dropped them off in front of their hotel. Turning left, she walked to the pharmacy next door. She strolled down the aisle with feminine hygiene products and picked up a box of her usual brand. A perfect ruse, if ever there was one. The pharmacy also had a mailbox, located near the cash register. While she waited for her turn to pay, she nonchalantly dropped the envelope into the outgoing slot.

The next morning, Robyn went to work as usual, but she fervently hoped she didn't look as bad as she felt; it had been a sleepless night. Who did she think she was? Jane Bond? She was no super-spy; she had zero stealth in her genetic makeup. Her skin itched like it was being studied under a microscope. Her nerves were completely and truly shot. As the morning wore on, the document on her computer screen began to blur. She rubbed her eyes and sipped the dregs of cold coffee from the bottom of her cup. Her head pounded and, with the number of times she glanced at the time, she would give herself a repetitive strain injury. Would this day never end?

It was almost a relief when the security guards entered her office.

***

There had been no word from Robyn since she and I had talked about the benefits of obtaining engineering plans. This was worrisome, but it had only been a couple of days.

I'd called Maguire but only got his answering machine—fourteen times so far. I'd keep trying. Maybe he was just crawling around inside another cave somewhere. I had a feeling, though, that I would never reach him.

The boys were getting ready to go into town. Joe was good at picking up gossip and Bob was good at making sure Joe didn't get caught.

"And maybe little Ben is around," Joe said.

Bob's ears perked up. I swear that coyote understood human.

***

The bike rumbled through the back-streets. There were rusted pieces of playground equipment in a corner lot where the urchins sometimes played. No sign of them. Bob jumped out and dashed into the narrow space between two ramshackle houses. Joe turned off the bike and waited.

Less than three minutes later, Bob hurtled out, soon followed by the shrieks of his admirers. He watched them chase each other around the pair of A-shaped pipes supporting a third, thicker bar that, at one time, must have had swings hanging down from it. They had found a rope long enough to throw over the bar and had tied its ends together, and then had added about ten more knots up its length. They would grab it as they raced by, swing around in a circle just missing the side pipes, and leap off, seeing who could fly the farthest. Their feet barely touched the ground as they raced around again re-building momentum. The whole structure swayed ominously at this vigorous activity.

Although Joe knew he could do something to make it more stable, he also understood the pride it had given to the kids. They had made this fun thing by themselves. He would never take that away from them.

Fifteen minutes into this extreme sport, Bob butted one of them as he was reaching for the rope and soon the four of them were wrestling in the dirt. Joe pulled out the big bag of goodies he had picked up knowing that Bob would hear the rustle of the paper. The coyote immediately shook off his

176

assailants and sat up, tail around his feet, tongue lolling out the side of his mouth. The kids tried to do the same thing, and sat on their heels, big grins on their faces, and tongues sticking out. Joe stared for a minute and burst out laughing.

He sat with them and doled out food and drink. Bob politely ignored any accidentally dropped food, which Joe admired.

Little Ben, who was their usual spokesperson, said, "The big trucks?"

Joe nodded.

"They's NOISY!" The other two growled like an engine. Bob, of course, joined in.

"My uncle says they's goin' to the wrong place."

They all pointed northwest, where Richardson had his site.

"Why is it the wrong place?"

Little Ben shrugged and ate his seventh cookie.

"Did your uncle say anything else?"

Ben chewed for a while and guzzled some orange soda. "Somefin about... bad water." He chugged the rest of his pop, leapt to his feet, and raced down the street. The others followed; there were new adventures to be had.

Joe sat and considered this piece of information: bad water where Richardson dug. This was worth pursuing. He walked back to his bike, marvelling at the energy of children.

He parked on a side street near the *café* where he and Flotsy had gone. He'd gotten a good tip that first time, which was why he was going there again. He sat against the wall about half-way down the narrow room and pulled out the paperback he always carried for just such occasions.

There was the usual gathering of moms and babies, a couple pouring over maps, three locals at the counter—you could tell by their easy familiarity with the staff—and a few scattered singles intent on electronic devices of one type or another. He understood their usefulness. What he didn't like was the way they seemed to take over some people's lives as though their very breath depended on them. Oh, well. He'd had this conversation with himself many times. He just preferred to experience life in person.

On the other hand, it sometimes helped in covert surveillance. Like the call that had just come in to the woman two tables over. The words 'can't find her' and 'camping?' dropped into a lull in the ambient noise of his surroundings. The woman typed something into an electronic notepad. She listened some more and disconnected. Joe turned his head further away from her and kept his nose in his book. She packed her things and left. Joe left a tip on the table and followed.

Because he knew where to look, he spotted Bob in the shadow between two dumpsters. His gaze followed the woman, and then, so did Bob's.

Joe had a good idea where she was going and took a short-cut to the hotel where the project people stayed. She entered the hotel a few minutes later. This was enough confirmation for Joe and he hurried back to his bike. Bob was already in the side-car. They had to get back to Flotsy.

***

The campsite was arranged to my satisfaction, but I couldn't settle, and a walk through the trails around the campground felt like a good idea.

Most of the sites were filled; the owner must be pleased. I waved at some of my fellow campers; it was what was done. The place was nicely maintained, and the washrooms cleaned at least daily. I would complement the staff when next I saw any of them.

Even at mid-morning, the sun was strong. I pulled my new hat forward so that it shaded my poor nose; the rosacea seemed to flare if I even thought of letting the sun hit it. The trees were dusty as was nearly everything. The least breeze wafted it in from the desert that was all around us. It was, supposedly, a temperate desert which meant that a wee bit of rain fell, unlike, say, that one in Chile, where it could have zero rainfall for years. What must that be like? In photos, it looked like the surface of an alien planet. Of course, to an alien, Earth's entire surface would look like an alien planet. Huh.

I'd been walking with my head down to keep the reflected sunlight from an Airstream motorhome off my face and automatically stepped off the road at the sound of a vehicle behind me. A black sedan with tinted windows glided by—not the kind of car one usually sees in a family-oriented campground. I watched it turn in Harvey's direction. My scalp tingled, and not from the instant perspiration that sprang out on my head. I kept on walking and tried to act naturally. Knowing full well the limit of my acting skills, the small maze of cacti on a low rise beckoned me as a possible hiding place. I wandered over to it and bent to study the plants more closely. Peering out from beneath my hat, I could see the top of Harvey's antenna. It shook, like it always did when someone stepped into the vehicle.

The sound of Joe's motorcycle made me jump. Still bent double, I scurried to intercept him. Bob saw me and nudged Joe. He detoured to pick me up, barely stopping while I clambered on behind him, and continued out of the campground at the same slow speed. At the highway, he turned towards town, and, once there, sped down the first side street, and turned again and again until I no longer knew exactly where we were, only that the quality of both roads and buildings had deteriorated. He stopped in a decrepit neighbourhood and pulled up to an abandoned shed. He motioned for me and Bob to disembark, turned the machine off and carefully navigated the bike into the enclosure. He shut the door as best he could, given that it hung loosely from the top hinge. Bob had trotted off as soon as the bike stopped to do whatever it was that Bob did.

Grabbing my hand, Joe and I ran, twisting between the shacks and debris. In the shadow of a fence, he stopped, and dropped to his knees bringing me down with him. I was glad I had worn long pants—such a trivial thing to think at a time like this—but when you're scared, the trivial can be a great comfort.

The sedan cruised by. It looked like no one was in the vehicle, so dark were the windows. Anyone or anything could be scanning the area.

We remained in our crouch for a long time. Joe whispered that Bob would let us know when it was safe. It was getting dark before the coyote silently re-appeared.

I stretched cramped muscles and would pay a

180

great deal of money for a drink of anything. Money. I checked my pockets. Nothing but a crumpled tissue. Damn. Harvey was off limits and the nearest casino was an hour away. Double damn. Joe opened his wallet. It looked like our total combined wealth was a single ten-dollar bill and some loose change.

We could drink water at the gazebo's fountain, buy gas for the motorcycle, and drive to the casino. I said as much to Joe.

"Too risky."

Oh, yeah. They probably knew about the motorcycle. I sat down on the ground. Bob sniffed my cheek and leaned against my side. I put my arm around him.

The first giggle startled me. Bob kept very still, eyes straight ahead. As soon as the small hand reached for his tail, he pounced, and the scuffle began. Giggling and squealing, creating a ruckus that alarmed me, kids and coyote chased each other in the small clearing that had been our hiding place. Joe seemed content to watch, a glint in his eye indicating that he wasn't worried about this turn of events.

At last, little Ben, panting, hair stuck in spikes to his sweaty forehead, dropped to the ground, grinning at Joe.

"You got a great dog, mister."

"Thanks, but he isn't really a dog you know."

The three children glanced at each other. "O' course, we know that. We just ain't stupid enough to say. They's some as would shoot 'im if they knew. Thing is, they don't know nufin'." His gang nodded.

How does a child of six get so jaded? I couldn't

see their faces clearly in the meagre light from a distant lamppost, but I suspected their eyes looked a lot older.

We sat around in a circle; the only thing missing was a campfire. The little girl bounced up and scampered off to return a few seconds later with a battered canvas carry-all. She first extracted an old towel which she placed carefully on the ground ensuring that all the edges were flat. Next out of the bag were a mostly lint-free handful of gummy bears, half a submarine sandwich (ham, I think), assorted pieces of bruised fruit, a two-litre bottle of water, and an unopened bag of chips. The two boys looked on but did not grab at anything. The ritual was apparently not over yet. They bowed their heads.

"Thanks for the food," she said. The boys, unleashed at last, dug in.

Wherever did she learn such niceties? Why ever did she choose to continue practicing them? And, even more unexpected, why on Earth would the boys go along with her ways? I would love to speak with her, find out her story. I reached for the water and sipped, grateful for the bounty of children.

Bob sat politely, waiting for his share, which was given to him as was his due. They treated him like a fourth member of the gang.

Supper over, Joe spoke.

"That black car today," Joe said. Small heads nodded.

Nodding started at a young age.

"Are there more cars like that?"

The second boy spoke for the first time. From a

182

brief exchange during the meal, I'd learned that his name was Arthur. "Yup."

"How many?"

Arthur looked at his hands and extended seven fingers.

This was bad. I know I shouldn't be surprised. Richardson had nearly unlimited resources. But why would he expend them on us? What could we do to him? Especially now that he doubtless had all our research and plans from ransacking Harvey, and that it was all too depressingly likely that Robyn was under close surveillance, or even under arrest. If I was an outsider looking in, my impression would be that we were a bunch of crackpots. Visions from rocks? Superhuman powers? Who would swallow that? Of course, this Richardson might be slightly un-hinged—not a good thing.

I stiffened. Joe, discussing the niceties of building a fort from tumbleweeds with Ben and Arthur, touched my arm. I looked at him.

"Richardson will stop at nothing," I said. Joe nodded. "And I just realised that he is probably crazy." Joe nodded again.

He pulled an envelope from his pocket. "I picked this up at the campground office and was bringing it to you when we had to leave in a hurry."

I looked from him to it. "Robyn sent us the engineering plans?"

He nodded.

This time, I welcomed the gesture.

We slept that night in a dilapidated barn-like structure not far from where we'd stashed the motorcycle. It was one of the many hiding places the kids used. Over time they had scrounged blankets and clothing from various backyards that came in handy as bedding. Bob kept watch near the broken panel where Joe, especially, had trouble squeezing through. This was also an excellent vantage point from which the coyote could pursue anything of interest for a late-night snack.

I was too wound up to sleep. My brain wouldn't stop filtering through the fragments of information we had gathered. Robyn was likely compromised, Smythe was up to something, bad water (what was that about?), The Mouth remained a mystery but was definitely worth pursuing, and Richardson was a powerful, psychotic wild card. Good thing we had an arsenal of one coyote, two adults, and three kids. It had a kind of symmetry: one, two, three. And on that frivolous observation, I slept.

***

Maximillian Wendall Richardson observed the interrogation from the comfort of his town office. The girl was babbling. He glanced at his watch. Fifteen minutes. His people were performing as they should.

He raised his hand. Jones quietly appeared and handed him the pertinent data of—he checked the name—one Robyn McMaster. Her entire life boiled down to half a page. The words 'participated in marches' stood out in his favoured orange highlighter. She was supposed to have been a harmless nature journalist, published in the right places, and credible enough to lend his project the verisimilitude he required. He despised upstarts. How did this get past the screening stage? Jones would find out.

184

"The status of her friends?"

"Nothing yet," Jones said, and handed him two additional sheets of paper.

Richardson glanced at the information. Joe Gallant and Olivia (aka Flotsy) Ducharme. He carefully crumpled the pages. He also despised the leeches of the world.

He stood. The hotel was low calibre and his staff had had to make many adjustments. The view, however, soothed him. Under the bleak, ugly landscape lay a project so vast that even he, in his avaricious and vicious nature, found spellbinding.

***

The sun had not yet cleared the horizon when we crawled out of our hiding place and meandered through back streets. The kids had already disappeared to do whatever street kids did.

Bob pranced around, ready for anything; I envied him his energy and joie-de-vivre. Joe led the way and I followed in a kind of zombie-like daze. The last several hours of my life (was it only yesterday?) had been one long moment of running and hiding and being more scared than I'd ever been in my life. I hadn't realised just how afraid I was until now. My small world had exploded. I had been thrust out of the comfort zone I had worked so hard to create for myself and landed in the middle of a B movie. Joe played the lead role, Robyn the damsel in distress, and Richardson the bad guy. What did that make me? The side-kick? The comic relief? The dispensable extra? When I looked at it like this, what did I really bring to the table? She-rock used me as a conduit for messages—messages that no longer seemed to be needed; I was good at getting money—if we could only make it past the cordon strangling our movements; and I could gather information—if we could make it past the cordon strangling our movements.

The bottom line was that I was another person Joe had to worry about. The next steps were his job; my job was done. So why didn't I just leave? I let that thought bounce around inside my head like a pin ball, the flippers spinning it from side to side, ricocheting off tender parts—tender parts like the part where we were friends and the part that I liked having him around. But when one of the friends was more of a burden than a help, wasn't it better for that friend to just make a quick exit?

I stopped walking, struck by the revelation. I was very good at making quick exits; I'd been doing that most of my life. But how could I make an objective decision when that decision looked a whole lot like my standard knee-jerk reaction?

Joe touched me on the arm and pointed his chin in the direction of the back door of one of the diners.

"Wait here."

The nearest wall provided a good leaning surface and I slouched against it. Bob sat beside me, tongue hanging out; he knew what was coming.

We feasted on yesterday's lasagna, cold out of the fridge. It was marvelous and, best of all, it was free. Joe knew the guy. "He said we could drop by late tonight for more. He hates to throw food out."

"What about water?"

"I know a place."

Of course he did. This only proved my point to myself: Joe had everything he needed. What he did

186

not need is me to slow him down.

He took us on a circuitous route, avoiding the centre of town. "We can't keep this up much longer," he said.

This was harder and more depressing than I thought possible. If I could get to the main highway or, better yet, to one of the big-rig truck stops on the main highway, I could be far away before dawn. It was a good plan, if I could avoid Richardson's men.

We arrived at the water place, which was a pipe sticking out from a warehouse wall. I did not want or need to know what kind of warehouse it was or why they would ever allow precious water to trickle out into the desert air. I cupped my hands together and lapped at it like, but not nearly as efficiently as, a coyote.

Refreshed, Joe turned us toward the desert. Our objective was the industrial wasteland on the outskirts and, specifically, a derelict shack surrounded by the rusting carcasses of various pieces of machinery.

"You sure know how to show a girl a good time," I said, as we found the least oil-stained part of a bench to sit on. Misplaced humour was my usual way of handling a hard situation.

"You're leaving." Joe looked at me. His eyes were dark and sad.

I shrugged and turned my head away. "I think it's for the best."

The silence lengthened as can only happen with Joe.

"The best for whom?"

"Well, everyone obviously."

"Everyone, who?"

"You, me, Robyn, the kids, Bob. Everyone." I was starting to get annoyed. Why did I have to spell this out? The sun was hotter and the smell in this filthy place was making me sick.

He knelt in front of me and put a hand on each shoulder. My discomfort at this most gallant of gestures was shoved aside, and I stared back at him, determined.

"Just because you're not a warrior doesn't mean you're not needed."

What?

"Every fight has a thinker, a planner—a person who keeps it sane. That's you." He shook me ever so gently and stood. He scraped his fingers through his hair.

Almost as good as a comb, I thought. My vision blurred. Damn. It was not a good time to get weepy; there was no nice box of tissue around. I turned my head and surreptitiously wiped my nose on my sleeve; these clothes would have to be burned at the end of this escapade anyway. The abrupt thought that this was one of perhaps many escapades both dismayed me and lifted my heart. But if Joe thought I had value, then maybe I did. Somebody says one nice thing to me and I fold. Sheesh. But it was a good kind of sheesh.

"Okay, then." I straightened my shoulders. "Time to think and plan."

Joe smiled.

"Disguises. We need disguises, and good ones. The kids can help. How do we contact them?"

Joe went to the doorway, sniffed the air, and slipped outside.

I spent time gingerly examining the junk in the

shack. There were a surprising number of possible weapons: the business end of a hammer, several rusty nails, a couple of long handles for who-knew-what that were mostly intact, and, best of all, a two-foot crowbar. The glass from the window was too shattered to be of use and all else appeared to be scrap, at least to me.

Coyote preceded man by a few seconds who was in turn followed by our trio of waifs. They were giggling.

I raised my eyebrows.

Joe shrugged.

The little girl (I must try to find out her name) began the ritual of 'setting the table.' I knelt on the other side. She looked at me and gestured for me to assist. This simple act of domesticity was soothing and, once the provisions were laid out to her satisfaction, she and I looked at each other. A smile flickered on her small face. "Thanks for the food," she said, still looking at me.

***

"You won't like it," Joe said as he reached for my head.

The bleak motel room had the bare essentials of bed and bathroom. A chipped dresser held up a lamp with a stained, ripped shade, and two kitchen chairs were jammed beneath the small window allowing a person to scuttle sideways between them and the bed, if you had skinny legs. Strewn on the bed was what would be transformed into our disguises: skirts, pants, shirts, jackets, hats, and other accoutrements including an array of accessories. The kids and Joe had acquired the booty from various establishments that donated

189

things to orphanages, homeless shelters, and other places that had little or no money for simple things like clothes and food.

"I won't like what?"

He slipped my glasses off.

I blinked at the suddenly brighter view of the motel room. It was not an improvement. I grabbed for the glasses. "You don't understand. I need those."

He kept them out of my reach by the simple expedient of raising his arm. I hated people who did that; they made you feel like such an idiot just because you were short. "Bully." I glared at him.

His eyes never left mine. He didn't even flinch. It was probably something he learned because of something his so-called gift had put him through.

"You can't make me go around with my eyes visible," I resorted to logic, "because then no one will look at me."

Joe waited.

I stomped my foot. "Didn't you hear me? How can I find anything out if no one will even look at me?"

Joe waited some more.

I needed to think. The dinky bathroom would have to do. I slammed the door, which immediately bounced open. Gods, after all the exits I've made, you would think I could make a good one.

I sat on the edge of the tub and fumed. He knew how people reacted to me—I had told him often enough. Why would he make me subject myself to that look of primal fear mixed in with a liberal dose of extreme distaste? Wait a minute. This would be my protection. I slapped my palm to my forehead. I could be so dense. I wondered if I was as dense about other things too. Who was I trying to kid? I went back into the room as though nothing had happened.

While I had been having my snit, Joe had pawed through the clothes and now sported what can only be described as a down-on-his-luck salesman look: black dress pants, shiny with age and wear, a pink dress shirt frayed at the sleeves and collar, a grey and blue herringbone sports coat, and the pièce-de-résistance, a bolo necktie fastened at the collar with a gaudy bit of red plastic that looked sort of like a horse's head and embedded in a chunk of chipped gold-painted metal. He was currently trying on a hat that had likely been donated by a theatre troupe. It was lime green with a stiff circular brim. He turned his head this way and that, bending over slightly to see himself in the tiny mirror nailed to the wall above the dresser. "The hat's not quite right," he muttered and turned to his second choice—a faded brown fedora. The look actually suited him, if you only ooked at him from the neck up.

"Can you cut hair?"

The question startled me from my survey of what he had chosen for me. I couldn't take my eyes off the popping red of the T-shirt and the neon-pink of the capri pants. They reminded me of the candy floss at a carnival. The glitter was worn off in places and a couple of the rhinestones were missing from the ace-of-hearts design on the front of the shirt. The pink pants had silver stitching in swirls up the outside of the legs. There was also a small bottle of hair dye with a tube of gel, make-up that I decided

191

to ignore, and a pair of horn-rimmed sunglasses that would dwarf my face. All that was missing was a stick of gum.

"Can you cut hair?"

"Uh, sure." I looked at him. He had tucked his shoulder length black hair up into his hat. Joe was transformed.

"I'll start growing a mustache. Shouldn't take long."

He brought one of the chairs over to the widest available space and put scissors and comb on the dresser beside it. He took off his jacket and shirt.

I was briefly mesmerised at his cavalier attitude towards disrobing in front of me. It was not as if I hadn't seen him before given our living circumstances. But somehow it was different in a squirmy kind of way to see his bare chest and back in a motel room.

"Would you mind getting a towel from the bathroom?" He turned the chair around and sat, his arms resting on the backrest, and waited.

Right. Cut his hair. So much easier to think about. I grabbed a towel, slung it around his shoulders, and picked up the comb. "How much do you want off?"

"All of it."

Seemed I was in charge. I had cut my family's hair from the time I was big enough to hold the scissors. My own too, though the back of my head was, shall we say, not quite right until I got the hang of it. Jacinthe had even asked me to do hers too. It seemed I had an eye for what would work and proceeded to cut and style Joe's hair. It was a lot softer than it looked.

"So. The clothes," I began. What do I say about the clothes? He had given our outfits a lot of thought. There was no doubt that Joe looked quite unlike his usual self, which was a long-haired slightly dangerous man in scruffy jeans and a plaid shirt hanging out. I noticed that he still wore his boots but that he had cleaned them. It was my middle-aged hooker look that I sincerely hoped was a joke.

Joe waited for me to continue. Of course.

I worked on his hair, which did not take much concentration; my hands knew what to do. There was no denying that the 'look' Joe had picked for me was entirely different from my usual subdued, loose-fitting style. Could I carry it off? It would also mean an entirely different way to act, to talk, to walk, to be.

"It will be impossible for me to be convincing."

"How so?"

How to explain? "I've never, you know, walked the way a woman wearing that outfit would walk."

Joe pointed to the shoes.

They were three-inch strappy sandals, fire-engine red with glittery bits here and there.

How had I missed those? I would break an ankle in those!

"You could practice," Joe said.

I snipped one last time and surveyed the result. The shorter cut enhanced the sharp features of his face, making him look predatory—perfect for sales. I reached over and took the mirror off the wall and handed it to him.

He stared. "You're good."

I gathered all the hair in the towel and opened

193

the door, scattering it to the wind. It would make fine nesting material for the birds.

It was time to change his mind. "Okay. I get the no-glasses and I will dye my hair. After that, we'll see."

Joe nodded.

A short time later, I emerged from the bathroom as a brunette with a short, pixie cut. Little wisps of hair framed my face. I quite liked it.

Joe smiled.

After rummaging through the clothes, I found something that was different and suited my new do. I returned to the bathroom-cum-hair salon-cum-change room; it was a busy place.

I felt like a forest elf with the dark green hippy-top embroidered with gold and orange leaves, and the loose knee-length brown pants. The taupe-coloured floppy hat was perfect. Footwear was a problem, though; a sturdy pair of sandals was needed. In the meantime, I chose a pair of brown socks to wear with my sneakers. Not bad.

Joe nodded.

Thank the gods.

We were ready for our first foray. I just had to figure out which of the multiple pieces of our puzzle we should attempt first. The bad water seemed the safest item to pursue. We could ask the kids to point out who had made the comment in the first place as well as enlist them to reconnoitre.

Joe pondered. "They'd be willing, of course. Anything for an adventure. I'm uneasy about it, though." He looked up. "And it's not The Nuisance."

Right. It must be male intuition. I'd heard about

this but knew it was not a good time to discuss the likelihood of its existence. Right now, it was far too risky to ignore any gut feeling.

"How about if they just give us clues to his whereabouts?"

Joe nodded.

We had not yet discussed the most worrisome item on our list of worrisome items: Robyn. She was the only person who could have told Richardson about us, and about the campground. Unless Richardson had goons in the Library checking on what people were reading…

"Robyn," I said.

"I know a guy."

"What guy?" How did he do it? How did he learn the things he learned? Maybe it would be better for my nerves if I never knew. "When will you be able to talk to this guy?"

He looked at me with distress and fierce determination in his eyes. "Tonight, and the less you know, the better. At least, for now."

***

The sun had set. We were hungry, and it was time to test our disguises. Joe left to saunter down the main street; he would meet me in forty minutes by the kids' sleeping place. I would leave in eight minutes to peruse the two head-shops in town. I hoped I didn't scare anyone with my bare eyes.

It was hard at first. How do you not walk like you usually walk and not look like you're trying to not walk like you usually walk? I glimpsed my awkward motion reflected in a store window and immediately changed my approach. Better if I moved naturally and trusted that the rest of the disguise would suffice.

The chimes tinkled, and my nose was assaulted by a miasma of incense wafting through the air in smoky tendrils. It burned my eyes, but then I thought that 'bloodshot' would be a perfect addition to my sham. The tiny shop was packed with all manner of trinkets and books and music and posters. A glass case on one wall held various means of inhaling whatever the happy buyer chose to burn in them. Beside it was a construct of shelves inserted into the carcass of a saguaro. On the shelves were an array of elves and sprites and other forest creatures created from pewter and pottery and glass and steel and wood. I spent some time gazing at this display.

I was beginning to think I had wandered into another world, one which had no end, when in a far corner, propped against a beat-up case, was the guitar that belonged inside it. It was battered and had three strings missing, but I had to have it. The purse that suited my disguise was a cloth sack and I rummaged around in it for money. I always had some. I think that the realisation that I had exactly zero money showed clearly on my face.

"Hey."

In my peripheral vision, I registered someone approaching. My paranoia erupted. This so-called disguise of mine didn't fool anyone. I was caught. I had no illusions about myself and would sooner-rather-than later tell them everything they wanted to know even if I had to make it up. Joe should have let me leave. Better yet, I should have been strong enough to have done the right thing in the first place and just left without telling him. I knew it was the right thing to do. Why was I so weak and stupid?

"It's a steal at fifty bucks," the voice said, "and I'll throw in the case."

I've said it before, but it bears repeating: I gotta get a grip.

The young man beside me stood hip shod in tattered bell-bottomed jeans embroidered in neon flowers. His Nehru shirt was festooned with beads and feathers. The scarf around his forehead threatened to dislodge the tiny round glasses perched on the end of his nose. He shoved them up with his middle finger. Even through all this sensory overload, I noticed that his fingernails were painted black.

I shrugged.

He shuffled his sandaled feet. "Okay. Forty-five bucks. But it will have to be cash."

I sighed.

"Forty, and that's my last offer."

I started to walk away and had reached the door. It was then that I saw the 'Help Wanted' sign. Mmmm. I slowly turned to face the clerk. "How about I work for a few hours? We'll trade. My labour for the guitar and case. And a new set of strings," I added as an afterthought.

He shuffled his feet some more. "You ever work in a store?"

"Sure, lots of times," I lied.

"Great!" He reached over the counter and punched a button on the cash register. It pinged open. He extracted a set of keys and tossed them to me. "Close up at nine and be here tomorrow by ten. Bye."

The chimes tinkled, and he was gone.

Slightly dazed, I stared around. There were three customers in the shop. Gods, what if they wanted to buy something? Panicked, I hurried around the counter and stared at the mayhem. This would never do. As was my reaction to many kinds of stress, I immediately began to organise the work area. I found the small manual for the cash register jammed beneath it. There was a brief overview at the front and I felt reasonably confident that I could put through a sale. But what had I gotten myself into?

At precisely nine o'clock, I announced that the store was closing. The two people remaining in the store slowly made their way to the door never once taking their eyes off the merchandise. I bid them good evening and hoped they hadn't pilfered anything. The door was locked, the 'Closed' sign turned facing outward, and the main lights dimmed in record time. In a moment of panic, I raced around the store to be absolutely positive that no one lingered and finally leaned my back against the door and closed my eyes.

The light tap on the glass was like a gunshot. My entire body froze. A scratching sound on the wood part of the door accompanied by a soft whine brought me to my senses. Shaking, I turned and unlocked the door for Joe and Bob, fiercely hugging them both for a brief second.

Joe sauntered around the shop and Bob sneezed.

"So," he said.

What was I thinking? We had had a rendezvous and I blatantly ignored it, all because of something I wanted. The heat in my face burned and I deserved it. I had done a stupid thing.

"Sorry, Joe. It's just that I saw the guitar…" I couldn't go on with this lame excuse.

He walked over to it. "This one?"

I nodded.

He picked it up and tuned the three remaining strings. The chord he strummed was thin, of course, but the tone was good. With a little attention, it would suit me very well.

"So. You traded a bit of your time working here," he waved a hand around the store, "to pay for it. What's it worth? About fifty bucks?"

I blushed again "Forty, including the case and a set of strings."

"Not bad bargaining, Flotsy. But how many hours will it take to work off your debt?"

What had we agreed? Oh my god! We hadn't named a specific number of hours! What was the minimum wage here? Couldn't be more than ten dollars an hour—I'd have to work two more hours.

"On the bright side," Joe interrupted my internal conversation, "we have a relatively secure place to spend the night, complete with indoor plumbing. Not a bad deal, all things considered."

While he spoke, Joe gathered ponchos with zig-zag patterns, and little multi-shaped cushions covered in imitation plush velvet. He glanced through to the tiny washroom and into the jam-packed storeroom at the back and decided that where we were standing offered the best space. He layered the ponchos on the floor, reserving some as covers, and tossed the pillows to one end.

"Our accommodation for the night." He sat down and pulled off his boots.

Just like that, my thoughtless and selfish act was turned to our advantage. I used the facilities and lay down next to Joe.

Bob sneezed again; he was not happy with the incense-laden air and made it clear that he wished to spend the night elsewhere, most likely where there was also a chance of either cadging or catching a bit of food. Joe let him out the door at the back of the shop.

As we settled ourselves to sleep, Joe told me about his evening.

"Nothing blatantly unusual, except for a certain tension in the air. Richardson's black car patrol is making everyone nervous. You can't help but see them slink about." Joe harrumphed. "It's an arrogant and stupid move to think that the locals have no power. We might be able to use this to focus negative attention on his project. And maybe take some of the attention off us."

"What about the guy? The guy about Robyn?"

"Too early."

"Too early for what?"

"He may be available later." Joe turned on his side and, shortly, his breathing slowed and deepened.

***

I woke bleary and disoriented. Joe was gone, but that was no surprise. He would show up again with (I fervently hoped) breakfast. I did my usual clear-up and clean-up routine and was standing at the cash register when Joe returned. He had spent the last of his cash on coffee and an egg sandwich. Maybe I could talk the shop clerk into letting me work a bit longer, just enough to get us by. We ate in amiable silence, like an old married couple.

"So?"

"He's unavailable at the moment."

"Any other ideas on how to find out about Robyn?"

He sighed.

I took that as a 'no.'

I had given a plan a lot of thought and one possibility was quite simple, even though I had tried hard to come up with a more complicated one—one that would suit the level of danger we were in. I looked at him. "You're a salesman, a talker, a spinner of tales." His eyes widened. "Spread a nice bunch of icky rumours about Richardson around town. You know. At the coffee shops, the grocery store, the gas station. Everywhere people gather. And where people gather, they talk. I've even come up with a few starting lines for you, because that's all you'll need. People love to fill in the details with their own ideas that, believe you me, would be more fantastic than we could ever invent." I sat back and smiled.

Joe was not smiling.

"What? It'll work, I'm certain of it. Everything I've read and observed about human nature says it will work."

"It's not that. It's that there's a black car across the street."

I glanced up. Were the windows reflecting the street back at them or could they see us inside? They probably had special equipment to see through anyway. I glanced at my watch—nine fifty-five. I looked down both sides of the street. The store clerk was two blocks away, ambling along, on the same side of the street as the car. I grabbed Joe's arm.

"I see him." Joe ran through to the back of the storage area and peered through the grimy window to the alleyway. Empty. He slipped out and moments later he had caught up to the clerk.

What was he doing? He pulled a cigarette stub from his jacket pocket and appeared to ask the clerk for a light. The young man rummaged around in more pockets than I thought were possible in a pair of pants and produced a book of matches. They were chatting and smiling throughout this innocent-looking encounter.

There was no movement in the black car—at least that I could see.

Bob trotted around the corner, stopped to urinate on the back tire of the car, and continued into an alleyway a few yards beyond. What was that about? Who knew with Bob, but it made a good distraction. When I looked back to Joe and the clerk, Joe was gone, and the clerk had crossed the street, his hand on the door handle of the shop. This time, the sound of the chimes was not so annoying.

"Hey," he said.

"Hey."

He wandered around the store, perhaps noticing that I had organised a few things but perhaps not.

"What's your name anyway?" he asked.

"Petal."

"Cool."

I shrugged. "Parents."

"Any sales?"

I shook my head.

"Slow time of the year."

I nodded. This was going to be a long couple of

202

hours. I brightened. "Maybe I could put the strings on my guitar."

He rummaged through under-counter drawers and containers for a while. "Must be in the back somewhere."

Distracted as I had been by our conversation, I hadn't noticed when the black had left. This disturbed me more than I thought possible. I should be more vigilant than ever but all it took was a triviality to break my focus. Maybe they had left because of the very fact that I could so completely dismiss them? Then again, there were at least seven vehicles creeping around town, so how could my not knowing where one of them was make me afraid, when I didn't know where the any of them were? I sucked in a breath: because they had seen Bob and just might decide that the 'salesman' and/or the 'clerk' were teamed with the coyote. I had to assume that Robyn had told them everything. I had to assume that Richardson's people would follow every lead. Time to get out of town.

The shop clerk returned covered in dust and other debris. With a big smile, he handed me the strings. Thankfully they were the ones individually wrapped so they would not be corroded. I stuffed them in my pants' pocket and walked to the back of the store. I placed the guitar in the case, closed it, and kept on going through the back door and out into the alleyway. I felt a little badly about leaving him, but the less he knew the better. I pulled my hat further over my face and chose a random direction, careful to keep my pace slow.

Buskers could be found everywhere there were people. I would set up in the square on the bench that offered a bit of shade. I spent some time cleaning the guitar and putting on the new strings. I gently strummed a chord and smiled. The sound was rich and mellow, and I segued into my first song.

It had been a few weeks since I'd played, and my fingers were tender, but that didn't matter; it wouldn't take much time before the old calluses reasserted themselves. When the first coins clinked into my case, I jumped. By the end of the lunch hour, there was enough money to get us through a day or two. As quietly as I had arrived, I left, figuring that Joe would either find me *en route* or that we would meet as originally planned—at our first overnight spot.

The guitar case had a couple of long straps so that I could carry it like a backpack, leaving my hands free. There were convenience stores along the way and I gathered provisions. I strolled along and munched an apple. As dusk descended, I angled towards the not-so-nice side of town.

Something cold and wet inserted itself into my hand and I stifled a shriek. Bob's nose. "Geez! You could give a girl a heart attack." He smiled as I rubbed his ears; it was hard to stay mad at Bob.

He dodged into an abandoned and very smelly tenement. I followed. He led me on a twisty and awkward path through the underbelly of the town. By the time he pushed his way into a familiar barn-like building, I was tired and dirty, but there was Joe, handing me a cool bottle of water. Ambrosia.

After I had taken the edge off my thirst, I looked around. Joe had retrieved his cached motorcycle, but it didn't look quite right. "What did you do your bike?"

"Oh, this and that." He turned back to the machine and studied the spot where the attachment for the side-car had been. He ran a hand across it; it looked smooth and blended well with the rest of the metal. The colour of the gas tank was now bright red and there were other red highlights on the spokes of the wheels.

It looked completely different and, genius that I am, deduced that this was what he intended. I had given it to him; it was his bike and he could do with it what he wanted. But it made me feel sad and hurt that he would change it so.

"I know someone who will take it in trade for a car. I meet him," he glanced at his watch, "in thirty minutes."

We sat and ate sandwiches in silence. I tried valiantly to suppress my distress that he would trade my gift. How could he do this? I thought he loved that bike, and Bob certainly enjoyed the side-car. I wondered what he had done with that. Probably dismantled it into components and sold them. My distress became an angry simmer.

"I'll be back," Joe said.

He wheeled the bike through a newly-made opening at the back of the building. I listened as his footsteps and the crunch of the bike's tires faded, then all was silent. Bob padded over to me and put his head in my lap. He, too, mourned the loss. We sat like that until Joe returned an hour later.

He seemed pleased with himself and even the sight of Bob and me obviously hurt and mad did nothing to dampen it.

"It's perfect," he said, without further

205

explanation, "and the forecast calls for a dark night with a bit of wind to toss the sand around. Ready?"

He picked up my guitar while I gathered the rest of our worldly wealth, which took all of twenty seconds. It was remarkably easy to move when you had nothing to move.

We walked in silence. "How far is this... vehicle?" I whispered. I had walked a lot today and was tired but knew myself well enough to know that it was more than that. My weariness was more about what he had done to the bike—to the first real present I had given to anyone—than about anything else. I stumbled. I didn't look forward to Joe bringing up the subject as he was bound to do; he could interpret my moods very well.

The sight of our new 'ride' startled a laugh out of me. It was a faded, sickly-green station wagon. It was one of those older models that looked more like a freezer than a car. Square and boxy with room for the whole family. There were even a few dents in the body and a shabby tartan blanket complete with fringe thrown over the back seat. Joe opened the door and Bob leaped inside, rucked up the blanket and lay down, head up, tongue out, and smiling.

Huh.

Joe opened the tailgate at the back of the station wagon and placed my guitar inside. He gestured for me to hand him the groceries and he stowed them as well. With a gallant bow, he opened the front passenger door for me. Resigned, I settled myself inside. If Bob could do it, so could I.

It started on the third try—not a reassuring sign—but Joe paid it no mind. He put it in drive and smoothly pulled out of the junkyard and onto a back street at the edge of town. No businesses were open and there were few streetlights. I refused to get my hopes up. Who knew how persistent Richardson would be?

Chapter 16

Maximillian Wendall Richardson fumed.

He could refuse the request from the town council to clarify a few points regarding his project, but his marketing staff strongly advised that it would be to his benefit. He had avoided the dirty little town as much as possible, concentrating solely on his vision of the future, a future where he would control virtually all North America. With the west under his thumb, he could make demands from the east and they would be met. They would not let their fellow citizens suffer. Such altruism. He sneered.

If winning meant he had to appear once more at a council meeting, then so be it. He would devise some way, or perhaps many ways, in which they would pay for discomfiting him. Their families always provided opportunities for effective blackmail and revenge. The beauty of it was that nothing, ever, could be traced to him or his company. He would start with the Mayor himself. As Richardson recalled, he had two—or was it three? —darling daughters. He signaled for his assistant. Maximillian Wendall Richardson was a man of action.

The meeting began in its usual plodding way. Richardson seethed with impatience.

"There is talk in the town of disruption to our water table and perhaps even the quality of our water." This comment was from the proponent for the environment.

Richardson nodded his understanding and

arranged his face into one of concern.

The speaker continued. "Experts have been consulted and they have questions about your project."

This would never do. He could actually hear the small 'p' in 'project' in the man's voice—an insult to everything that Richardson had brought to this backwater town. He would sneer at his little internal witticism later, in private; his public face never showed any trace of what he thought. That these inferior creatures chose to disrespect his work was most annoying, and they would pay more than they ever thought possible.

Richardson raised a finger indicating that he would speak. He stood to impress them with his grace as well as to use body language to its full effect. His assistant dimmed the lights, except for the one bathing Richardson in a warm glow. The screen behind the podium displayed a beautifully rendered chart.

"As you can see," Richardson swept his arm and pointed to the chart, "I, too, have consulted experts, experts in a great many fields, in order to ensure that just the things you mentioned would not occur. The quality of the water and the table upon which it rests are pivotal to my Project. But why listen to my words," he chuckled, "when the results speak for themselves? I would, though, beg your indulgence and ask one of my staff to assist me by explaining these results in language that everyone can understand. It seems I tend to get a bit technical," he bent his head and looked down for a moment, "and that is because I am so very devoted to this Project." He let the conviction in his voice ring through the chamber. "I needed to understand how it affected everything before ever embarking upon such an undertaking. I am a businessman, not a risk-taker." He scanned the room. This won them over; none of them were risk-takers. "And now, I will pass the floor to the Manager of my Desert Project who will explain everything and answer all your questions. Please welcome Julius Bell." He clapped the man to the podium and sat, gathering himself to endure the doubtless long and tedious meeting. Oh, yes. They would pay.

His assistant placed a glass of water before him. It would contain something which would assist him to remain calm. Perhaps he wouldn't fire the boy just yet.

210

Chapter 17

We drove for what was left of the night on well-travelled roads heading towards Nevada. We took turns behind the wheel. It was definitely not my still-mourned Monte Carlo, but it handled well. Joe was at pains to explain the maintenance as well as the upgrades that had gone into the vehicle over the years. He especially liked the numerous cleverly hidden compartments throughout the wagon. He didn't say, and I didn't ask, what they had been used for, but he assured me they were all empty.

The only tense moment was when a very fast car overtook us and passed us like we were driving backwards. It continued at breakneck speed and we breathed again. Bob didn't even open an eye. I promised myself to pay closer heed to his reactions. On the other hand, Richardson would likely be fooled for only a short time and we had better make the best of our reprieve.

Of course, I knew where every casino was and with my disguise could return to some of my favourites. We needed to lay low for the day and the sky was already streaked with bands of colour. The next town boasted not only a nice, medium-sized casino but also the usual somewhat down-on-their-luck motels on the outskirts. We pulled into one among a row of seven or eight, none of which stood out from the other.

We hauled in our meagre luggage and Bob disappeared into the scrubby desert that stretched into the distance. Joe volunteered to scout the neighbourhood for food and I took the opportunity to avail myself of the bathroom. The marvelous sensation of being clean and the smell of coffee as Joe came back into the room, brightened its shabbiness considerably.

We ate in our usual silence. It was comfortable, and I almost forgot that he had defaced and traded in the motorcycle. And what had he done with the side-car? And what was happening to Robyn?

He looked up from his food and sighed. "It had to be done."

Great. The guy could read my mind now.

"And, no, I can't read your mind. But your face says everything."

I turned my head. I could feel my mouth tightening and forced myself to relax. "It's just that it was a present, and, I know, I know, you can do anything you want with a present. It's just that it was the first present I had given to anyone in a long time." I ran out of words and looked down.

He covered my hand with his. "Flotsy. Olivia. Look at me."

I could be a big baby and refuse. Or I could mature just a little. I looked up.

Joe studied my face. "You know I loved that bike, don't you?"

I nodded.

"And you also know that I would do anything to save you and Robyn and She-rock, don't you?"

He was setting me up. But his logic and sincerity broke through my bitterness. He was right. Again. "I get it, Joe, and thank you. I'll be okay." I tried a watery smile. By the look on Joe's face, I wasn't very successful.

I tried again. "It's a great station wagon.

212

Especially the colour. What's it called, anyway? 'Baby-drool-after-eating-spinach'? 'Avocado-from-the-wrong-side-of-the-tracks'? All-purpose-puke'?"

He raised his hands in surrender.

"Besides, Bob likes it," I added. "It's probably better for his ears that they're not in the wind all the time like they were in the side-car." I had tried to talk Joe into a leather pilot's helmet I found on the Internet. It was for children, but it would be perfect to protect Bob from getting an ear infection. There was even a matching set of goggles to go with it. The look they had both given me spoke eloquently of what they thought of that clever idea; they wouldn't even consider trying it on. Sheesh. "By the way, whatever happened to the...."

Joe interrupted. "It's not what you think. The guy I traded with is keeping the side-car safe. We'll get it back when we can."

I felt better and smiled. "Time to plan our next move." I yawned. "After a short nap."

It was dusk when we emerged from our motel. No sign of Bob but he could take care of himself.

We decided to leave the station wagon at the motel. It was a long walk to the main street, but the cooling day made it pleasant. If we had to, we could take a cab most of the way back.

The casino I wished to target had not yet reached the peak of business that I preferred so we strolled along the short strip. I had some busking money left and we scouted the buffets for the one that looked the freshest and ate our fill, taking our time. When the bustle of happy gamblers filled the sidewalks, we returned to the casino. Joe continued past the doors and lingered in one of the souvenir shops. His slightly tacky salesman disguise worked well with the gaudy décor.

I went in and was nervous at first; it had been several weeks since I'd tried my luck. I closed my eyes and took a deep breath. It would either work or it wouldn't, and better to find out quickly. I put a small bet on black and, to my dismay, lost.

"It's not the end of the world, sugar." The alcohol-laden breath was way too near my face. I scuttled sideways, like I'd just seen a cockroach. "Oh, don't be like that, sugar. We all lose some of the time." He reached into the breast pocket of his dress shirt. "Here, place this one for me." He smiled, displaying his nicotine-stained teeth. "Right there, on the red." He boldly took my hand, put the chip down, and pressed my fingers to it.

Stunned, I pulled away, rubbing my hand on my pants. His bet won. Thrilled, he grabbed my arm and hauled me closer. "That's it, sugar. Now do it again." This time, it hurt when he shoved my hand down on the chip. Enough of this, and where was a bouncer when you needed one? I stomped on his foot, he let go, and I ran. His raucous laugh and sudden shout of triumph when he won again were swallowed by the noise of the casino as I put more distance between his disgusting self and me.

Back on the street, I slowed. My nerves were tattered, and I needed to gather myself before a second attempt. The smelly bozo was bad, but he didn't bother me as much as had my loss. Was it one of those backward things where when you expected something to happen, you decreased the possibility for it to occur? Had I jinxed myself? Determined, I strode into the next casino. I chose black again. And lost again. This was bad; this was very bad. *Well*, I thought, *best to know the worst*. I placed my last dollar on red and won. I felt a tiny thrill of excitement, but this could be just the usual odds. Taking a deep breath, I put a dollar on red again. And won again. Okay, this was better.

Soon, I cashed out with about three hundred dollars inside my shirt. Elated, I wanted to find Joe but knew better than to be seen with him. Instead, I chose my next target and continued down the strip, winning a little at each casino for the better part of two hours. Satisfied, I began the trek back to the motel by the route we had agreed on. Four blocks later, Joe was at my side. I hadn't heard a thing.

"Sheesh! You're as bad as Bob! Sneaking up on a girl like that!" I whispered as harshly as I could.

Joe shrugged, and we picked up our pace. The neighbourhood was not conducive to an evening stroll. We didn't speak again until we had, separately, entered our room. A few minutes later, a light scratch on the door announced Bob. Good thing I had stopped to pick up more food.

A low whistle was Joe's only comment as he gazed at the just over five thousand dollars in a neat pile on the side table.

The boys ate some of the convenience store bounty, but I was tired and crawled under the covers. Bob, always happy to nap, curled up on the floor beside the bed.

"I think I'll stay up for a while."

Joe turned on the television set with the volume way down and stared at it. I would have bet my entire winnings that he didn't pay any attention at all to what was on the screen.

The next morning was a typical desert morning. I was keen to leave, still a little worried about the sleaze who had accosted me. It was hard to tell how much a person could remember and I definitely did not want him to remember me.

We drove about an hour before stopping for breakfast. It was time to plan our next move.

I dropped Joe off at the local second-hand electronics store. His task was to procure a computer that could read Robyn's memory drive. My job was buying food and a few articles of clothing for us—there had been no time to waste on such a mundane task as laundry. Bob didn't like this town and stayed with me. On impulse, and certainly matching my disguise persona, I dropped into an outdoors store and spent too much money on a tent and sleeping bags, a small cook stove and utensils, some dried victuals, and other paraphernalia for camping out. I had a strong sense that we may need to disappear without notice.

The beauty of a station wagon is its enormous storage area at the back of the vehicle. My purchases fit easily, and I discovered that the back seat folded. In an emergency, we could sleep in the space it made. Mind you, Joe would have to fold himself a little. Not as cozy at Harvey was, but it would do. Pleased with myself, I paid a nearby casino a short visit to top up our cash supply.

Bob was getting a bit anxious for a run. I pulled over beside a vacant lot and he jumped out. Never one to hurry his business, Bob cruised the perimeter of the lot until he found the perfect spot (how did he know it was the perfect spot?). Finished, he roamed along the edges of the buildings surrounding the lot. I was getting nervous. There was light traffic and he was, after all, a coyote. Worse, pedestrians had just turned a corner and were headed our way. I pulled a bright red scarf out of one of the clothing bags. Bob came over to me, likely thinking a new game was afoot. He was not pleased when I tied the scarf around his neck and led him back to the car. He hopped in, circled on the blanket and lay down in a huff.

"Nice dog," the man in the group commented as he walked by.

"Thanks," I answered, giving him my brightest smile.

The paranoia about Richardson finding us and about Bob being shot was getting to me. We had to be continuously on guard and I wanted it to be over. Joe and I would have a serious discussion. Today.

He was not at our rendezvous location and I was too anxious to wait. I circled around and drove past a second time. Still no Joe. If I did this a third time, it could look suspicious, if, of course, anyone was watching. What do I do now? What did they do in the mystery books I'd read? Why couldn't I think of a single ploy?

Oh, no! She-rock gripped my mind and I swung the wheel hard, slamming on the brakes at the same time. Bob yipped, and I passed out.

A sense of desperate urgency pummeled me. She-rock screamed and screamed. Her hopeless despair scraped along my nerves. A jumble of rock shards fell from her eyes.

I spun into a deeper part of her. Rock formations flashed like bleak strobe lights. Over and over again, the formations assaulted my vision. It must be a message if only I could grasp it.

Alas, the human body is no match for She-rock's intensity. I lost all connection with her and a heavy blackness took me under.

***

Bob was assiduously licking my face, whining at a painfully high pitch. I tried to push him away. He persisted. My eyes would not open on their own and I had to raise the lead weight of my hands to pry the lids apart with my numbed fingers. Not much time had passed.

The station wagon was partly on the sidewalk and skewed at an angle. I reached vaguely for the ignition and on my second attempt engaged the engine. I put it in reverse and slowly backed off the curb. The thump was solid and, to my ears, sounded like nothing was broken.

I looked around. The episode must have been very short; I had not yet attracted attention. The water bottle in the holder proved a challenge. My hands had no strength and I started to cry. I decided I could live without a drink and deemed it more important to use what little strength I did have to drive to a more secluded spot in which to recover. We crawled down the street. Only a couple of vehicles chose to blare their horns at me.

At last, the edge of town appeared with its usual array of mostly vacant strip malls. I chose one at random and inched into the parking lot. I stayed well away from other vehicles. Stopped at last, I tried the water bottle again. Success. Bob panted at me. Yeah, yeah.

In slow motion, I got out of the car and opened

the rear passenger door. A bowl for his water was on the floor mat. Dizzy, I sat down and slopped water into it. To the sounds of Bob lapping, I put my head back against the seat.

By the time Joe found me, it was late afternoon. The car was steaming hot and my body was sore. I had slumped onto my side and had slept like that. Bob, smart coyote that he was, was nowhere in sight. Probably resting in some cool, shady dirt. I think I cried a little.

Joe helped me to sit up, gave me more water to drink, and got into the driver's seat. He drove us out of town and down a ramshackle road that led nowhere. Perfect. Too dazed to help, I watched Joe set up the tent, toss the sleeping bags inside, and start the stove. He woke me to eat some soup and helped me into the tent. No one had said anything.

The next morning, I felt better except for the headache. Joe, being his usual excellent self, handed me a mug of coffee and two pills. Over the small fire, he toasted bread and handed me a hot slice.

"You're..." I stopped to cough and took a sip. "You're good at this."

Joe smiled. "And you're a good patient—most of the time. By the way," he continued, "the camping gear was a stroke of genius."

I felt inordinately proud of myself. Bob appeared out of the surrounding scrub and proudly dropped his catch at my feet. I gulped. He was just doing what a coyote does to show gratitude. So what if a bloodied rabbit was his idea of a bouquet of roses? I scratched his ears upon which he immediately flopped down and rolled over onto his back for a belly rub. Some people were very easy to

219

please.

The laptop Joe pulled out from his carry-all had seen better days. Joe, a 'be prepared' kind of person, also had extra battery packs. He inserted the memory drive into its socket and I shuffled closer to see what happened.

He looked over at me. "She-rock?"

I grimaced. "She's bad. We have to do something very soon." My voice caught, and I had to swallow before going on. "She's being torn apart."

"I wonder if Smythe is behind this? Maybe we should take a closer look at him. But first, let's find a backdoor into the project." He clicked open the only file on the drive.

I thought it would be relatively easy to read a plan of what must be essentially an underground construction project—floors, walls, plumbing, electrical bits, unknown large spaces for Richardson's surprise, and so on. But this was so far beyond any kind of plan or map that I had ever seen that I couldn't see any pattern at all, let alone figure out a way to get in. Who knew engineering drawings could be so obtuse? Lesson learned: never underestimate something of which you know nothing.

Joe went around the edge of the drawing to get a sense of its totality. It may have made more sense if we had a gigantic screen, like at a professional ball game.

"Go to the middle," I suggested. She-rock was our focus but not necessarily Richardson's. But if she was there, at the centre, we could look for 'spokes' leading to her. However we proceeded, we would study this schematic inch by inch.

Sometime much later, bleary-eyed, we took a break. I was still sore and headachy from yesterday's encounter and opted for a short walk to stretch my muscles. Bob opened one eye, closed it, and went back to sleep. Digesting a rabbit or two tired out a fella.

Joe and I wandered around the arid desert landscape, careful not to step on pretty much anything but sand or rock. You never knew what you could damage or what could damage you.

"Robyn," Joe said.

Succinct opening gambit. "I'm worried about her too, but nothing is more important than stopping Richardson. Everything else just has to wait."

Joe put his hand on my arm. "I know that, but she could be in pain because we let her do something for us."

I looked down at his hand on my arm, making what I had to say more difficult. "It is hard for us to think about what might be happening to her, very hard. But we didn't 'let' her do anything. She saw what we were reading in the Library and came to us, remember? She wanted to help."

"I know, I know." He got up and walked a few paces. With his back to me, he continued. "You and me, we're different. We have to do this; we are driven to do this. Would we even have known about what is really going on without our special guides prompting us? It's just that I don't know many ordinary people who would do what Robyn was willing to do, and I think we owe her for that."

He was right. I would ever have known the need to stop Richardson and, even if I did, would I

221

be this involved without She-rock's dilemma? "What do you suggest we do?"

He turned and looked at me. Oh, yeah. I was the planner. So. Save the girl, then save the world. Easy, peasy.

We studied the engineering drawings late into the night and found nothing that meant anything to us. Neither of us had a contact who could help; Robyn was the one who knew someone, but he was the person from whom she stole the plans. She was the one who had also found that article by Sam Maguire, the cave guy who had disappeared.

"I think we should go where the spelunkers hang out and find The Mouth."

Joe nodded.

"And on the way there, we could sneak into the project and free Robyn."

Joe smiled.

Geez. "Well, since that first guy you were trying to contact didn't work out, how about the guy you traded the bike to. He wouldn't be averse to a little illegal activity, would he? He may even be able to arrange a distraction for when we're ready to spring Robyn. After we find out where she is, of course. Oh. And I think that the hidey holes in the station wagon might come in handy later."

Joe looked thoughtful. Good.

I lay down, and notwithstanding the hard ground digging into my bones, I slept.

The vision gently insinuated itself into my natural dreamscape. The colours became brighter, the lines more delineated, and the smells pungent. I struggled to wake up; I could tell that this would be a bad one.

***

I was gagged. I couldn't breathe, and my heart pounded. A key turned in the lock. I tried desperately to scream and, even more desperately, tried not to cry. Crying made things so much worse. My nose plugged up and my tormentor loved to see me panic as I struggled for a sip of air. I forced my breathing to slow and attempted to remove myself from myself—become disembodied. It was the only thing that kept me sane. My sight dimmed as the shadowy figure stalked closer and closer, so close that I could smell his expensive cologne. It blended with the stench of his morbid lust, making me ill.

***

I was being shaken. My head hurt. My throat ached.

"Come on, come on." Joe sounded terrible. "Wake up, Flotsy, wake up!" He shook me some more.

I moved my arms. If I didn't let him know very soon that I was awake he'd do one of us an injury. I moved my arms again. "Stop." I formed the word in my mind and I'm pretty sure I moved my mouth. "Stop." I tried again. This time, Joe was looking at my face. He gripped me to him in a fierce hug, pushed me away so that he could look at me again, and gripped me in a second fierce hug. This time when he released me, he eased me onto the sleeping bag. He gathered his own and covered me with it. I was shivering.

"Stay right there."

As if I was going anywhere. Bob nosed into the tent and lay down between me and the tent wall. As I've thought many times before, he was one smart coyote.

Joe returned with lukewarm broth that smelled revolting. Bastard that he was, he forced me to drink it. All of it. Bastard.

It was mid-morning when I next awoke. The tent was empty of both man and coyote and I relished the solitude. I had nearly fallen back to sleep when Bob came in, yipped, and raced out. Squealer.

At least the mug that Joe brought in this time was filled with decent coffee, and the bread had a good smear of honey on it. I choked on my second bite when the memory of my vision thrust itself into my consciousness. I had been inside Robyn's head like that time I had been inside Joe's when he met She-rock. Would these visions never reach their worst possible manifestation?

I struggled to extract myself from the bedding, spilling coffee along the way. Joe deftly took the mug and the bread from my hands and set them outside the tent.

"We have to go! Now!"

He patted the air in front of me. "We'll leave soon. Just take it slow, all right?"

I squinted my eyes at him. "If I do, will you give me back my coffee?"

Relieved, Joe smiled.

I hadn't realised how distraught he was until he unclenched his face.

"It's Robyn."

"I know. You screamed her name until you lost your voice. That's why your throat feels like it's been sandpapered. Good thing we were way out here." As he spoke, he gathered up pieces of clothing and put them in my hands. He picked up other odds and ends and backed out of the tent. "Take your time, but hurry."

A man of contradiction.

It was late in the day when we pulled onto the highway. Joe had made a cozy bed for Bob and me in the back of the wagon. I would rest for a few hours after which I would, hopefully, feel alert enough to drive. There would be no scenic route this time; we would reach the town where the project staff stayed as fast as we could.

Our stops were brief, and we arrived in the vicinity late the following day. We set up the tent well beyond the outskirts and I proceeded to reinforce my disguise—my white roots were showing.

Bob also had to be disguised in order to play his part and he didn't like it at all. The scarf I had used on him earlier became part of his ensemble—Pirate Bob—and a little of my brown hair dye did wonders to subdue his distinctive coyote markings. However, he did not accept these changes gracefully. Joe had to have a little talk with him when he would not stop licking the dye from his coat.

"It's just until we get Robyn," I consoled him. He wouldn't look at me. "I'll get you one of those gigantic bones you love." His ears perked up a bit. "Maybe two." His ears perked up a bit more and his right ear flopped forward. A good sign.

The worst part was that we could not stay together. Richardson's people would be looking for a man and a woman with or without a coyote. I had no doubt that Robyn had been forced to divulge everything she knew about us. Joe and I also knew, however reluctantly, that the kids had to be involved— Robyn hadn't yet met them and couldn't have given them away. This was the whole reason for making Bob look a little more like a German shepherd, at least from a distance. The coyote could help protect them and we were desperate for any information they could glean.

"I hate to put them more at risk than they already are, out there on the streets, but we have to use everything we have and everyone we know to find where Robyn is being held. All I could see in the vision was a dirty basement window." I was anxious about this whole escapade—anxiety fueled my sense of urgency and likely clouded my judgement. But if the kids found where Robyn was, they could be captured themselves. I was making myself sick.

"Your busking makes you visible and invisible at the same time, and we need a way to communicate with each other. How about when I drop a five-dollar bill in your case, it means 'meet me at the barn at dusk' and if I drop a twenty, it means 'get there now'?" Joe pondered his own idea, nodding to himself.

"And what will you be doing?" I asked sweetly. This whole communication scheme smelled like a plot to protect me and I did not like it one bit.

He pondered some more. "Me? I'll ask my acquaintance if he can find out where Robyn is being held, and if he can help with her extrication." He looked at me. "I'll need a lot more money."

Ah. That's what I was good for. I could feel the flush rise up my neck and into my face. As suddenly, it receded. What else did I think I could do? Rush past Richardson's security and single-handedly free Robyn? I knew better than that; it was that vision of her unnerving me. Oh, no…

***

My throat closed, and my hands and feet felt like icy blocks. I wondered if they would turn black and simply fall off my body. I shuddered and tried to cough. Something foul was stuffed into my mouth! Panic sent its insidious tendrils into my chest. I had to stop it! I had to breathe through my nose. I had to stay alive.

***

My eyes snapped open. While I had been incapacitated, Joe had driven us closer to town and now sat with me in the back seat, his arm supporting me while I tried to sit up. There was no need to explain what had just happened.

"Change of plans. Bob and I will take a look around and find out if the kids have noticed anything. He'll stay with them while I go talk to a guy. It may take a few hours. Pitch the tent somewhere and we'll find you." He shook his index finger at me. "Your visions are unpredictable, and we have no one else to take care of you. Please," he gripped my hand, "please stay at the campsite."

Look who's the planner now?

Chapter 18

Joe melted from shadow to shadow leading to the ramshackle place of business he studied from the cover of a narrow alleyway. Curtains were drawn over its grimy windows through which a sickly light emanated. Three vehicles of various makes were parked along the curb. From the occasional glow of a cigarette, two of them held occupants. He would wait. He was good at waiting.

When the last vehicle pulled away, Joe waited a while longer before moving to a position where he had a clear view of the dark lane separating his target building from an equally squalid building beside it. The man he sought would not leave by the main entrance but, even so, he almost missed the movement when a black door opened into the lane. A tall form slipped through and hurried towards the rear of the building. Joe took a step to follow.

An iron grip squeezed his biceps.

"Not a sound," his captor hissed, and backed them further into the alley. The explosion a few seconds later flattened them both to the ground but the man never lost the hold on Joe's arm.

Joe was hauled to his feet and, without further persuasion and knowing he had to get far from this place, Joe let himself be led away from the scene of the crime, ears ringing from the blast. Minutes later and several blocks away, they heard the distant sound of sirens. They ducked into a doorway, indistinguishable from a dozen others they had passed. The man produced a key and after a quick look around, unlocked the door and hustled Joe inside. They walked down a long hallway, through a second door, and into a dingy room. Joe recognised the man seated on the other side of a table; it was not a happy moment.

"What you doin' skulkin' 'round in my town?" The face of the man who spoke was shrouded in cigarette smoke, but Joe would know that voice anywhere. "Speak up, boy."

"I'm looking for someone," Joe answered. He was frisked thoroughly by the man who had brought him in, who then shoved him into a chair facing his interrogator, the whole while keeping a nerve-numbing grip on Joe's shoulder. Out of the side of his eye, Joe glimpsed that his other hand held a nasty-looking knife, the blade serrated to inflict maximum damage.

Joe studied the leader. Once a bully, always a bully. Good name for him, Joe decided, 'The Bull,' but he would call him that only inside his head. He even looked like a bull: short, squat, with a flat-ish head wedged onto shoulders the width of the doorway. His bare forearms rested on the table, the better to display the garish tattoos intertwined around scars that looked remarkably like teeth marks and—what a surprise—outlined muscles he casually flexed. A cigarette dangled from his fat, moist lips and Joe hoped it would burn him. This was one of the thugs who had beaten him and left him for dead in Las Cruces. This was the member of the gang who had taken particular enjoyment in making sure Joe hurt everywhere. This had been the same time that the coyote had first saved his life.

The Bull pawed through Joe's wallet and pulled out a wad of bills. "Found someone." He poked a stubby thumb into his own chest. "What you gonna buy with this? A woman, for a change?" He said something rude in Spanish about Joe and his attraction to canines to which his cronies sniggered.

"Yeah. A woman." It wasn't even a lie.

With a speed belying his bulk, The Bull stood, reached across the table, and backhanded him across the face, knocking him to the floor. "You want a woman, you see me, understand? This is my town and all the women work for me." He strutted around the table to get a good angle on the kick he gave to Joe's ribs. "Understand?"

Joe grunted, trying to protect his head by curling into himself.

Another man hurried into the room and whispered something to The Bull. He bellowed orders and his lackeys dispersed until only he and the guy who had brought him in were left. Joe didn't like this turn of events at all. The Bull could indulge himself and, this time, finish the job he had started way back when. Joe tensed, ready to make a break for it.

The Bull made sure Joe was looking at him when he swung his leg back for a second kick. He grinned in sadistic anticipation, his cigarette wobbled. His grin widened, then changed subtly as though he had had an inscrutable idea. A trickle of blood stained his teeth and the cigarette sagged so that the lit end grazed his chin. He began to topple, landing heavily, inches from Joe, giving him an excellent view of the knife protruding from The Bull's back. His captor knelt to pull it out—a sound Joe hoped he never heard again—and wiped the blade on The Bull's shirt.

"Name's Chevy," he said, "and you're Joe." Joe struggled to his feet. "Word on the street is you're out to take Richardson down. Word is you have a man," he paused and tilted his head, "a woman, on the inside." He looked around the room and reached for the bottle of Mescal on a window ledge. He took a healthy slug and passed it to Joe.

The fiery stuff blunted the throbbing in his cheek bone but did nothing for the pain in his ribs. He kept the bottle and held it loosely in his hands, waiting.

"That building, the one that blew up. You do that?"

Joe shook his head.

"Too bad." He pulled out his knife and studied the blade. "You have to pay more attention if you want to live much longer; my little sister could sneak up on you. There's a real nice bounty on your head and it doesn't say how many pieces you have to be in."

Where was The Nuisance when I needed him? Typical. "So. What's your interest in Richardson?"

"Where's the other one, the one you travel with?"

Joe shrugged.

Chevy surged towards him, murder in his eyes. Joe could get maybe one good punch in. He raised his forearm to fend off the knife. Chevy stopped, fist clenched.

"If you don't tell me what I need to know, I'll put you back outside," he paused. "You won't like it."

They were at an impasse. As far as Joe could tell, his options were to die now or die later, and how was that different, really, from every other moment in his life? He needed help and here was help, albeit not quite what he had had in mind. Time to deal.

"We don't know each other, and we don't trust each other, and we don't have time to do either. But it sounds like we might want the same thing and I'm willing to share knowledge for knowledge. I'll start." His former captor-turned-saviour perched on the side of the table and continued to toy with his knife.

"I'm listening."

"You know about the aquifer?"

He nodded.

"Good. That makes it a lot easier." Joe told him about what would happen if Richardson breached the cavern ceiling. He told him about the plans he had acquired and about The Mouth. He did not mention She-rock or Flotsy or Robyn, even though it seemed that Chevy knew about at least one of the women.

Chevy's eyes glittered. "You have plans?" He wagged his hand in front of Joe's face so that the iron engineering ring on his baby finger was unmistakable. "Do you have them with you?"

Joe sneered, just a little. "How stupid do you think I am?" He put the Mescal bottle down taking the risk that he no longer needed it as a weapon and perhaps eliciting a small measure of trust. "I was looking for someone to interpret them when you grabbed me."

"As this piece of trash," Chevy shoved The Bull's body with his booted foot, "pointed out before, found someone, didn't you?" He rifled

232

through the rest of the room, unearthing assorted weapons and some cash. "Time to go. The rest of Alejandro's gang will wonder what's taking him so long to finish you."

Alejandro was far too grand a name for the thug cooling on the floor.

We ghosted through industrial wasteland and out into the desert. It was late and Flotsy would be worried. No help for that now; Bob would keep an eye on her while the kids slept.

Chevy moved like a wraith, or at least how Joe imagined a wraith would move. Blending, silent. They were deep in the desert in minutes. He crouched, and Joe followed suit. There was a cluster of boulders ahead. *A secret desperado hideaway, just like in the movies.* Joe smiled in the dark.

"I saw that."

Moves like a wraith and sees in the dark like a cat. Joe could learn a lot from this man.

A dim glow blinked on and off. Chevy stood, and we walked towards it. The light had come from a tiny battery-powered flashlight. Chevy picked it up and we squeezed through a crevice. We inched around a gaping black hole in the floor and on its far side was another crevice. Beyond that was a second black hole but this one had a rope ladder descending from its lip. Joe could simply be shoved in and left for dead down there but why go through all this trouble?

Chevy tucked the flashlight in his waistband and manoeuvred himself onto the ladder. He didn't wait to see if his captive-turned-fellow-conspirator followed.

This could be the point of no return, Joe

thought, as he watched the man disappear further down the shaft. It seemed crazy that anything useful would come of this, and maybe equally crazy not to take it. What they were trying to do was highly improbable for one man, two women, and one coyote—adding another man to the team just didn't improve the odds that much, and it might mean having to reveal his and Flotsy's gifts to another person—a big risk to take. Joe watched as Chevy stepped from the ladder and through an opening in the wall leading to what must be a tunnel. A few seconds later, the flashlight lit the rough wall across from where Joe stood.

"You coming?"

It was a hard thing for Joe to admit that he needed help. Most of his life he had been alone and done some impossible things alone, but that had always been under The Nuisance's umbrella of protection, who had not made his Asshole-self known for some time. To make matters a hundred times worse, there was Flotsy and Robyn and Bob, and the kids. And, oh gods, She-rock. But what would happen if Richardson was not stopped? When he thought of it like that, there really wasn't much choice at all. He got on the ladder.

Ribs screaming, Joe descended the ladder and crawled onto the floor of the tunnel. He lay there, facedown, taking rapid, shallow breaths until the pain had subsided enough for him to get to his knees and then to his feet.

The tunnel led to a wooden door wedged into a side opening. When Chevy saw Joe approaching, he opened it and went in. To Joe's disappointment, there had been no secret knock. Whoa. Maybe this whole escapade was bringing out another side of him. Or maybe, he was just exhausted and hurt, and grasping for anything to keep him going.

The small cavern beyond the door was provisioned as for a siege: crates of food and barrels of water lined the walls. On top of these were blankets and assorted clothes, and, in a niche that receded into darkness, he could see stacks of wood, likely for cooking fires. He continued to survey the 'hang-out' when his eyes stalled on the neat pile of guns and ammunition. Wrenching his attention away from the ordnance, Joe felt a morbid certainty that if he was not of value, he would never leave these caves.

Seated on cushions around a small fire was a hodgepodge of men and women ranging in age from twelve to seventy. The intensity with which Joe was examined made every hair on his body tingle as though he passed through an electric current. Whatever he had gotten himself into, it was becoming weird enough to comfortably fit into the weirdness that was already a big part of his life.

Chevy produced a state-of-the-art laptop and held out his hand to Joe. Even though he had been frisked thoroughly, there was no chance that Chevy could have felt the tiny storage device secreted in his left boot. Joe looked around at the people who, on the surface, appeared calm and contained. This did not in any way reduce the scrutiny to which they subjected him. He could feel it probing him but not in a bad way—if there was even such a thing as good probing. He sighed. They could detect whatever they chose to detect and didn't have to physically see the device to know that it was here.

His boot had been on for a long, hot, active day and the pungent odour that briefly wafted into the cave gave Joe a moment of juvenile satisfaction. He handed the memory storage drive to Chevy.

Chevy's eyes glittered as he gently pushed the device into the slot. The light from the screen shone on his features that he supposed Flotsy would describe as handsome. What was more objective and certain was that he was immediately engrossed in studying the plans.

The discussion their arrival had apparently interrupted began again. It soon became obvious that they were united in their anger that this businessman could simply do whatever he wanted to do. They had been watching Richardson prior to the first time he attempted to buy the land. They had spies on the town council and spies in the hotel where the project employees were housed. For a short time, they even had someone in Richardson's personal coterie, but the masseuse had disappeared.

"She was my mother." The young girl who spoke held a small knife. She eyed the slender weapon in her hand and returned somewhat more vigorously to sharpening its blade.

The talk quieted as the night passed. A spattering of tales and legends were interspersed among the ideas of how to stop the project.

"I have a story," Joe blurted. Heads swiveled in his direction. He cleared his throat, nervous in front of an audience. They were fighting the same fight and needed to know everything that he knew, and vice versa. But they should also know the full extent of what they were protecting. It was more than the land and the water. He would tell them about She-rock, and if they thought he was a lunatic, well, maybe he was.

As he spoke of She-rock, he forgot about the cave and the people in it, he forgot about the ache in his side and the puffiness of his cheek. The misery and desperation of She-rock remained clear in his mind. He told them about Flotsy and how she was the conduit of communication for She-rock, about Robyn and how she must be rescued, about Bob and how he had an uncanny knack to be where he was needed, and about the three kids and how adept they were at hearing and seeing things. He did not even try to hide his extreme anxiety and worry for them.

When Joe was finished, his throat was dry, and someone passed him water. He was sore and more tired than he could ever remember. Sometime during his soliloquy, Chevy had closed the laptop and sat in silence, listening like the others.

They probably think I've lost my mind; won't be the first time.

Abruptly, the questions began. Where, exactly, was the She-rock phenomenon located? Where, exactly, was Flotsy? Where, exactly, was Robyn? What kids? Who else knows about this? What can we do? Does Richardson know what he will destroy? How do we stop him?

The initial outburst abated, and Chevy stepped into the momentary lull. "These plans," he gestured to his computer, "are useless for our purposes." The murmur of voices rose again. He raised a hand. "The Mouth may be a better way, and some of us know the area surrounding it quite well. It's where we'll start." He turned and began to stuff items into a backpack.

Joe sat bewildered, his exhaustion and pain choosing that moment to engulf him. He needed to save Robyn, Robyn who had sacrificed everything, and wobbled to his feet. A familiar hand landed on his shoulder and pushed him back to the floor.

"Rest. I have people looking for her. We'll get her back. You need to heal before you can be of any use to us."

"Flotsy? Bob? The kids?" Joe's eyelids were drooping closed; they must have added a little something to the water he had gulped down. Or he could just be that drained.

Chevy hitched the strap of the pack to one shoulder and headed for the wooden door. "Rest," he said again, and was gone.

Joe's knees wobbled, and a kind hand helped him to sit. He gently toppled sideways, muzzily thinking that he would catch up with Chevy later.

Chapter 19

The campsite I chose was mostly hidden by rubbish bins and the rusted- out hulks of vehicles. The tent blended rather nicely with the muted greens and browns, and seemed to disappear altogether when I studied it from a short distance.

I slept through the night. I woke, ate, and waited.

Well, Joe said it himself, my busking made me visible and invisible at the same time and he would surely remember the five-dollar and twenty-dollar codes. The sun was approaching noon, and the main square would be busy. I gathered my guitar, water, and hat, and wandered in what I hoped was a haphazard way into the centre of town.

My fingers were sore from playing and the sun was hot. Most people had finished lunch an hour ago and had left for the coolness of their homes or workplaces. Still no sign of bills, fives or otherwise, in my guitar case. There were a few coins, though, which I gathered and shoved into a pocket. Joe was just delayed, I repeated to myself. I wandered down the street like I usually did, stopping to gaze into shop windows.

"Hey, Petal!"

What kind of a name was 'Petal?' Oh, crap. I had stopped in front of the head-shop where I had worked for a very short time and had left in somewhat of a hurry. "Hiya," I answered. I had never learned his name.

"How's the guitar?"

I smiled. "Just lovely. I've been playing in the

square."

"Yeah. I heard. You're good."

I blushed. Gods.

"You busy?" He ushered me into the shop. "I could use a break. There's even some chips."

Drove a hard bargain, this boy. "Hey. I forgot to ask your name."

He shuffled his feet. "Balthazar. You know like the angel, or like the big bottle of wine," he explained.

"No kidding?"

"Most people call me 'Bizar.' You know, like the name of my shop," he said as he walked out the door.

"Oh, yeah," I said to his back.

Business was slow, and I used the time to clear my mind by straightening out the merchandise. The chimes tinkled, and I banged my head on the shelf where I was working. My nerves were not up to what they had been exposed to lately.

The man was tall and rangy but with the windows backlighting him, I couldn't make out his features.

"Need any help?" I asked, being the consummate salesperson that I was.

He walked over to me. He was very tall, at least in comparison to me.

"Just looking," he answered.

He continued to stand there, and I felt the air shimmer. He had the blackest eyes I'd ever seen, and I couldn't look away. I didn't want to look away. He stepped closer, studying my face as I studied his.

"Flotsy?"

240

I grabbed the shelf beside me and the caftans that I had so carefully folded and placed there tumbled towards the floor. Quick as a snake, he caught them before they landed and laid them back in their spot, ensuring that they were squared-up and even with the edge of the shelf.

Wow. I smiled.

"Chevy," he said, by way of introducing himself.

"Like the car?"

He did not smile. I guess he'd heard that one a few times.

I jumped at the knock on the alleyway door.

Chevy put up a hand to stop me. He slipped into the storage room and pressed his back to the boxes beside the door before opening it a crack. Bob and little Ben came in, unsurprised that a stranger greeted them. Ah, perhaps not a stranger. I relaxed my clenched muscles and joined them.

"Seen 'em," little Ben said, "through a basement window, over to the hotel. Always a man around," he tried to lower his little-boy voice to a conspiratorial whisper, "with a gun." His job done, Ben went into the shop, deftly pocketing an item or two, and came back munching the chips Bizar had left on the counter. Bob appeared beside him and they both sat on the floor enjoying the treat.

Chevy rifled through his small carry-all and gave the boy a plastic bag. Ben's eyes lit up. He wiped his hands carefully on his shirt and took the bag reverently from Chevy and gazed inside. With the tips of his fingers, he lifted out the brightly coloured comic book and devoured its cover with eyes as big as his ears. He heaved a huge contented

241

sigh and gently put it back inside the bag, leapt to his feet, and scampered out the door, Bob close behind.

Chevy and I smiled at each other and my heart gave a little thump. Wait. How did he know my name? From Joe? I looked at the floor, desperately trying to think.

"My name is Petal, by the way." I turned and walked back into the shop. Just because he knew my name and Bob seemed to accept him did not necessarily mean that he was a man to be trusted. He made me nervous. I would play it cool.

"Joe's safe," he said from directly behind me.

I started. He was another one of those move-without-making-a-sound types. My poor nerves.

"He's with some friends of mine." He paused. "Look. I have to go now, but I'll find you later." He disappeared out the back.

Great. I get to worry while the men-folk do the work. Has it always been the way? Not for me, it hasn't. I was not going to sit idly by. I knew how to be careful. I knew how not to be seen. I just needed a plan.

The jewellery case was a messy jumble. Excellent planning activity.

By the time Bizar returned, I had gotten exactly nowhere with my plan. My heart demanded that I rescue Robyn, but my head firmly overrode that impulse. All that would happen is I would end up being another source of Richardson's sick entertainment. What I could do was reconnoitre The Mouth. I would be the woman enamoured of spelunkers, those brave men who tested life and limb in an underworld fraught with danger and

242

discovery. A smidgen of hero-worship could do much to entice tales of their exploits.

"Hey." Bizar was back.

"Hey," I said back, and left the store.

The barn was empty when I arrived. Good. I stuffed a few things in my capacious handbag. I'd leave the station wagon and camping gear for Joe and Bob. The bus would be my choice of transportation: public, busy, and anonymous.

Guitar in hand, I ambled towards the square where I busked. Siesta time was over; people would begin circulating, ready for some entertainment. If anyone saw me, it would look normal.

The bus terminal was a few blocks off the square. I turned down a side street and stopped at a mediocre diner. I sipped coffee and nibbled a bland sandwich. My surveillance skills were amateurish, but I did not detect anyone paying special attention to me. I left a tip appropriate to the poor service and bad food and continued away from the square.

There was a bus heading in the right direction scheduled to leave in forty-five minutes. I bought a ticket.

It was the longest wait of my life. My shoulder and neck muscles were locked with tension. I breathed deeply and rolled my head around. I eased the grip on the handle of my guitar case and stretched my fingers. The first call was made for my bus and I headed for one of the terminal's washrooms before embarking. Anyone who peed in a moving vehicle had to be far more desperate that I would ever be.

The handicap cubicle was free. I struggled to open the door with my guitar in one hand and my bag slipping off my other shoulder. Awkward, but I made it in doing the sideways shuffle.

A hand clamped over my mouth and I was pulled against a solid chest. I dropped my things and clawed at my attacker's hands.

"It's me. Chevy," he whispered.

I continued to struggle, flailing and kicking wildly. He circled his other arm around my waist to stop me from trashing about, but it only made me fight harder.

"Cut it out," he hissed, "they'll hear us."

That broke through my panic. But how did he know I would go to this bathroom and to this bathroom stall? Who was this guy? One thing was certain: if he did not want me to get away, I would not be getting away. I stopped my useless attempt to escape and sagged. He immediately loosened his grip but did not let go of me. He brought his mouth close to my ear.

"Richardson's men are waiting for you in the terminal. We have to leave this place."

"How do we do that?" I whispered.

He knelt and dumped my belongings on the floor of the cubicle, sorting through the clothes. "Here." He handed me a scarf, pants, and a shirt. For himself, he chose nothing. I put the outfit on top of what I wore and tied the scarf around my head like a gypsy.

"You'll have to leave the guitar."

I sighed.

He shoved my bag and most everything else inside his own carry-all, leaving me some cash. I put the cash in my bra. "Now what?"

He turned his head, listening. Boarding

244

announcements blared over the speakers.

"Now you leave. Don't go back to the barn. Go to the centre of town. I'll find you there."

He ushered me out ahead of him.

"What about you?"

"Go," he said.

I hesitated at the bathroom door and looked back. No Chevy. The men in my life just kept disappearing.

The terminal was busy with travellers and their baggage. I waded in and joined a raucous group on their way to Las Vegas. I drifted to the middle and smiled and laughed along with them. They turned for their bus and I kept on walking, keeping to a slow, steady pace. I did not look around even though it felt like a hundred pairs of eyes were stabbing into my back. I was quite proud of myself.

Chevy intercepted me a few blocks away and hustled me into a condemned building. We picked our way through the first floor and down a flight of stairs into a dank basement. I ignored the skittering noises and clutched the back of Chevy's jacket. We exited by an old coal chute and continued into the bowels of this no-man's land. The road was cracked, and litter was pasted on remnants of chain-link fencing. Abandoned cars, stripped of anything useful, were haphazardly strewn about in vacant lots. If there were any people squatting in the dilapidated buildings, I did not see any.

It was a relief when we glimpsed the pristine desert landscape. Chevy increased our pace. We continued out into the desert and did not stop until a rise in the land would hide us from any surveillance originating in the town. Chevy dug out a water bottle and handed it to me. He returned to the top of the rise and lay there, looking back the way we had come. And lay there some more. At long last, he rejoined me.

Twilight stretched the shadows around us. As always, I found it beautiful. There was something about the dry air that crystallised what you saw through it. Sharper edges, vibrant colours, distinct textures. Even the smell was honed to a precise fragrance. I closed my eyes and breathed it in, instantly flashing back to the marvelous aroma of the shawl Joe had left for me at that campground three years ago. Three years. He had been part of my life longer than almost anyone, even if we didn't meet up again until recently.

"You love the desert."

"Mmmm." I opened my eyes. His face was close to mine, those black eyes unreadable. I stepped back. "What now?"

He looked aside. "We walk. It's not much farther."

"What's not much farther?"

"You'll see."

Whatever happened, I was committed now. More like I ought to be committed now. Where were those blue pills when you needed one?

Chevy's idea of 'not much farther' was radically different from mine. By the time the primitive encampment came into view, I was limping and ravenous. The cold desert night had seeped through my two layers of clothing and the tiny campfire drew me like a moth. I crouched, extending my hands nearly into the flames.

Someone cleared his throat, no, her throat. I

looked up and into the oldest face I had ever seen. She could have been the prototype for those dried apple people that you see in craft shops. Her deep-set eyes all but disappeared in a nest of wrinkles, like black holes at the bottom of a woven funnel. She blinked and seemed to disappear altogether. I shook my head. I needed something to eat.

Like magic, a steaming cup was handed to me. Chevy crouched beside me with his own cup and we drank the savoury broth in silence. Feeling more myself, I looked around. Primitive, yes. Without comforts, no. I could see inside one of the tents through an open flap. Bedding was piled high and the flickering light bespoke a candle or, more likely, a lantern. I yearned to crawl in.

"We have to talk," Chevy said.

More people had gathered around and, just so I could make a lasting first-impression, I was flung into a vision.

***

She-rock gathered her remaining strength into a tight ball and held it deep within herself. The perspective soared dizzily, and I was witness to Richardson's desecration of her body. She contained her agony but could not repress it all and pain arrowed through me. It was far worse than physical pain—it was the pain of excruciating loss, of eternal helplessness.

***

The pile of blankets on which I lay gave me no solace. I wept and could not stop, the sobs wracking my body. Chevy held me, rubbing my back. The old woman sat on cushions beside him, eyes closed, and worked beads through her gnarled fingers. I took a shuddering breath and feebly worked my hands up between our bodies. Chevy looked at me and pulled a pristine, white handkerchief from an inside jacket pocket. He placed it gently in my hands.

I smiled a little.

When I awoke the second time, it was full day. I just wasn't sure exactly what day. Biological needs—drat them—often drive one from one's warm cozy nest. I forced my stiff aching body onto its side and pushed myself up. I sat for a few minutes until the dizziness subsided. Some considerate soul had left water as well as a very delicious looking cookie within easy reach. Fortified by both, I located my sneakers and stumbled outside. A composting toilet was in a small tent of its own set up a short distance from the other tents. Ah. Modern conveniences.

Word that I was up had spread and a contingent of people awaited me. I hoped they had more of those cookies. They were a mixed assortment of young and old, male and female, light and dark—just like most other places I've been. There was no sign of Chevy, but the old woman was there and beckoned me to her. Among all these strangers, I felt very alone and missed Joe and Bob terribly. She placed a hand on my elbow and encouraged me to sit on the camp chair next to hers. Miserable and uncomfortable with all the strangers around me, I sat.

It was later in the day than I thought. A wonderful aroma escaped the big pot set on one side of the campfire. My stomach growled, and I blushed. Everyone laughed a little. I had just done something Bob would have done. I smiled.

The old lady gestured. Dishes were filled, and utensils passed around. Hot stew, chewy bread, and as much water as I could drink. Conversation was light as befit a meal. The bowls were then whisked away by a young boy and girl, tittering as they brought the dirty dishes inside another tent.

The old lady cleared her throat and silence descended. She introduced herself as Yavapai and went around the circle saying everyone's names. There were a dozen people and I fervently hoped I would remember at least some of them. Yavapai looked at me.

Oh, yeah. I hadn't had the chance to introduce myself earlier, what with the vision and all.

The vision. I started to shake and, to my dismay, cry. Again. Yavapai took my hand and pressed gently on various parts of my palm. The shaking subsided; the tears took a bit longer.

I blew my nose and took a deep breath. "I am extremely grateful for your help and for the delicious food." They smiled and nodded. "My name is Olivia Marie Ducharme," I said, "but I prefer Flotsy." Was now the time to tell someone besides Joe and Robyn about my visions—my curse? My gut told me that these people would listen, even if they could do nothing to stop them from happening. But would speaking about them help me? Give me insight? What did I have to lose?

"I have had visions most of my life, visions about tragedies about which I could do nothing. But, lately, the only 'visions' I have are not visions at all but instead a sort of communication from an entity I call She-rock. It is her existence that is most urgently threatened by Richardson's project." I

249

looked around expecting at the very least scepticism but more likely disbelief or a 'you got to be kidding' look. But it was as if I had been talking about bad weather; their expressions only showed concern. Perhaps Chevy had brought me to some sort of cult, sympathetic but which had lost its hold on reality. If anyone had told me such a thing, even a short time ago, I would have quietly slipped away.

The silence lengthened. I sighed. Here it comes—time for me to move on. But I really would have liked a second bowl of that stew before I left.

"Yes, Cheveyo spoke of this." A man of indeterminate age, skin leathery and darkened by the desert sun, spoke. "It is a thing among many things of which we have some knowledge. But he said to first tell you that Joe was resting and recovering from minor injuries, and that the children had found where Robyn was being held. She will soon be rescued."

In the cooler evening air, I felt hot tears roll down my cheeks. Where had all these waterworks come from? I hadn't even cried at my own father's funeral.

Yavapai patted my hand, trying to make it all right. My first inclination was to shake her off; nothing could *ever* be made all right. But I was so tired, so tired of trying and failing, so tired of moving from place to place, so tired of being alone all the time. Besides, it was obvious that I couldn't be left on my own anymore. Who knew when the next communiqué would come and flatten me? Maybe the next time I would be driving on a highway and hit a school bus and kill everyone on board? Maybe I would be walking along a canyon

250

wall and tumble right in, landing broken and bleeding at the bottom, never to be found?

The old woman stood and beckoned me to follow her into her tent. The light inside was softly flickering and the air redolent with the herbs and other paraphernalia she perhaps used for healing. There were delicate pieces of woven art sewn into the walls, and a variety of small bottles and other containers stacked neatly in shelving made from unusual pieces of desiccated saguaro. She beckoned for me to sit across from her, the small fire between us.

"You have the gift," she began, and smiled at my sour expression, "or curse of sensitivity to certain energies, energies that surround us always, but of which only a few become aware. Or allow themselves to become aware, and we must agree to this awareness. Also, it is possible to stop the awareness altogether."

"What? I never agreed to anything!" As least I don't remember agreeing to anything. My first vision was so long ago, but deep inside I had had an inkling that my mother knew what was happening to me and chose to let it continue. I'd think about that later, much later.

Yavapai stirred a small kettle and poured a measure of dark liquid into two cups. She handed me one. "It is just plain tea," she assured me and smiled with her entire wrinkled face.

"Time itself is fluid," she continued. "It can flow swiftly like a flash of lighting, or slowly like the majestic dance of the stars as they glide through the universe. It can swirl; it can zigzag. It can be everywhere at once. It can be nowhere at all." She took a sip of tea. "The idea that time is only past, present, and future is a fabrication, conceived by the unenlightened."

I swirled the dark liquid in my cup. The magnitude of what she was saying was worthy of some sacred fiery elixir reserved for just such an occasion, not mere tea.

"Yavapai," I said in a small voice, "are you saying that my visions and She-rock and Joe's experiences are all caused by special energies in the air?"

She nodded. "There are ways to create a buffer to protect yourself from the effects as well as from the after-effects of these energies. I will show you."

Just like that? I felt like I was going to pass out. I had to take several deep breaths to steady myself. The answers were here, in the middle of the desert, in a tent in the middle of the desert. Yavapai passed me a beautifully embroidered handkerchief and waited patiently while my latest crying jag wore itself out.

***

I was sitting outside when a cold, wet nose inserted itself into my palm. Bob. My heart lifted, and he and I did a little hugging dance. He raced around in circles, daring me to catch him, then leapt up at my face, leaving a slobbery kiss in his wake. Laughing, I wiped his drool from my cheek.

Shortly afterwards, a small group of people entered the circle of firelight. Two men supported Robyn between them, her ravaged face pale and sweaty. Little Ben, Arthur, and the little girl came next, dragging their feet, but perked up considerably at the smell of something to eat. They waved to me

252

and made a beeline to the woman who beckoned them with bowls and bread. I watched to see what would happen to the girl's ritual of 'setting the table.' The boys, amazingly, waited for her to take a bite before they dove in.

Yavapai stood and led the two men with Robyn into her tent. I followed, anxious to help. She turned to me. "Her body is not badly injured, but I will give her medicine to rest her mind. You should stay with the children. They know you and this will be a comfort to them."

I went back to my chair and watched the kids stuff themselves. Bob gnawed on something crunchy. Nearly the whole gang was here—everyone but Joe.

Robyn had a little colour in her cheeks the next day. Her eyes downcast and shuffling her feet, she let Yavapai guide her to the outhouse. She was in there a long time. When she emerged, Yavapai brought her to a folding chair next to me and gently helped her sit. One of the young girls brought her a cup of something that smelled of herbs and Robyn mechanically took sip after sip until it was empty.

The little girl put her hand on the arm of my chair. "What's wrong with her?" she whispered. "She doesn't have a band-aid or even any scabs." Reminding herself, she absently picked at the one on her knee.

How do you explain psychological trauma to a six-year old?

"Someone said very bad things to her," I began. "It makes her not want to be with people until she can forget the bad things."

She thought about this, scuffing the toe of her

sneaker in the dirt.

"But what if she never forgets the bad things? What happens then?"

How did I get myself into this? I looked at her, really looked at her, and wondered what had made her run away from home. What had been worse than what she had now: living on the meagre food she could beg or steal, sleeping in grimy blankets, and always on the alert for danger? Or had been abandoned on a street somewhere?

I took her hand in both of mine. "Sweetie, are there bad things you would like to forget?"

The tiniest of tears tracked through the dust on her face. She rubbed at it smearing it into a little mud.

I picked her up and held her and wandered away from the camp so she could have a good cry without anyone noticing. She cried and cried. I rubbed her back and muttered all the soothing words I knew. Eventually, there were longer and longer intervals between sobs and she began to hiccup. I chuckled a little, and then so did she. I put her gently back on her feet and rubbed my aching arms. How did mothers do it? How did they hold their children for hours and hours at a time? Maybe their bodies produce a super-mom hormone to compensate for the agony of labour and the ensuing carrying-about of the child.

She sat on the ground and drew circles in the dirt with her fingers. Without raising her eyes to me, she whispered that her name was Shirley, which she hated, so would I please call her Arabella. It had been the name of her favorite princess doll, she added. Somehow, this was Bob's cue. He raced over from wherever he had been lurking and licked her face free of dirt and mucus. She laughed and hugged him, holding on for much longer than Bob usually allowed.

Robyn was seated next to me again at lunch. She furtively glanced at me; I assiduously avoided making eye contact. I wanted very much to hold her hand or put my arm around her—comfort her in some way—but instincts told me to wait for her to come to me. She glanced my way a second time and a flicker of a smile briefly softened her face. Progress.

As we watched the kids and Bob play, it recalled again how very different that second vision of Robyn's torture was from my previous visions, She-rock excepted, of course. It's not that I hadn't noticed the difference at the time it happened, it was just that I hadn't had much time to consider it and what it meant, if anything. That second time with Robyn, I was with her; it was like I was inside her head. A similar thing had happened with Joe when he and Bob had visited She-rock. I had felt his sorrow.

Could I have helped Joe and Robyn? Could I have comforted them in some way? I distinctly remembered the last vision experience with Robyn: I couldn't feel my hands or move any part of my body; my breathing was ragged and panicky. When the door opened, the onslaught of terror and loathing had shoved me out of the vision. For me, it was not a moment too soon, but for her it would have gone on and on. I wanted to ask Robyn if she had felt my presence and what it had been like from her point of view. The coward in me reared up its yellow head. Maybe my presence had made it worse, maybe she was ashamed at having been 'seen' in such a vulnerable state.

Guilt swept through me like a familiar scouring brush. Could it be that the one time I could have helped someone, I scurried away as fast as I could? Wasn't that what I had been so desperate to do all those years—help the people in my visions? I hated it when I couldn't fix everything. As if anybody could. Maybe it was time to become my real self— the one who isn't perfect, the one who can't do everything right, the one who is just me with flaws and frailties. Huh.

Robyn was staring at me. "Are you alright?"

I grinned and nodded. "Just meeting myself for the first time, is all."

She raised her eyebrows.

I held out my hand to her. "Olivia Marie Ducharme. Most people call me Flotsy. Pleased to meet you."

"Robyn Elouise McMaster," she put her hand in mine and we shook. "Most people call me Robyn," she grinned.

I put my free hand on top of our joined hands, and she added hers on mine. The kids—ever vigilant—raced over in case a new game was afoot and added their small and not-so-clean hands to the growing pile. Not one to be left out, Bob gave a huff and laid his chin at the very top, tongue hanging out sideways, dribbling drool down our stack of hands like a unifying glue. That Bob.

Chapter 20

He arrived late at night after a cross-country ride in a 4-wheel drive Bronco. He gave thanks to the kind soul who had given him pain killers before he had left the cave. That was not the only gift either. He had a small tent, sleeping bag, assorted caving equipment, clothes, and a bit of dehydrated meat, all inside a medium-sized, well-worn backpack. Rope and karabiners hung from its sides, and sturdy pockets held a powerful flashlight and extra batteries. The boots were a little loose—all the more room for extra socks. It would be cold in the next caves he entered.

The driver dropped him off at the outskirts of town and continued on his own business. Joe guessed a population of about four hundred based on the number of buildings, and it might provide services for about that same number again. He could see marquees for three bars from where he stood and heard the rumble of music and voices that would be deafening inside. It would not be a good idea for a stranger to show up right about now, at this time of night. He'd likely walk in just as some stupid altercation broke out and find himself in the middle of it.

He turned from this unappealing scenario and walked into the desert. He would set up the tent and rest through what was left of the night and, from the way his body felt, through much of the day as well.

The bar, went he went in late the next day, was top-of-the-line dive. The blue-yellow bruising on his face and his limp from sore ribs added a nice touch of authenticity. Joe fit right in.

The barkeep swiped at circles of condensation in a slow, mesmerising, motion. He had likely been doing that for some time. The inevitable pool table gathered dust at the moment, but the juke box blared some twangy western drivel that Joe was hard-pressed to ignore. Why did it always have to be about the tragedies of love lost or love-never-had. It didn't even have to be about a person—they could be singing about their dog or their horse or their grandmother or their favourite shotgun. As mystifying as it was to him, it certainly seemed to work for the patrons scattered about the dingy room. They hollered out the words and kept the beat, mostly, with their hands and feet.

Joe hobbled up to the bar. It took a couple of minutes for the barkeep to notice him, but he didn't take Joe's order until the song was over. No sense in complaining. If he did that, odds were his beer would be warm or worse.

No one approached him, but he knew he had been noticed. These were not the nice, guide-led weekend spelunking kind of people; these were the 'I've got a hunch about something and I'd better not catch you spying on me' spelunking kind of people. These were the kind of people who would know more about the layout of the underground cave systems than anyone else. Especially about The Mouth. Joe was woefully inexperienced and would likely get himself killed, but finding a back door into Richardson's excavation was the only way to get inside to stop him.

He was driven by She-rock's anguish. He had stopped wondering 'why me' a long time ago. She-

258

rock wasn't the Boss Man. Her plea for help had burned into his brain without her need to reinforce it over and over again. Nevertheless, Joe's modus operandi had always been to get the job done as soon as possible; The Nuisance had drilled that into him. Most importantly, it would only be then that he could return to Flotsy and Robyn and the kids and Bob, their safety guaranteed. It seemed he had acquired an entire ready-made family which he felt a deep need to protect. The fleeting suspicion that She-rock had planted this thought into his brain in order to move him along dissipated as quickly as it had formed. He just didn't believe it was true.

As the sun set, the room began to fill. A group of women came in breaking the monotony of dour men who, like a light had been switched on, became more animated. The juke box was constantly playing now, and a small space was cleared for dancing. Betting was heavy at the pool table and Joe predicted that a fight would break out in the not-too-distant future. He had done what he came to do tonight, which was to make himself known, and quietly left the building.

The hand around his biceps was no less startling than it had been the first time, and Joe cursed himself that it had happened again. He really was not very good on his own and he blamed this completely on the Bastard.

Chevy let his hand drop, crossed the parking lot, and got in the driver's side of a dilapidated pick-up truck. Joe noticed that an oily tarp had been thrown over whatever was in the back. He got into the cab.

They drove in silence to exactly where Joe had

259

hidden his pack. Chevy retrieved it and stowed it under the tarp, careful to move things around just so. They continued for another hour, weaving in and out of dirt side-roads, travelling deeper onto the Coconino Plateau. By some landmark invisible to Joe, Chevy slowed the truck and carefully picked his way to the bottom of an arroyo. Joe pressed his lips together and cradled his abused ribs. In a mercifully short time, Chevy turned into a wide cleft in the rock wall and turned off the engine.

"First," Joe began, but Chevy silenced him with a sharp gesture. He listened intently for something, then nodded. Joe hadn't heard a thing; another skill to add to this guy's list. How did it go? Can hear like a bat.

They wormed their way around fallen rock, squeezed through yet more rock and descended a ladder, wooden this time, to arrive at, ironically, what looked exactly The Batcave from the old TV series. Well, not exactly. This one had more rock and fewer gadgets, but was impressive, nevertheless.

There were people working at various tasks, while others were wrapped in sleeping bags close to a small fire that had burned down to coals. The light in the cave was from work lamps powered by a small generator.

Chevy had continued to a table and sat with two men. One of them poured coffee for him without interrupting the other man who studied the material spread out over the surface.

Joe wandered over, keeping his distance, and took the time to look around more carefully at what was going on in this cave. He noticed many of the

260

same supplies that had been stored in the other, smaller cave, but in much greater quantity. The cave was separated into distinct areas, the largest of which was the work space. In addition to where people slept, there was a place for cooking and eating, and a sign propped against a tunnel entrance pointing to the composting toilet. In a sectioned-off area were mysterious lumps covered with tarps. His gaze returned to Chevy. He sauntered closer to the table. Noticing his motion, one of the two men waved him over and offered him a seat and a cup of coffee. Joe accepted both and sat, facing Chevy.

"First," Joe began again, "Robyn, Flotsy, Bob, the kids?"

"Safe," Chevy answered, and turned back to the discussion.

Joe breathed heavily. That was not enough of an answer to satisfy him; he needed details. At that moment, one of the men unrolled a map, distracting Joe from his burning need to pummel more information from Chevy. The map was likely of the nearby area. It seemed odd though. He stood up to look at it from a different angle, but that made no difference; it just did not look right.

"If we set a charge here," the man marked a small 'x' with a pencil, "the water will travel like this." He made light pencil marks in an array that reminded Joe of the body's circulatory system. "And when it reaches this pocket," he made a second 'x', "it will breach this instability." He circled an area that looked like rocks in an arrow-like formation.

The map suddenly came into focus. The contour lines on the map marked layers of rock under the ground. Topsy-turvy topography. The finer lines, like the streams and rivers and lakes above ground, identified similar waterways below. Whoever these people were, they seemed to know the lay of the land very well and were serious about stopping Richardson.

He re-wound the conversation. Had they really said, 'set a charge?' He abruptly sat back down. He couldn't stop himself from glancing at the tarp-covered bundles. Were they certain that this was the best option? How could anyone know all the effects of an underground explosion? Even though he had planned to do the same thing, he hadn't understood the extent of possible ramifications until he saw the underground map. He stared at it. His Handler had never allowed corollary damage to occur, except to Joe's own body, of course. Could these people possibly be as competent, as omnipotent? Joe felt sick. No human could do this right.

Joe looked around at the sound of a machine starting up. To the left of the entrance, a winch lowered a steel mesh cage to the floor. The man guiding it signalled to a worker overhead indicating it had touched down. Another worker glided in with a battery-operated forklift, gently inserted the forks into the pallet, and lifted the goods. He turned the machine around and drove in near silence to the sectioned-off area to deposit his load.

Joe's pack thumped to the floor next to his chair, but the person who had brought it over had already turned back to perform his next task. At the sight of his sleeping bag, Joe yawned. He had many questions and doubts whirling around in his head, none of which could be easily answered. He yawned

262

again. One thing was certain: if he was to begin to understand any of the answers, he needed a nap. In a few moments, he was stretched out on the hard floor with the others.

The aroma of brewed coffee made an excellent alarm clock. Joe assumed it must be morning. He used the facilities and snagged a quick breakfast at the kitchen. Steaming coffee cup in hand, he looked around for Chevy.

This took all of three minutes. The cave was an open space with no stalagmites or stalactites, nor were there any other type of rocky outcroppings to impede his view. The only line-of-sight obstacles were man-made, and these were mostly cabinets. The population of the cave had tripled overnight, everyone busy. The tension was thick in the air; something was about to happen.

Chevy huddled over a bundle of wires, soldering. Joe walked over to him. "What's going on?"

Chevy did not look up from his work. "Richardson moved his blasting schedule forward. That parapsychologist, Smythe, convinced him that the rock was alive, and Richardson decided he must have it all. Every last shard."

"Is that detonator ready yet?" Chevy asked the technician across from him.

"Any minute."

"Good. Set it for," Chevy looked at his watch, "fourteen hundred hours."

Joe glanced at his own watch. That was six hours away. "How can I help?"

Chevy pointed to a group at the edge of neat rolls of wire. He went over to see what he could do.

"The thing is," a young woman was saying, "he's in a rush and that is how we win."

"What do you mean?" Joe asked.

She looked up at the unfamiliar voice. "Oh. You're the guy who came in with Cheveya."

"If you mean Chevy, yes, that's right."

"Same thing. Richardson is not listening to his people, more luck to us. And the stupidest thing is, he hasn't looked beyond the immediate area. And by that, I mean several hundred square miles. If he had, he would know what we know, what we have known for decades," she smirked. "The water we're going to re-direct to cover and protect the ceiling of the aquifer is bad. Really bad."

Little Ben had said the same thing. "But how, exactly, is it bad?" The woman did not answer at first. Joe hoped that it wasn't because it was such a lame question.

"You can work and listen at the same time," she finally said. "Here. Strip the ends and connect two rolls together. Be sure to use a lot of electrical tape; we don't want any moisture to get in."

Joe selected tools and tape from a nearly supply shelf and began to work. Finally, a use for all the pieces of equipment that His Eminence had made him acquire and learn how to use.

"A few generations ago," the woman said, "there were many active mines throughout the area. Coal, gold, silver. The usual. But there was also uranium. Back then, the war effort was heating up and the military didn't care much about safety protocols, especially when their workers were mostly local natives."

She worked silently for a few minutes.

264

"The first sicknesses did not cause alarm even though our healers could not help. But then the sicknesses became much more frequent and the symptoms spread from the lungs to the kidneys and, later, to the bones. It was a painful, slow way to die." Her great-grandfather had been one of the first victims. The story-tellers kept the vision alive of his end—crippled, every breathe a gurgling struggle—so that the people would never forget what had been done and never let it happen again. She rubbed her eyes with her forearm.

"We know this land and this water. We know what it can do."

"It is time." Chevy did not have to raise his voice to be heard.

Quickly and quietly, every person stopped what they were doing and gathered closer to the makeshift blackboard. A map, similar to the one Joe had already seen, was taped to it. Twisty lines made with different coloured markers had been added to it. Other symbols were interspersed here and there but Joe did not know their significance and there was no convenient legend for reference.

"So that we do not overwhelm the thin layer of stone protecting the aquifer, we will implement our plan when Richardson's construction equipment is shut down to minimise as much vibration as possible. We will set off low energy charges at these three locations," he pointed to bright red dots, "allowing the flow to disperse evenly and quickly. But to bring enough water to the target area, we must first re-direct water from these other sources." This time he pointed to an array of green dots in a rough arc and located some distance from the red dots.

Chevy continued with a more technical discussion of timing, return routes, and emergency contingencies.

Joe knew only one thing for certain: he would be the sacrifice, the kamikaze, the crazy person to set and blow the red ones. That was what he was here to do. His life had been one long training session for doing an insane thing like this. The number of ways that this whole scheme could go wrong was mind-boggling. The what-ifs were innumerable. No one could possibly know all the variables with certainty. He was the only one who had put his life at risk dozens of times. He was the only one who could get it done. He was the only who had had a Dip-Shit, Crazy-Ass, Bastard, The Nuisance, Handler. If he died, well... there was that.

There wasn't time to explain all this to Chevy. He raised his hand.

Chevy stared at him. The cave seemed to contract upon itself until only the two of them existed.

"Joe and I," Chevy whispered, "will look after these." His large hand covered the red dots. "You know what to do," his gaze took in the others. "Let's get this done."

That was it. None of the psych-up, yelling, stamping, clapping, and hugging you see in the movies. This was on another level altogether. This was total commitment. This was intelligence and planning. This was redressing a wrong. This was honour regained.

Chapter 21

The bony hands on my head were annoying. Yavapai had claimed she could help smooth communications with She-rock so that they no longer bludgeoned me with their power.

"You must concentrate on her," Yavapai said.

If she only understood how it felt, she would not ask this of me. Or maybe she would. The feeling of urgency was becoming oppressive, demanding. I closed my eyes and let myself empty of everything but the thought of She-rock.

She-rock's pain was subdued, like it had been wrapped in cotton balls. This must be Yavapai's doing. I'd better not waste a moment.

***

They were very close to her core. She-rock whimpered, losing hope with every blow that struck her, with every moment that passed. There was a tiny flicker in the stygian blackness of her subterranean world, but She-rock did not have the will or strength to investigate.

***

I almost preferred the excruciating physical pain to this well of dark depression. Robyn, resting in a nearby tent, started to weep, raw and sensitised as she was by Richardson's torture.

Yavapai gave me a cup of tea; it warmed my chilled hands. I began to recite my experience to her and stopped. *'A tiny flicker'? What could that be?* Excited now, I stood a bit too quickly and steadied myself against Yavapai's shoulder.

"She-rock thought, 'a tiny flicker'!" Excited, I

scooped Arabella up and danced around with her. She giggled. Still carrying her, I exited the tent to tell the others. We must discuss what it could mean.

I put Arabella down and watched the smile fade from her face. "Oh, sweetie. Don't be sad," I crouched and smoothed her hair back. "That was just the first of many dances." Her smile returned, and she reached for Yavapai's hand, helping the old woman to a seat around the campfire.

The image of the little girl and the old woman brought a sudden spurt of tears to my eyes. This is what they meant by familial love. It didn't matter one whit if it was your real family or not, or even if it was for just a moment. Enlightenment swept through me.

The others gathered. One of the men, Istaqa, said, "It has begun."

I held my tongue for thirty long seconds, knowing that sooner or later he would elaborate. I cursed the virtue of patience that so eluded me. Breathing deeply, I stopped twitching.

"They have begun to bring the bad water to thwart the work."

A little cryptic and I needed to understand. "What do you mean, exactly, by 'bad water?' What makes the water bad?"

The silence smothered me. I would not like the answer.

His deep-set eyes met mine. "'Bad water' is a phrase we use to be vague to those who do not know, a phrase instead of using 'uranium-poisoned water.'"

My eyes opened wide. So much made sense. "The other group, with Chevy and Joe, is going to dynamite bits of underground rock in order to guide the... bad water to where Richardson is digging?"

He nodded.

"And this will make him leave."

He nodded again.

"Why? Couldn't he just pump it out and carry on?"

He shook his head.

I waited.

"There will be much water. It will continue to flow until the great wound he has made in Earth is filled."

The group around the campfire nodded in satisfaction. Dubious that Richardson would give up, but willing to follow their lead, I smiled.

"There is much danger in what they do," Yavapai said, spoiling my fragile optimism. "We must hold them in our hearts and minds to give them strength."

She folded her hands on her lap and worked the beads I had seen that first night. The others emulated her, and the camp grew still and silent.

I wondered where the boys and Bob were and moved as quietly as I could to the edge of the campsite.

The sun shone in the bright-white way it had in the desert. No shadows offered a cool spot. High noon. Bad things have been known to happen at high noon. I shoved that thought aside and thought about Joe instead. He was a resourceful man and had incredible experience to draw on. I didn't know much about Chevy, but he had the aura of a man capable of anything. I felt a little tingly just thinking about him. Sheesh. Here were two men undoubtedly about to risk their lives to stop a madman and here I was having a little fantasy about one of them. And that one wasn't even Joe. How interesting. I thought about the fledgling connection between him and Robyn. I thought about it some more. Nope, not even a twinge of jealousy. It felt more like hope that they would emerge from this incredibly dangerous exploit and find each other again.

Bob's silhouette appeared on top of an outcropping, his floppy right ear clearly identifying him. Two little-boy heads popped up. They carried something between them that I was pretty certain I did not want to see but waved at them anyway. If I could dance with Arabella, I could express my amazement at their find even if it was the desiccated carcass of some poor reptile.

Chapter 22

Godfrey Smythe listened through his apparatus. It remained primitive but had sufficed to convince Richardson that something was alive way down here. He moved his sensors further to the left, careful not to touch the rock with his bare hands. He did not like its texture and the way he thought he felt pain emanating from it. How could you feel pain from a rock? It was unscientific.

The footfall of his employer caused him to break into a sweat even in this chilly vault of rock.

"Well?" Richardson demanded. "Any more activity??"

Smythe swallowed. He desperately wanted to deliver a less bleak answer, but he had learned that Richardson could tell when he skirted the truth. "No. Only more of the same moaning-like sound." He extracted his less than pristine handkerchief from his jacket pocket and wiped his brow. Richardson pursed his lips in disgust and Smythe shoved the material out of sight.

They stood there: Richardson scowling and Smythe sweating some more. Smythe knew what was coming.

Richardson hefted the pick-axe leaning against the wall and hammered the sharp end into the basalt surface. A small piece was dislodged, and it dropped to his feet.

Smythe cringed at the sudden increase in the volume of the moan.

"There. That got its attention." Richardson rubbed invisible dirt from his hands, turned, and disappeared beyond the flood lamp that lit Smythe's work.

It was then that Smythe registered a remote tremble through his sensors. Puzzled, he adjusted them toward the direction from which this new reading had come. There was another tremble, and a third following closely afterwards.

"What is it?" Richardson hissed, standing much too close to Smythe.

Smythe could not think of how to phrase such a thing so that Richardson would not strike him. He hated it when Richardson struck him, not only because it hurt, but because you never knew where the strike would land—you had to brace your entire body. Sometimes, Richardson kept him in this state of painful tension for minutes at a time.

"Give it to me." Richardson tore the headset set from Smythe and, after wiping it thoroughly, placed it on his own head, his eyes never leaving the parapsychologist.

Richardson waited, and he was not a patient man. Suddenly, he must have heard something. Smythe could tell from the way his body jerked ever so slightly. Quick as the viper that he was, Richardson gripped the front of Smythe's jacket close to his neck.

This is it, Smythe thought, *the psychopath is finally going to kill me*. It was a relief; he was debilitated from knowing it would happen, but not when.

Richardson shook him a second time and tore off the headset. "What is this? And you'd better be right."

Smythe moistened his lips. Richardson slapped

him, open-handed, across the face. The sting brought involuntary tears to Smythe's eyes. Richardson slapped him again.

"They're... they're tremors, likely caused by explosives," he blurted and hunched his head into his shoulders.

Of course, Richardson didn't slap his face this time; he kicked him in the knee. Smythe dropped to the stone floor, falling on his side. Like everyone's on the work site, Richardson's boots were steel-toed. Smythe couldn't breathe through the pain; black dots swam before his eyes and he sincerely hoped he would pass out.

Richardson was yelling something into his walkie-talkie. He was not happy, and this made Smythe feel somewhat better.

He lay there, unable to move and unable to lose consciousness. His side and especially his shoulder and hip were losing all feeling. He dared not move his injured leg at all. The first plop of water on his hot face did not even startle him.

Chapter 23

Joe flicked his head-lamp on for a few seconds. The slime was not a putrid green as he had imagined. Worse, it was black as tar. Run-off from a mining project? Was it toxic? Joe had thought it couldn't get much worse after the near-asphyxiation at that last junction. He had had to exhale all his breath to make it through, not knowing for certain when and if he would be able to breathe in again. It had been the longest forty-two seconds in his life. To think: some people actually went spelunking for fun.

He dug his toes into the gunk and pushed himself along inch by inch, sliding his body atop the rock and goo in total darkness. Chevy had warned him a dozen times to turn his head lamp off whenever it was of no use. A lamp with dead batteries was to be avoided at all costs, Chevy had said. No argument on that one.

The route he was to take was imprinted clearly on his mind and this stretch was relatively straight. He pushed himself another few yards, his movements arduous and repetitive.

What would Bob do? Joe smiled. That coyote was a true friend. It comforted Joe to know that he was out there in the desert doing something amazing, like protecting the kids and making them giggle with laughter and shriek at the same time. Bob would be where he had to be, of that Joe was certain.

Robyn was surely freed by now and in the hands of healers. He only hoped that he would have the chance to be nearby to support her as she struggled with the damage Richardson had done to her mind. There was something about her that, well… there was something about her.

Flotsy was someone different altogether—someone he had never expected to meet. Someone who understood what it was to be manipulated by something out of your control. Someone who could sympathise with his apparent immortality just as he could sympathise with her prescience. He was slightly in awe that she could suffer such abuse and still always have the hint of a laugh close to the surface. She was his first true friend.

He had an epiphany. For the first time in his life, he had a friend and a woman he cared about. And he had Bob. On second thought, it could be that Bob had him.

The cold of the rock-and-slime combination penetrated through the layers of protection he wore. How long had he been still, daydreaming? If he had any energy to spare, he would give his head a good whack for allowing himself to be distracted. He began to shove himself along again as fast as he could. Even on the verge of hypothermia, he broke into a sweat.

He had to be getting close to the location where he was to set the charge. He groped ahead, feeling for the ledge that would indicate the next step in his route. Nothing. There was no help for it: he turned on his head lamp again. Solid rock walls caged him in. He had nowhere to go but back the way he had come, and there wasn't enough room to turn around.

***

Chevy set the timer for the first charge,

calibrating it to the second. He wondered about Joe—a rookie—thrown into a dangerous world to do an even more dangerous task. But the elders had insisted that Joe be the one to set the final charge. Chevy had had little choice. The entire mission would rest on the shoulders of a novice. He shook his head and turned toward the gaping hole leading to his second target.

***

No reason to panic; every reason to move with alacrity.

The fleeting thought that going backwards through a path he had already made would be easier had been naïve. His boots were getting heavier as muck accumulated on them. The borrowed gear he wore fit reasonably well and protected him, but he could feel the knee pads move a little. Abrasions and blisters were in his near future.

With his arms spread away from his body, he kept in continual contact with the sides of the tunnel. He could not risk missing the cue a second time.

He stopped. He thought he had heard something. He kept perfectly still. There it was again, like an echo, reverberating everywhere. He closed his eyes, not that it made much difference considering that there was zero light, but it helped him focus. A high-pitched squeal seared the very edge of his senses. *Bats? This deep in a cave system?* Whatever it was—and he didn't care if he was hallucinating—he'd be happy for something, anything to point him in the right direction.

It was at that moment that his right leg dropped into nothingness, dangling over an abyss like a tiny

276

morsel of flesh teasing whatever lay in wait.

If ever there was a time to use his head-lamp, it was now.

The beam of light made a valiant effort to illuminate the massive darkness. Joe forced himself to look down. There was indeed a ledge protruding from the wall, which continued in the direction he hoped it would. What he had not expected was the chasm. The map had indeed indicated a drop on the other side of the ledge, and Joe had not been too concerned about it. After all, this was the final leg of the journey and the ledge, he had been told, was wide enough for him to navigate. He would ask more questions next time; he would make sure that he knew all the small and, as in this case, large details.

He checked his watch; there were four minutes until the first charge blew.

Time stood still. He slowed his breath, envisioning the ease with which he would reach his designated target. He had survived much worse under The Nuisance and he would survive this.

He shifted his body so that he would be facing the cave wall and pushed himself into the cavern until both legs hung down. With his hands gripping the sides of the opening, he lowered his torso. His hands and arms, already beyond abuse, howled in pain at this new insult. As soon as his body could bend enough, he eased his hands from the sides to the bottom edge of the opening. Even when his feet felt secure on the ledge, it took Joe a few seconds to unclench his fingers and lower his arms.

He stood there, not looking anywhere but at his two mud-caked feet. With one hand on the wall of the cavern, he ever so slowly knelt, and, leaning forward, placed his hands on the ledge. Remaining on hands and knees, he traversed the final distance.

His gloves were pasted on by multiple layers of sludge. On reflex, he raised his hand to his mouth and was about to close his teeth on a fingertip, which was the usual way he helped himself take off a glove. He gaped at the filthy material and gagged; he used the grip between his arm and ribs instead. His bared hands were cold and trembled; he vigorously rubbed them together to restore some semblance of circulation.

The charge and its various attachments were nestled in a side-pack. He carefully extracted them and connected them in the order in which they were to be assembled. Taking a moment to breathe, he gazed at where he was. Spectacular was an understatement even in the paltry light.

He stared at his watch, counting down the seconds like a lunar launch. Pressing the button to start the timer was a disappointment after all the build-up. On the other hand, he was very grateful that he had a full twelve minutes to get clear of the area.

The return route was convoluted but had the advantage of moving in the opposite direction of not only his blast, but of all the blasts. He felt sudden pressure in his ears. It was the first charge, right on schedule. Joe picked up his pace.

***

Chevy did not often pray but did so today. Waiting was always the worst part. His continuous pacing had driven the others to the far end of the base. They, at least, had work to occupy them.

278

Constant monitoring of the tremors and their effects was critical. If catastrophe struck, they would know and sound the alarm, giving everyone a few critical minutes of warning to evacuate.

He didn't know Joe very well but admired his tenacity and loyalty—excellent traits in anyone. It was more the fact that he, Chevy, could not plant all three charges himself. There just wasn't enough time to travel the distances no matter how well he knew the cave systems. It irked him. Pride played a part, he knew this much about himself, but he was by far the most qualified. It had never been easy for him to delegate jobs to others. *What if they didn't do it right?* It was easier to do it himself than to fix what their ineptitude left in its wake.

The first charge should go off—he didn't have to look at his watch—now.

Chapter 24

Something had happened to his perfect Project that could not have happened. He would see for himself and entered the giant maw of the cavern.

At first, he ignored the frantic voices directed at him, but soon tired of them, and his sleek, matte-black revolver silenced the annoyance. He spared a moment to admire the craftsmanship of his weapon.

The Project cavern was empty, which also could not happen. Security guards were nowhere to be seen. *How could this be?* He may have eaten something which disagreed with his constitution and had put him off his usual control over everything. His chef would pay a heavy price for this.

He walked through his jewel of a Project, the culmination of years of planning—his ultimate vision being made into reality. And there it was: his beautiful machine. It made his eyes water and, luckily for them, no one was nearby to witness this. No one would ever know how his Father had humiliated him that childhood Christmas. And he, Maximillian Wendall Richardson, had had the brilliance to reshape that infantile yearning into an empire in which he could have anything he wanted. No, in which he could *take* anything he wanted.

He climbed into the control centre of the enormous bucket loader and pressed the ignition. The rumble of the engine soothed him, obliterating any remnant of unease he may have had about the inactivity that surrounded him. He, Maximillian Wendall Richardson, would take the machine down the spiral to check on progress. The action on the gear lever was as smooth as silk.

Before the machine was fully engaged, his ancient nightmare engulfed him.

...The wrapping paper could not disguise what was inside. Max came very close to wetting himself in his excitement. He glanced sideways at his Father, but he hadn't noticed. Weak with relief, Max waited for permission to open his very first gift. His father gave him a shove towards it.

Nervous, he took a small step. His Father had been known to change his mind and beat him for obeying what he had just been commanded to do. It was very confusing. His Father nodded again, this time impatiently.

Max ran to the box and ripped off the wrapping. The picture on the outside was fantastic and he was trembling with excitement. He missed his Father's snicker.

He pried the lid open and eagerly looked inside. He didn't understand what he was seeing.

His Father snickered again. "What did you expect? Something a real boy would want? A cry-baby like you?" He clouted Max on the back of the head and again, as the power of his Father's fist turned him around, on his jaw. Disgusted, his Father kicked him in the groin and stomped out of the room.

Max rubbed his stinging face with one hand and cradled his genitals with the other. He could not take his eyes off the mangled doll. One of its eyes hung from the socket. Its hair had been torn out leaving only a few clumps. There was dirt smeared all over her and she stood in yet more dirt.

281

It smelled bad, like the old outhouse on the hot days when his Father would lock him in there.

He heard his Father open a bottle. Max quietly left the house to hide in the woods. If he was lucky, his Father would be too tired later to look for him...

Richardson sneered. If only his father could see him now. On the other hand, if he saw his father, he would kill him again. He would keep killing him as many times as it took for him to stay dead.

282

Chapter 25

A wave of relief washed over me. *Now what?*

I looked around the campsite. Nothing was amiss. The wave came again, this time exponentially stronger. I sat down.

Yavapai was at my side in seconds and lifted my chin to better see my face. She studied me for a long minute. Her smile widening until it was beatific.

I didn't know what had happened, only that She-rock felt better. I felt light as air. I felt unafraid that a vision would lambaste me. Right now, right at this moment, I felt safe; I wanted to curl up and blissfully sleep, certain that there would be no vision to disturb my rest.

The others had gathered, eager for any details I might be able to provide.

Sighing, I brought myself back to the reality around me and pondered how we could learn about what had happened. My wave of relief was sadly devoid of particulars. The only way to find out was for me to go there, to the cave where Chevy and Joe were. I said as much to the group. It would be a long walk. Fortunately, I didn't have much to carry.

A bright yellow school bus chugged its way over the landscape. *What the...?* The kids raced towards it, Bob in the lead.

Yavapai took my hand. "We all go."

The camp was disassembled with such speed and precision that it resembled a well-rehearsed dance. It likely was. The best thing I could do was stay out of the way. Tents were cleared and flattened, cooking equipment placed into canvas bags, and everything piled into the back of the bus. Lastly, the area was swept with soft rakes. The campsite had vanished as if it had never been.

Before boarding the bus, we gathered in a circle and Yavapai offered a brief prayer of thanks to Earth for keeping us safe upon Her.

I shuddered at the thought of traveling desert back-roads in a school bus. Even with Harvey's extra-strength suspension, it had rattled my molars. I took a deep breath and stepped into the mayhem of thirty-eight men, women, and children, an assortment of dogs and hunting birds, and one coyote settling themselves and their baggage for the trip, which, thankfully, should only be about three hours.

Bob had secured a seat at the front of the bus, the three kids distributed nearby, and they had saved a place for me. Gotta love that.

Yavapai was a few rows behind us with Robyn, who was dressed like a queen in regalia the tribe had given her. She had colour in her cheeks and even smiled at Bob who had, of course, raced back, given her a quick lick, and returned to the front—the best seat in the house.

With a minimal grinding of gears and excited whooping from the youngsters, the driver—distinguished by his lime-green, neon-bright headband—eased the loaded bus forward.

Chapter 26

The machine was a marvel; it responded to the slightest touch. He pressed the pedal. *Just a little faster*, he thought to himself.

The spiral road descending into Earth was itself a marvel. He wasn't the least surprised since it reflected his vast imagination and ingenuity. It was his Project and he had to, once again, sort out the mess that his oh-so-educated-and-experienced staff failed to prevent. He visualised the heads that would roll, after they had been punished a great deal.

That girl, what was her name? No matter. She had told him everything. At any rate, she had been getting boring and he would soon toss her away like a grimy rag, unpleasant to the touch.

A drop of liquid splashed onto the windscreen. He pressed buttons and pushed levers up and down until he found the wiper control. There was only one wiper, but it was a beauty. Black and long, extending from top to bottom, cleaning the window in one sweep of its elegant self.

He felt a sudden and powerful wave of relief. Strange. He, Maximilian Wendall Richardson, had no need of relief. Everything and everyone in his life did exactly what he wanted it and them to do. He postulated that this odd sensation could be caused by a combination of gases from the explosives and vehicle emissions. He opened the side window of the cab but could smell nothing unusual. He did, however, feel dampness in the air.

He was approaching the site where, in a few days, he, himself, would detonate the barrage of explosives, releasing the vast aquifer and guiding its contents to his secret underground reservoirs. He would have a high-profile camera crew there so that the entire world could witness his power and genius. Maximillian Wendall Richardson would be honoured and respected, deserving of all accolades—as if he needed their petty praise.

Another few drops of liquid splashed on the windshield. This was a dry area, chosen for that property because it was easier to work in and, more importantly, had good access to the aquifer.

The corkscrew of road was well-lit by the powerful headlights on the loader. Ahead, a sheen of water lapped against the rock wall. Perhaps that combination of gases also caused hallucinations. He drove further, as though nothing was amiss; useless to waste his attention on something that could not be possible.

He still had the window open and could hear the murmur of water over the sound of his engine. *Audio hallucinations as well?* This perhaps deserved closer inspection.

As he throttled down to bring the machine to a stop, a white globe bobbed to the surface a dozen feet ahead. He released the brake and eased forward to get a closer look at what likely wasn't even there.

The backwash of water caused by the loader's movement made the globe float closer. Richardson clenched his teeth in rage; his blood rose to a boil. It was that repellant Smythe.

The loathsome creature had whined on about 'voices' in the rock and had excavated samples. He had said there were tremors. It was now obvious to Richardson that the parapsychologist had been the cause of the tremors so that he could force an evacuation of the Project staff and carry out his own nefarious plans undisturbed.

He inched the loader forward and lowered the bucket. The bucket splashed into the water, spinning Smythe in slow circles until he snagged on a rocky outcrop near the wall of the cavern. Perfect.

Richardson revved the engine. Blue smoke poured out of the exhaust. He released the brake and slammed the gear lever forward. The loader rumbled inexorably towards Smythe, his pallid face and blind eyes delightfully clear in the bright beams of the headlights.

The impact against the wall threw Richardson into the windscreen; a gash in his forehead bled copiously. He wiped at it, licked his hand. He had never been so happy.

He manipulated the bucket to scoop Smythe into it, then lowered it so he could gloat over his victory. He clambered from the cab and waded through the waist-deep water to view his catch of the day, his mouth widening in a smile. Smythe would have recoiled if he could have.

It wasn't as gruesome as he had wished but it would do. He shoved Smythe's head underwater for the simple pleasure of doing it. The loader's engine would soon be inundated, and, with regret, Richardson pushed Smythe's head under one last time.

The rumble of the loader could not mask the screech of rock sliding over rock. Richardson peered into the darkness; he could see nothing but more darkness.

The wall of water hit him in the back like a

sledgehammer and pinned him to the side of the bucket. He looked over the edge at Smythe's body bobbing about like a drowned rat. The bucket tilted. Richardson gripped it to keep his head above water and so was in the perfect position to see the jagged, gaping hole through which his beloved bucket loader majestically fell. He would never let go. It belonged to him.

Chapter 27

The Batcave looked the same as when he had left it, except for the champagne and the music and the dancing.

Exhausted and exhilarated, he sat where he stood. Someone handed him a bottle of water and a sandwich. He took a long swig, thirstier than he could ever remember.

Chevy sauntered over and clapped him on the back, making him spit out his bite of bread.

"Sorry." He dropped into a squat and examined Joe's face. "Glad you made it." He rose and made to clap him again and grinned instead. "Oh. Your friends should be here in about an hour. You might want to consider a wash."

Breathing what seemed like the first time in days, Joe smiled.

Chapter 28

The ultimate thrill of flying on his beautiful machine, the world at his command and nothing to stop him, had been the best moment of his life. Maximillian Wendall Richardson relished the memory and jealously guarded it. No one else would *ever* experience what he had.

His people would soon find him. How could they proceed without his steady hand at the helm? He tried to chuckle. It sounded more like a wet gurgle. That would never do. He tried to clear his throat but found he could not. Then he remembered, somewhat mollified, that he didn't have to say a word to silence his people. They would never reveal his secret because they would be dead. He tried to chuckle again.

He opened his eyes; the darkness remained. Perhaps he had not opened his eyes at all. He blinked again and again. No change. Was he hallucinating again? If so, it was boring. He tried to move something else, but no part of his body obeyed him except for his eyes—which he wasn't entirely sure about—and his ears, judging by the constant and erratic drip that annoyed him.

His people would arrive any minute.

Chapter 29

The kids had a great time in the bus until one of them vomited, which, in turn, caused a number of people to feel unwell. They stopped for a time while the messes were cleaned up and various potions administered. The rest of the trip went by in a daze, Arabella fast asleep in my lap.

The entrance to the secret hideaway was disappointing; I had hoped for something straight out of a Bond film. This was just a short trudge down a rutted road too steep for the bus and a squeeze between some rocks.

A steel cage, also known as the elevator, descended to the floor of the hideaway. It was a nice dramatic touch but could not compare with Joe and Chevy standing there, alive, looking up at us as we descended. Bob leapt out as soon as the barricade was opened. He raced to Joe and ran in circles around him. The kids bulleted towards the smell of food and, Bob, with his tongue lolling out, happily followed them. Robyn stepped gingerly onto the cave floor, swaying. Joe was there in a flash to steady her. When he was sure Robyn was stable, he turned to me, swooped me in his arms, and twirled us in a joyous circle.

"We did it!" He grinned.

Breathless, I said nothing for a moment. "I just couldn't believe it until I saw you," I began, "relatively unscathed." His hands and forehead were bandaged, and there were likely other wounds hidden beneath his clothes.

"Just a few scratches. But what about you?"

His question was directed at me, but his eyes swiveled to Robyn. I raised my eyebrows and gestured for him to go to her. "We'll talk about me later."

Chevy had held back, uncertain of his welcome. I walked over to him, stood on tiptoe, and kissed him on the cheek. "Thanks," I said into his ear.

He took my hand kissed it. Wow. A man of few words but excellent actions.

The party continued for many hours, with new people arriving all the time to add their congratulations. At one point, I gathered Arabella, Arthur, and Ben—he had decided he was not 'little' anymore—and made them a cozy nest; they tossed and turned for about three seconds. They looked so peaceful and the nest so welcoming that I joined them. Bob trotted over with a blanket he had been given, I hope, secured in his jaws. He dropped it strategically to keep an eye on the ongoing activity, and did his usual 'ruffle the blanket, circle three times, and lay down' routine.

The smell of coffee has a way of seeping into the most restful of sleeps. I breathed deeply and opened my eyes a sliver. A steaming cup had been placed beside my bedroll. I looked around, but no one was nearby; I raised the cup in thanks towards a group of people gathered at the far end of the cavern. I sipped, amazed at how good I felt.

The kids remained fast asleep and Bob briefly opened one eye. I eased myself out from under the covers and went in search of the washroom facilities. In addition to several composting toilets, there was also a separate washing-up area and, refreshed, I stepped back into the main cavern.

People were milling everywhere and what first appeared to be chaos was, in fact, a reasonably well-ordered rout. "What's going on?" I hadn't meant to say it out loud.

A young girl turned to me. "We're going home," she said and grinned.

"Where's home?" I asked.

She thought for a minute. "Outside." She grinned again and scampered to the line-up for the elevator.

I watched her go and thought that 'outside' was a terrific place to live. What had my home been in the past few years but a means to move from one 'outside' to another. It certainly was easier if I stayed in warmer climes but, as a girl who had grown up in Canadian winters, the cold and snow didn't bother me all that much, at least it didn't used to.

The events of the last few weeks had been all-consuming and thinking about afterwards hadn't even occurred to me until now. It was not as though I thought we would all die—although there were way too many tense moments—but rather that things were changing so fast I couldn't assimilate them all.

I certainly hadn't thought about Harvey lately and I wondered how many of the people around me had a traveling home. Likely all of them, given the portability of the camp I had just experienced. It was comforting to know that a nomadic life was not only more prevalent than I had thought, but that it also could be rewarding in many ways, ways I hadn't thought possible, as in, you could make friends. They valued me, and this warmed me in places I hadn't been warm in a long time.

I forced my thoughts back to practical matters. According to Chevy, Harvey had been towed from the campground and torn apart by Richardson's people. I was angry at first but knew it could never be my home again after my things had been pawed through. I also knew it wouldn't take me long to win the money for a new motorhome and could visit my new friends, which was when it struck me that I now had more friends than I could count on one hand. I cried a little. Sheesh.

I would also like, for once, to grow a garden through to its maturity, edible and lush and vibrant with colour. Maybe if I thought about it hard enough, I could travel and have a pied-à-terre. Hard thinking was something that would have to wait for a much quieter time and place.

I heard my name. How was it that you could hear your own name through such hubbub? We must get hard-wired to its vibrations or something. I looked around and the waving arms guided me to a cluster of work tables arranged into a breakfast nook. The gang was all there: Joe, Chevy, Robyn, Arabella, Ben, Arthur, and Yavapai. I looked for and spotted Bob under the table. It seems they were waiting for me to arrive since no one was touching the food piled high in platters and gently steaming. I glanced at Arabella who nodded at me. I sat. We all held hands while the little girl said her junkyard grace.

The boys carefully watched how Arabella served herself a little of everything before she began to eat. We all did our very best to emulate her, a few of us with small smiles on our faces. The boys had

294

second and third helpings before asking permission to leave the table. I tried not to laugh but I think a chuckle may have escaped, which I promptly disguised as a cough. Yavapai patted the girl's hand before she ran off to join them.

The cavern was much quieter; most of the families had left. The scientist types would stay for quite some time to monitor after-effects, and, as the water and assorted debris stabilised, plan careful forays into the system of tunnels and caverns to take samples and measurements not only of contaminants in the water but also of new rock faces that had been exposed.

"She-rock," I muttered under my breath. She was the reason for this whole escapade. She was the reason we had to stop Richardson. She was the reason why Robyn was tortured, and why I had suffered so much. She was the reason we were all nearly killed, even the kids. That last was unforgiveable.

Joe took my hands and unclenched them. In a soft voice, he said. "We saved thousands of lives."

"We prevented a major quake," Chevy added.

"We stopped a monster," Robyn whispered.

"We did the right thing." Yavapai smiled wider and wider, until her eyes were enfolded by wrinkles.

Wouldn't you know she would have the words that would jolt everything into perspective. That would ease our consciences. That would validate all the choices we made. That would convince us it had all been worthwhile. That would do so much—except let us go back to who we were.

We all needed time to heal, each in our own way.

The kids were easy. To them, life had always been one hair-raising adventure after another. Yavapai encouraged them to stay with her for a time, to which they happily agreed.

"The food," Ben solemnly said, "is very, very good."

Yavapai confided to me later that teaching them reading and writing was at the top of her list.

"You know they will do whatever Arabella wants to do."

Yavapai smiled. "And she will guide them well, although there will come a time when they are independent young men with minds of their own."

I hugged her. "That will be a good day."

Robyn was fragile and Joe was protective. This, too, was a no-brainer.

"We'll stay around here for a while to be near the healers," he squeezed Robyn's hand, "after that, who knows?" They smiled at each other.

Love was a beautiful thing. No sense in asking them what they would actually do during this 'while.'

Bob's head popped up in between them. Robyn giggled. That Bob—— better than any psychoanalyst.

Earlier, Chevy had said a quick goodbye to each of us and left with one of the small groups. Their mission was to seek out any of Richardson's 'leftovers.'

"Good idea," I'd said. "There's no telling what a crazy man like that could have put into motion."

"Exactly," he replied, and squeezed my shoulder.

So much for the power of my sexual allure. I

sighed. He had never led me to believe there was anything between us. It was just wishful thinking on my part.

As for me? I needed time to think.

Chapter 30

I stayed around the area for a few weeks. I needed money and there were many casinos within easy driving distance. I was, however, in a bit of a conundrum: I needed money to buy a vehicle but needed a vehicle to obtain the money.

The desert bus driver's name was Topojeejo. Before I could ask, he told me that his parents were big Ed Sullivan fans, and had changed the spelling of the name so that their son would not be confused with the big-eared mouse. He said, with a shrug, that they laughed raucously every single time they told that story.

Topo, as he preferred to be called, had a small and well-maintained fleet of vehicles he loaned out—if you had the right referrals, which I did. I told him why I needed a car. He mulled things over for a minute.

"You know," he said, "I could probably retro-fit proper suspension onto an RV. Not much different than a bus really." He went around to the back of his shop and put a twenty-dollar bill in my hand.

"What's this for?"

"You as good as they say, the winnings from this is all the payment I'll need for the loan and the upgrade."

He dropped a set of car keys on top of the twenty and wandered back into the garage. "Oh," he said over his shoulder, "fill 'er up before you bring 'er back." He chuckled. "Just like a proper rental-car place." He chuckled some more.

My casino luck was in fine working order and, more quickly than I had dared hope, my brand-new RV, with all the improvements Topo could add, cruised down the highway. It was good to be on the road again, alone and fancy-free. The breeze caressed my cheek. The copper sunset turned the landscape molten. The quietude soothed me. She-rock had shattered me what seemed like a gazillion times. In the painful process, she had given me insight into the depth of my strength and endurance. Yavapai, may the gods look kindly on her every single day, had taught me ways to mitigate the worst symptoms that manifested with my visions and gave me several recipes for soothing teas.

The visions still came to me suddenly and with power, and, although there was nothing I could do about what happened in them, I could control how I reacted. They no longer tore me apart with anguish and desperation, and the futile need to do something, anything. And, who knew? There may come another day when a vision of mine, or a visitation from someone like She-rock, would be useful. Until that theoretical time, I would continue to practice self-control during visions and try to analyse them at a deeper level. Maybe I could finally learn to predict them in some measurable way instead of always being taken off guard. Maybe there was more of a pattern to them than I could previously see, now that I could maintain more distance from them. That would be very useful.

A bar of melody drifted from House. I had briefly toyed with 'Harvey2' as the name for my new motorhome, but it was more than a bit cumbersome. And, anyway, House was, in fact, where I lived. The bar of melody repeated itself. I'd previously learned that it could and would do that for a very long time.

We'd chosen 'Witchy Woman' as a joke; it had had to be something catchy for me to even consider the cell phone Joe insisted I have, and the native-sounding drum-beat reminded me of the wonderful people I had met in the desert, especially Yavapai. How could he know if I was okay? he'd asked. How could he know if I needed something? he'd asked. How could he know if I was in trouble? he'd asked. He browbeat me until I took the device and promised him a hundred times that I would check it occasionally and keep it charged. Bossy guy.

I ran to House, tripped over the kindling, and charged up the steps just as the music stopped. Carry it with you at all times, he'd said.

I pressed the blinking button and he picked up.

"Did you hurt yourself running for the phone?" he asked oh so sweetly. "Sorry, sorry, I didn't mean to say that! Please don't throw the phone!"

There was panic in his voice. I kind of liked that.

"And how's Robyn?" This always derailed him from a harangue about the proper feeding and care of an electronic device.

"She's terrific! Hasn't had a bad dream in over a month!"

"And the kids?"

"Great! They come around with Bob now and again, when the tribe is nearby. They read everything in sight. They're going to rule the world, those three."

"And you?"

300

"I love my life so much right now that I'm…"
He hesitated.

"You're what? Happy?"

"Of course I'm happy, that's what bothers me."
He took a deep breath. "What if it goes away? I'm
just a little afraid, is all."

Astonished that he would admit fear of any
kind, I knew he was serious.

"Afraid it'll go away?" I hazarded.

The line was silent for the usual Joe moment or
three.

"I know it's unreasonable of me," he said.

"This is not my area of expertise by any means
but I'm pretty sure that 'reason' has little to do with
this. Love is a gift, a real bona fide gift. Hold tight,
but don't strangle the poor girl." This from the love-
expert who had never been in love.

"Hey, where are you anyway?" Joe asked.
"This signal is strong."

Back to the cell phone. Sigh. "Way to change
the subject, Joe. As a matter of fact, I'm outside."

"Ha, ha."

"Was there anything that prompted this call?
Like, say, you missed me and desperately needed to
hear my voice?"

He paused again.

"I guess I just wanted to let you know that, yes,
we do miss you, and, yes, you would be welcome to
drop by anytime."

I smiled. "You know? You have a great way
with words, even if it takes you a year or so to put
them together."

"Nice. Okay, talk to you later."

"You bet." What choice did I have?

My plan was simple. I would retrace my journey so that I could close all those post office boxes, which never had any mail delivered to them anyway. And, I grudgingly admitted, now that I had a cell phone, I could reach the people who mattered in seconds. It was liberating, something I would never tell Joe.

House was lovely inside and out. Topo's modifications made the ride smooth and quiet. He had even rigged everything so that it required less maintenance, especially in the dusty desert. He laughed when I told him he was a genius.

"No, no, no," he began, and dug his hand into a pocket to pull out a thick wad of bills, "you are the genius." He laughed again and patted House on his way by. "Bring 'er by anytime."

Maybe it was time I changed the RV's name to a girl-name. Nah. House was exactly what she was, and her name still made me think of my French kin and their abuse of the poor letter *haitch*. Unfortunately, it was the only thing about my family that made me smile.

It could have been triggered by my thoughts earlier in the day or not, but the vision that night was of home, of Prince Edward Island. Since my father's death, I had seen nothing of the Island in a vision and it startled me into losing my newfound focus.

***

She lay in the same living room and in the same place as her first husband. Her silver hair made her waxen skin appear thin and surreal. She was dressed in a black so dark it was like looking into the vacuum of space. Her hands were crossed at her

302

waist and held her five-decade rosary. She never went anywhere without it.

***

I opened my eyes. Tears dripped down the sides of my face and into my ears. I knew that my mother was on her death-bed and that this vision would very soon be reality. I also knew that no one would want me to be there. My appearance at such a time would bring back the whispers and suspicions about how I had killed my father. And now, the rumour would be that I had also killed my mother and had come back to gloat.

Reasoning and proof and facts would never work. The prejudice and fear ran too deep. In fact, the juicier the story, the more they clung to it as truth. Was it simply because their own lives were so tedious that they had to fabricate outrageous stories about other people's lives in order to consider theirs more satisfying?

I used my laptop—Joe had also bought me a laptop; he really loved this tech stuff—to see if an Obituary had been published. Not yet. I could, if I wanted to, make it to the Island in less than a week. What I would do when I got there, I did not know, but I was drawn to do this. I'd sleep on it and see how I felt in the morning.

Fat chance of sleep with this gnawing in my belly. Once I'd rolled around enough in bed to make myself slightly dizzy, I got up, made a big pot of coffee, and headed east.

It never took long to close a post office box— they were always in demand and the staff rushed my request through before I had the chance to change my mind—and I continued to do so even in the headlong rush to reach my destination. I had to do something to make me stop driving for a few minutes. Worse, my obsession to arrive did not diminish as I got closer.

At the end of the third day of nearly continuous driving, it was time to stop for more than just to close a post office box or to put gas in the tank. The lines on the road were starting to weave together in braids. Not a good sign.

I pulled into the next campground that accommodated motorhomes and paid for a spot. It was lovely. The lake was mirror-smooth and the surrounding forest smelled like heaven. This was what I needed. I had spent so long in the desert, I had forgotten how beautiful trees and open water could be.

By some combination of sight and smell, no doubt exacerbated by my fatigue, the memory came crashing back. The campground was familiar. I placed a call.

Joe answered on the second ring.

"Guess where I am?"

"No."

"You're no fun." I had been hoping he would give it a shot. "Do you remember that nice campground where you dumped me after breaking me out of the loony bin?"

Silence. "Seriously?"

"Yup."

Silence. "But why are you so far away?"

My turn for silence. "I had a vision…"

"Just a minute," Joe interrupted me, "I need a computer."

I waited.

"Okay. Go."

Joe had decided he would write a descriptive record of my visions. I had told him I already did, but he thought it would add a second perspective. Every little bit helps, I guess. How do I start? The beginning is usually a good place. I described the vision to him, and then how I seemed to have no choice but to return to the Island. I still didn't know what I would do when I got there the day after tomorrow.

Silence.

"Joe?" He was taking a long time even for him.

"Olivia. Are you sure?"

"Yes, and don't call me that."

Silence. "I just booked a flight to Halifax. Can you meet me there? There's no connecting flight to Charlottetown on the same day I arrive." He paused. "I know! I'll rent a car and meet up with you there."

Did I want Joe with me? Would it help or hinder? Would he be too much of a distraction or a shoulder to cry on?

"I just don't know, Joe, if your being there would be the right thing to do. I'm a little freaked by this and I want to keep a low profile. And with the ton of Gallants around, you won't remain unnoticed for long." Another thought flashed in my mind. "Oh, and my best friend when I lived there married a Gallant. Louis, I think, and they have three kids."

"Louis would be, what, the same age as you?" Joe asked.

"I think so."

Silence. "Your instincts are right, as usual. I should not be there. If I remember correctly, the

305

Gallants in North Rustico are cousins. But on the other hand, pretty much everybody is related to everybody else on the Island."

We laughed together at our first-ever-shared Island joke.

"Okay. You're on your own, but please, please, please keep your cell phone with you at all times and call immediately if you need me. Or if you need anything at all."

Joe. A generous man.

I slept that night and felt a little less gummy-eyed when I woke. I'd make breakfast and enjoy the view of the lake while I ate.

I stepped out of the motorhome and wandered over to the picnic table. I loved picnic tables: you could sit anywhere on them, even dance anywhere on them. As I shifted my hip to perch on top, I noticed movement under my House.

If better not be a skunk, I thought, and ever so slowly stood and backed away. The guy at the check-in would have to handle this one.

The whimper was faint. I stopped, turned my head, and watched as the mangy dog emerged, crawling on its belly. Its ribs were visible, and its nose was dry and cracked. He was a long way from Bob's vibrant health.

Maybe some family accidentally forgot it or maybe it lived nearby. I looked at him more closely and decided 'it' was a 'he.' He dropped his gaze, quivering. Whoever he had belonged to, had not done well by him. I decided I would change that.

I scrounged together something suitable for a canine to eat, which he ate like the starving animal he was. Once the bowl was as empty as it could

306

possibly be, he sat and looked at me, uneasy. I wondered what his coat would look like if it was cleaned and brushed. And smelled better.

It was my experience that if I paid enough, the campground guy would let me use the big dishwashing tub. I had soap that would not harm the dog, and an old blanket would do to dry him off. All I needed was a brush and some dogfood. At some point, I would take him to a vet for a general look-over, but that would have to wait until we had a much stronger and trusting relationship.

I found a piece of rope in House's storage locker and gently tied it around his neck. He whined, but walked beside me, head hanging down.

The bath was not fun for either of us. I added a doggie manicure to my list; he desperately needed his nails clipped. I lifted him out and he shook several times, water flying everywhere.

We were both wet and exhausted by the time we got back to the campsite. I filled a large bowl with water, gave him more to eat, and tossed a dry blanket on the ground, which—surprise, surprise— he rucked up, turned in a couple of circles, and lay down, asleep in seconds. I watched him for a while. He twitched and whined in his sleep. Poor dog. He sat up and looked at me.

I sat on the ground a few feet away from him and started talking nonsense. At some point in my monologue, I extended my hand to him. His nose twitched. I kept my voice low and soothing and moved closer to him.

Forcing a bath on him had been far easier than coaxing him to approach me on his own. We sat looking at each other as I continued my attempt to lull him with my voice.

At last, he inched his front paws forward until he was laying down, close enough to touch. I took this as a good sign and slowly brought my hand up to his shoulder. He quivered, but soon calmed. I gently patted his shoulder and eased my hand up to scratch his ears. I think this was when he fell in love with me.

The nice man who monitored the campground had been pleased to purchase a few things for me—I tip very well. My dog would have the latest in gear, and the healthiest of food and snacks. Odds were that he would eat better than I did.

We stayed at the campground for the rest of that day and night. I wanted to become friends before becoming traveling companions. He was nervous about the motorhome, but a little bribery convinced him that it couldn't be all bad. He was soon bounding in and out like a circus clown.

We went for a long walk. The leash seemed like a good idea at the beginning since there were other campers about. It soon became clear that the dog stuck by me like glue and, once we had walked beyond the grounds and onto a forest trail, I took the plunge and let him run free. He was like a maniac, racing back and forth between something only he could detect and me.

I left the motorhome door slightly ajar in case he needed to go out during the night. The door was wide open when I awoke. I reached for the glasses I hadn't worn much lately but decided I'd better get used to them again, and hauled on a sweater. I searched the site and the nearby area. The dog wasn't anywhere about. This was a definite déjà vu—a Joe move. My eyes prickled. How could such a short time with this dog affect me so much? We hadn't even decided on a name yet.

It must have been all that time with people. It had softened me, and I had let my defenses down. Served me right.

I quickly cleaned my campsite, anxious to be on the road after this delay. The engine turned over and its sound comforted me. I pulled out of the site and slowly drove the twisty way to the entrance of the campground.

There was a convenience store attached to the kiosk. This would be a good time to stock up on road food. I opened the door and a mass of fur accosted me.

"He's been visiting," the campground man said. "What's his name anyway?"

I was a little busy hugging dog and being licked by dog to answer immediately.

"His name?" I prevaricated. I looked at him, tongue lolling out of the side of his mouth, his eyes bright.

"Boy-oh-boy." I laughed, inspired. "His name is Roy. You know, after the cowboy guy, Roy Rogers."

The man looked at me and shrugged.

He must be too young to have heard of the western hero. His loss.

I finished my shopping, and me and Roy embarked upon our first 'happy trail' adventure together.

Chapter 31

The bridge was new to me, and scary, especially high up as I was in a motorhome. Roy was sniffing his brains out—the ocean a whole new world for his olfactory lobes to explore.

Joe had called yesterday. I told him about Roy and he laughed. At least someone got the reference. He was nervous for me; I was nervous for me. Lots of nervousness to go around.

"So, what's the plan?" he had asked, knowing I always had a plan or was working on one.

I didn't have a plan then and I still didn't have one.

I had been seventeen when I boarded the bus to escape from the only place I knew. It had, of course, changed in the years I'd been gone. The Confederation Bridge was by far the most dramatic. There were more roads, more houses, and more stores, but the landscape was much the same—red earth, rolling hills, and green crops and trees. The air smelled familiar. But my memory of the Island was shrouded in sadness and anger. It could never be home to me; it could never be cleansed of the past.

The campground was fine, and far from North Rustico, its best feature. I knew from the newspaper that my mother's service and burial had been yesterday. Her black and white photograph was one from about the time I was born, over thirty years ago.

I would wait a day or two to be certain that any out-of-town visitors would be gone, and then I would visit her gravesite. The compulsion to do this was strong and I had learned to trust my instincts.

I parked the motorhome a few blocks away. The juicy bone I had procured would occupy Roy while I did whatever it was I was here to do.

Shuddering slightly, I put my foot on the soil of my hometown. No bolt of lightning struck me dead. No specter of my father or mother appeared to damn me. So far, so good.

I pulled my hat down on my forehead and adjusted the dark sunglasses that fit over my grey-tinted ones. The short walk to the graveyard loosened my taut muscles a little.

Her grave was beside my father's. They had purchased a family plot when they started having children, and the price had been low at the time. No sense in wasting a good deal.

The epitaph read 'May the Lord receive you with open arms.' It was weird to feel nothing. She had been my mother after all. I chose not to beat myself up over it. I was finally getting the hang of liking myself.

I stood there, waiting, staring at nothing in particular. I was here but the compulsion to be here had not dissipated as I had hoped it would.

The footsteps were hesitant, stopping and starting every few yards.

"Hello?" It was a young girl's voice.

I turned. She was about fifteen, wore tinted glasses, and white streaks already showed in her dark hair.

"George's daughter?" I guessed. My brother had married young.

She nodded.

"Are you her?"

I smiled. "If you mean 'am I your long-lost aunt,' then, yes, I'm her."

"Olivia?"

"I prefer Flotsy."

Her faced flooded with embarrassment. "I forgot," she whispered.

"Let's go for a walk on the beach," I suggested. "Roy would love that."

She nodded, not even questioning who 'Roy' was.

My life was filled with people who nodded.

Roy was ever so happy to meet another human, and thought a walk was just the ticket.

We laughed when he had his first taste of salt water, spitting it out again and again. I hadn't known that a dog could spit. That Roy.

"My name is Stella, by the way," she said, "and I've wanted to meet you for the longest time. The stories they tell about you just can't be real. Is it true you lifted an entire dock and made it land on your father? That you wished it so hard that it happened?"

I chuckled. "My, how my powers have grown. Must be all the fertiliser they put on these fields."

She looked aghast.

"Sorry, Stella. I didn't me to make a joke of this, and there is a tiny nugget of truth about the stories they tell. I didn't cause anything to happen, I just knew that it would. I get glimpses of the future, which I can't do anything about, at least most of the time."

She put her hands over her mouth, her eyes wide. "Me, too," she whispered.

312

Was she ready to learn about her sensitivity to energies? Could anybody ever be ready to learn about this? Not likely. I took a deep breath of the salty air and removed my sunglasses as well as my tinted glasses. She may as well see everything.

"You see, the thing about some people," I began...

About the Author

PEGGY HOGAN is the award-winning author of *For a Song*, in which a minstrel stumbles upon an entire race of people that needs saving. In her second novel, *Milo's Burden*, a young boy inspires others to make it right, no matter the cost. Both novels are available from Fiction4All.

Titles by Peggy Hogan

For a Song
In which a singer saves the world

Milo's Burden
Sometimes you have to make it right, no matter the cost

Flotsy
Do what you can; forget the odds

What they are saying about...

Milo's Burden

Set aside some time when you pick up *Milo's Burden*, because you won't be able to put it down.

It's totally engrossing! The story will also haunt you long after you finish the last page.

Annette Campbell, Reader

I just finished your new book and was captivated by the cast of characters, and the pace and energy of the plot. This book has an intensity and rawness.... What a page turner!

RJL, Reader

I finished reading *Milo's Burden* late last night and let out a sound when reading the last paragraph... it was so unexpected and so brilliant! Bravo on yet another super enjoyable fantastical book. I read *Milo's Burden* never knowing what rich words you would put to pen in describing the lands, its people, and what was to happen next. I love that in your writing.

Dianne Deans, Reader

What they are saying about...

For a Song

For a Song imaginatively created an alternate reality, but one in which, like our own world, pure ideology takes those hungriest for power far from their good intentions, with disastrous consequences for everyone. The plot was suspenseful, funny, and was carried along with a beautiful sense of wonder from page 1.

Chris Benjamin, Author of *Drive-by-Saviours* and *Indian School Road*

You have such a lovely turn of phrase—paints pictures in one's imagination! A pleasure to read.
Karen Jans, Reader

I finished *For a Song* today and was mesmerized by the adventures of Blat. I could not imagine how you could conceive this diverse cast of characters and exquisite plot for the story. I just loved your book.
RJL, Reader

It's brilliant! I was hooked. I carried it in my purse, read it when I could, made excuses to be alone with your story. It was such a joy to read.
Dianne Deans, Reader